P9-DZA-529

A Door in the River

Other Hazel Micallef Mysteries
BY INGER ASH WOLFE

The Calling
The Taken

A Door in the River

a hazel micallef mystery

INGER ASH WOLFE

PEGASUS CRIME
NEW YORK LONDON

A Door in the River
Pegasus Books LLC
80 Broad Street, 5th Floor
New York, NY 10004

First Pegasus Books cloth edition 2012

Library of Congress Cataloging-in-Publication Data is available.

ISBN: 978-1-60598-420-9
10 9 8 7 6 5 4 3 2 1

Printed in the United States of America
Distributed by W. W. Norton & Company, Inc.
www.pegasusbooks.us

In honour of my grandmother,
Freda Strasberg, born Wolfinger

A Door in the River

Prologue

Saturday, August 6, 11:21 p.m.

She needed to get to the road. She knew it led away from here. Eventually, it connected to the highway that went all the way to Toronto, a city she'd once visited. But if anyone was looking for her . . . the road was two hundred metres away, and the parking lot in between was all lit up. She could stay in the woods, she supposed, and get farther south before exposing herself. That would probably work. But then from Toronto? She wasn't thinking that far into the future. And if she wanted one, she'd have to stay more than a few steps ahead.

By now, he would be missing her. By now, he'd know she was gone.

He was going to follow her. She knew he would. She could lose him in the city, change her looks. But if she did that, she'd never know if she was safe. He'd always be in the back of her mind. No matter where she went, she'd be expecting him to step out of a doorway and say hello.

Then there was the problem of the man lying at her feet. He was on the ground between the pickup and the Camry, flat on his back and breathing funny. She wasn't sure what was wrong. She wasn't sure it mattered now. He was out of view, anyway. She watched his lower jaw working silently in time to the movement of his hand, a pulsing motion, like he was operating a tiny bellows that worked his mouth.

She crept toward him cautiously and then leaned down and rifled the pockets in his jacket. His eyes were wild, following her, trying to communicate with her. She pushed him over onto his side and saw the bulge of his wallet in his back pocket. She wedged it out and opened it. "I . . . ," he said, and she saw the effort it took him to utter even this single syllable. She opened the wallet. There was a bit of money and some ID. His driver's licence gave the name *Doug-Ray Finch*, but he'd told her his name was Henry. Maybe that was a lie, too. She used her foot to settle him on his back again, and he puked violently and breathed it in and his chest rose up. He let out a deep *whoop* and fell back against the gravel. She put the wallet away undisturbed in his jacket pocket and took a step away into the darkness. But he knew she was still there. His hand was open, straining. His eyes were like starlight in his head.

This Henry complicated matters. This was way too many loose ends, too much unfinished business. No one was going to take care of it for her. It was up to her now.

She backed up off the asphalt and when she hit the grass, she turned and kneeled down behind the derelict pick-up. She peeled her rotten shoes off her feet and ran, crouched, back into the cover of the woods. Back into the heart of Westmuir County.

I

Monday, August 8–Friday, August 12

] 1 [

Monday, August 8, 10 a.m.

Emily Micallef was refusing to smile. Her daughter, Detective Inspector Hazel Micallef, had got her to agree to the photo session and to get gussied up in a fine dark-blue summer dress, and even to stand in the garden, but she wouldn't smile. The photographer, Jonas Greenlund, had resorted to sticking a quarter to his forehead, but all that won from Emily was a scornfully raised eyebrow and the rejoinder that she wasn't a fourteen-year-old in her first bra. She was a woman of eighty-seven who was entitled to look any way she pleased. And she wanted to look respectable. Serious.

"But you look stern, Mother."

"It's steely intelligence."

"But this picture is for me. If Martha or Emilia want a picture of you that looks like you've been constipated since The Beatles, then they can pay for it."

"Oh for the love of Mike," said Emily, and she bared her teeth in mockery of a smile, sticking her face forward on her neck. Her face looked white and drawn, a wilting flower on a dried-out stalk. Greenlund took a shot.

"If you don't give me a natural smile, Mrs. Micallef," he said, "I'll put you on my website."

The phone rang. "I'll get it," said Emily, practically leaping toward the house. "I may be back."

"We might as well do me," said Hazel. "She'll probably creep out the front door and drive to town." She took her position in the garden and stood turned one-quarter away from Greenlund. She'd decided against having her picture taken in uniform, as the Port Dundas Police Department already had an official photo for the station house, and it had been a while since a good likeness of her had been taken. If these turned out, she thought, each of her daughters could have one, and even her ex-husband, Andrew, might like one for his house. (She imagined it pinned to the wall, sharing space with screwdrivers and hammers, over his workbench in the basement. She merited that much.) Greenlund was waving her a step back and telling her to relax her shoulders. Hazel had dressed in a black blouse and forest-green cotton skirt that hung down to her shins. She was wearing her best shoes as well: a pair of black Italian flats she'd bought from Bally three years ago, on sale for $120. That these were her best shoes spoke volumes about her, and Hazel knew it. Not merely that she was frugal, but that she could never have seen herself in $500 shoes, no matter the occasion. She could never have carried it off. But this was one of the things about growing old successfully: you came to learn your own personal price points. She could spend more on trousers than tops, for instance (her legs were long for her height), but no matter what she spent, she could not wear bracelets, and every kind of hat but her OPS cap made her look like she'd taken the wrong advice from someone.

This ensemble (total cost: $385) was just right. It had the kind of elegance she could plausibly display, and she was comfortable in it. Greenlund had her turn this way and that, coming close and then backing away, firing off pictures. "These are going to be heirlooms!" he exclaimed and then took two quick pictures of Hazel's skeptical smile.

They were still playing with angles when Emily appeared at the back door, holding the phone at her side. She hadn't changed her clothes. "It's Melanie from the station house."

Hazel took the phone. "What is it?" she said to her secretary (whose actual title was *executive assistant*).

"Have you heard about Henry Wiest?"

"What about him?"

"He's dead."

"What?"

"He's dead. He had a heart attack on the reserve."

"Jesus. What time did this happen?"

"Midnight or thereabouts."

"In Queesik Bay?"

"Right. Cathy Wiest phoned Jack Deacon. Someone on the band police called her at home and told her they had her husband in the hospital on the reserve. They didn't tell her he was in the morgue until she got there. She agreed to let them do the autopsy."

"Why didn't she call anyone up here?"

"Isn't Deacon her uncle?"

"Maybe. But . . . god! Dead?" Both her mother and the photographer swivelled their attention to her. "And what was he doing in Queesik Bay?"

"Skip, I don't know!" said Cartwright. "Maybe he was going to the casino. But they found him in the parking lot of one of the smoke shops on the 26."

Hazel stood with the phone to her ear, shaking her head.

"You there?" said Cartwright.

"I'm here."

"Funeral's Thursday. I expect the whole town will be at the service."

"I bet," said Hazel. "Okay, Melanie. Thanks for telling me."

Hazel hung up and stared at the phone in her hand. "Henry Wiest is dead," she said, like it was a question. "Had a heart attack. At a smoke shop on Queesik Bay Road."

"Oh, poor Cathy," said her mother. Henry and Cathy had been married for fifteen years and everyone in the two Kehoes – Glenn *and* River – as well as in Port Dundas knew who they were. They were almost a famous couple, known by name to just about everyone who lived in those towns, and many more besides.

Hazel was retreating into the house. "We'll have do this another day," she said to Greenlund.

"I understand completely," he said. "I wonder if my wife knows." He put the lens cap on his camera and took out his phone.

The autopsy done on the reserve gave the cause of death as cardiac infarction brought on by extreme anaphylaxis. He'd been stung by a bee. That made it the second fatal sting of the summer. There had been news in May of a new strain in Ontario and Quebec and it'd been spotted for the first time in Westmuir in July. Every week now the papers had another story of kids stung on a camping trip or someone having a bad reaction to a sting in a village garden. All the local paramedic teams had tripled their stock of EpiPens and there were editorials on how to deal with the invaders and avoid their stings, from wearing shoes outdoors at all times to defensive soda drinking ("Keep the opening on your pop can covered at all times! Bees love sweet things and will crawl inside your sugary drink only to, *possibly*, sting you *inside the mouth*! Ouch!").

The one death had occurred in Fort Leonard, in the middle of July – a camper on a portage had been stung repeatedly while carrying his canoe – and Wiest was the second. It was impossible to know if you might have an anaphylactic reaction to a bee sting. The problem with anaphylaxis was that you could receive six bee stings in your life (or eat a dozen peanuts, or wear latex gloves twenty times) before the deadly reaction kicked in. And, sometimes, a series of mild anaphylactic reactions would lead to a fatal one.

Henry Wiest owned the hardware store in Kehoe Glenn – called, simply, Wiest's – and at one time or another most people in a fifty-kilometre radius had called on him for some reason. The family-owned hardware store in Port Dundas had closed in 2001 when the Canadian Tire had moved into town from the highway and expanded, and Wiest's reputation for driving out to fix a lock or get a chipmunk out of a wall was, by that point, legend. There were plenty of contractors and electricians, roofers and excavators in the region, but small jobs tended to flow Henry's way: he was reliable, friendly, and cheap, and he never did anything that wasn't necessary.

His wife, Cathy, owned Kehoe Glenn's best-loved café, The Frog Pond, which apart from having an excellent breakfast and lunch menu also boasted the best coconut cream pie in all of Westmuir County. Both husband and wife were the kind of local celebrities only small towns have: he could fix anything; she made amazing pies. Between the two of them, a childless couple, they made a fine living, but they lived in almost obsessive modesty. Sometimes people had gossiped that Henry Wiest had more than $5 million in savings. Yet they had occupied that pretty house on Church Road since 1986, the year they were married, and it was no bigger a house than two people needed. Henry drove the company pickup on business and otherwise drove a used Camry. Cathy drove a new one. Her Camrys eventually became his used Camrys and then they'd buy her a new one. Every five years, when the warranties ran out.

In the afternoon, people were going to pay their respects. Hazel went home first to change into civilian clothes and then continued on to Kehoe Glenn. The Wiest house was set back a ways, against a ravine, and there was a beautifully kept garden in the front. The smaller second storey of the house sloped down asymmetrically over the garage. Huge orange day lilies nodded against the front of the house below a big bay window, and blue delphinium, echinacea, and foxglove stood tall in their beds leading away from the house in serpentine patterns. Soft tufts of lamb's ear lined the edge of the bed. Hazel went up the walk, her attention drawn to the riot of colour and scent, and felt especially sad that Henry's widow had to cope with his death in the context of such rude and splendid life.

The house was already full of people – friends, relations, townsfolk – and Cathy's employees had brought over a groaning board's worth of food from the café. In a cynical part of herself, Hazel wondered how many of those who'd come to give their condolences hadn't just come for the food.

She gave a wide berth to the buffet. How people could eat at a time like this was beyond her. Cathy was sitting at one end of a couch, receiving people. She looked to be in shock a little, but it hadn't caused her natural warmth to flag. She was a beautiful, capable woman of thirty-six, and it was hard to imagine anyone bearing up with as much grace as she was.

There was a clutch of people standing around Cathy and not talking so much as they were emoting to each other. Professional criers, Hazel recalled, had once been hired by mourners to bring the proper gravity to a sad situation. It seemed the performance came naturally to some. She threaded her way eventually to the couch and took Cathy's hand in hers. "I don't know what to say."

"What is there to say?"

"I thought he was indestructible."

"Apparently not. It's unimaginable to me that he could have fallen off as many ladders as he did but be *killed* by something that tiny."

"Why was he down there?"

"He told me he was going to Mayfair to pick up some

filters. Maybe he got a call on the way back. I don't know. I didn't talk to him after he left the store."

"It's awful, Cathy. Just awful."

Hazel hung back for a while after that, and shook hands, and made the appropriate gestures to the family. She overheard quite a few Henry Wiest stories that she already knew. The time he came in the middle of the night and enticed a family of raccoons out of Robert Moss's attic with nothing more than a net and one of The Frog Pond's meatballs. His uncle was talking about how Henry had three wild years in his teens when nobody thought he'd ever settle down. He was obviously never going to take over Bill's store. His father, my brother, said the uncle, pausing. *But* there was always a lot more to Henry and he wanted to be able to be with that woman, there, he said, pointing at the couch. Hazel watched people coming up to the uncle, smiling and touching him. She'd never heard of a wild version of Henry Wiest, and she'd known him from babyhood. The Wiest family went as far back in Westmuir as the Micallefs. Hazel had been fifteen when Henry was born; maybe his wild years coincided with her child-rearing years. She filed it away, though. She had her own collection of stories. Her ex, Andrew, had once needed a hand to help trim heavy branches hanging over their roof: Henry had insisted Andrew go back inside and watch the football game, it was a two-man job he could do on his own. And once, when Martha was fourteen and alone at home, an attempt at teaching herself to drive had found her backsliding down the hill behind the house in their 1982 Volvo station wagon. Henry had answered her panicked call for help and he came to winch her back uphill and show her how to fill the tire tracks in the snow with cedar switches. (Martha told them the truth, anyway. They debated whether the elder Wiest would have approved of Henry's abetting. He'd been a Calvinist type, William Wiest.)

Both of them had been fixtures in the town. Cathy had sat on town council. If someone was having a party in Kehoe Glenn, there was a good chance they were at it. Henry had been fun to know. A party they'd had once at the house in Pember Lake had gone so late he'd fallen asleep on the couch with a blanket over his head. They'd left him there until noon the next day, tiptoeing around, and then decided to wake him. But when they pulled the blanket back there was a pile of pillows under it and a note that read, *Keep it down, please.*

She was going to miss him.

When people began to leave (and when the vittles began to dwindle), Hazel went up to Cathy a second time, to say goodbye. "There were a lot of people here," she said. "He was well loved."

"Thank you for coming, Hazel. You know it was your father's generation that set the example for Hank, once he was ready to come around to it. His dad, yours, all those nice old guys who used to curl together at the bonspiel . . . they were the template. I wonder what this place is going to be like when their influence is finally gone."

"Well, it's up to us to keep it alive. Henry was the best example of it, though."

Cathy half smiled at Hazel. "Thank you for saying that."

Hazel gave the mourning woman a huge hug. Then, gently, she said, "Do you mind if I ask you something, Cathy?"

"Like what?" Hazel's tone had put her on alert.

"I'm just wondering if Henry smoked."

"Oh, he quit years ago. But he bought the occasional pack. I sometimes found them."

"Do you think he would have gone down to Queesik Bay to buy a pack of cigarettes?"

"Hazel . . ."

"I know," she said, "Sorry. Force of habit."

She squeezed Hazel's hand and turned her reddened face to the next well-wisher. Hazel went back to her car. She drove home with the radio off, thinking. Why had Henry Wiest parked far in the back of the smoke shop? There was a drive-through there if he'd wanted to be subtle about it. But he'd parked. So maybe he hadn't gone for smokes. She sincerely doubted that he'd gone for souvenirs, either.

] 2 [

Late afternoon

Things were changing at the Port Dundas Police Department. Years of talk about amalgamating some of the region's smaller shops was turning into a reality, and the Port Dundas detachment was about to experience that in the form of Ray Greene returning to his old shop as the new commanding officer. Supposedly this was the beginning of a renaissance for Port Dundas: the detachment was going to grow, become more central to Westmuir operations. She wondered what Ray was going to be called. Probably superintendent. It made her skin itch to think of it. He'd been gone for almost a year, after quitting the force over Hazel's methods, as *his* CO, and now he was coming back, not as her deputy but her boss. Ray himself had informed Hazel of Commissioner Willan's decision in person back in May: he was going to be installed in January. So she had five months, five more months to do things her way.

After the gathering at the Wiest house, she called down to Queesik Bay to get a copy of the band police report on the discovery of the body, and a copy of the autopsy. The report was faxed up from the reserve police department. It was detailed and unprovocative. Under the details of time and place, the reporting officer, a Lydia Bellecourt, had written:

> I responded to the location at 12:35 a.m. in regards to a report of a body in the rear of the parking lot behind Eagle Smoke and Souvenir. Upon arrival at the time noted above, a customer of Eagle Smoke and Souvenir, full name LOUIS PETER HARKEMAS, directed me to the location of the body, which he first saw when he was parking his car and his headlights illuminated it. He reassured me that no one had touched or moved the body from when he first saw it. The victim was found lying on his back, on the gravel of the rear parking lot, between a red, 2003 Ford F-150 pickup with the licence plate AAZW 229, and a grey 1997 Volkswagen Jetta with no plates. The victim was dressed in jeans, a blue shirt, and was wearing black Blundstone boots. The victim had vomited.
>
> I ascertained that the victim was not breathing and

did not have a pulse, whereupon I radioed QBAS to state that the victim appeared to be deceased and that in addition to life-saving equipment that had already been dispatched, a coroner would be needed. The ambulance arrived on the scene at 12:41 a.m. and pronounced the victim dead. The coroner, CALVIN BRETT, arrived shortly afterwards and did his own exam and wrote his report on the scene (#38174490). He estimated the time of death at between 11 p.m. and midnight. A driver's licence and an Ontario Health Card confirmed the victim's identity as HENRY PHILLIP WIEST, of 72 Church Road in Kehoe Glenn, Ontario. DOB June 11, 1959. Contents of the victim's pockets were a wallet with $45 in cash, a cellphone, and a comb. All items were bagged. There was no damage to the victim's vehicle, and there was nothing of interest in the truck except for a load of home furnace filters, and a half-drunk Tim Hortons coffee in a cup-holder. There were no personal belongings in the truck except for a folded blanket. Papers confirming victim's ownership of the truck were found in the glove compartment. The victim's last name is also painted on the side of the truck and refers to a well-known business in Kehoe Glenn, Wiest's.

There appear to be no witnesses to the victim's death. There was no evidence of a struggle, no blood or bullet wound on the victim, no clear signs of strangulation or blunt force trauma. The victim had his truck keys in his hand. Nothing at the scene suggested foul play; investigation reserved until results of autopsy.

Signed,

LYDIA BELLECOURT, RC QBPS

The band police had sent a car to pick Cathy up and she'd given permission for the autopsy to be performed on the reserve. It had its own lab – Westmuir's chief pathologist, Dr. Jack Deacon, often just sent his tests there. The report said that Wiest had edema associated with an insect sting causing anaphylaxis and that a single sting to his face had caused his death. The toxicology had come back negative. So that was it. She called James Wingate, her detective constable, into her office and showed him the faxes.

"It was a wasp," she said. He was standing in front of her desk, studying the report quickly. She put her finger down on the *Cause of Death*. It read, *Anaphylaxis due to wasp sting*. "My luck."

"Why your luck?"

"No stinger. That would be proof of something at least." She took the police report back and sorted it with the other pages. The cover sheet read, *Please let me know if I can be of any further service* and was signed by Bellecourt. "Did you ever meet him?"

"I've only been here nine months, Hazel."

"You would have met him eventually," she said. "You've probably seen his pickup a dozen times without even knowing it. One day you were going to have trouble with the wiring in your living room, or you were going to find a leak under your sink, and you'd ask someone for a name and that name would have been Henry. Everyone knew him. That's why there were three hundred people in that church. I bet there were fifty underemployed contractors handing out their cards yesterday."

"So he was well liked."

"Loved."

He continued reading the stapled fax pages and felt backwards for the seat of the chair in front of her desk. "There were no cigarettes in his pickup," he said. He sat with a faint thud. "So he must have been stung just as he was getting out."

"Hey, does it *say* pickup? It does, doesn't it? He was driving the store's pickup."

"Is that a problem?"

"It kind of puts the kibosh on the cigarette-buying idea. He'd have gone down in his car."

"Why."

"Because he's buying cigarettes on the sly, dummy. You don't do that in a vehicle with your name painted on the door."

"I'm still working on my detectivating skills."

"But he must have gone down for a reason, right? If not cigarettes, then what?"

"Souvenirs."

"On his way home with a load of filters?"

"Why is the pickup so important to you all of a sudden?"

"I don't know," she said. "I want to know what he was doing down there. It would *help* me to know."

He leaned over in the chair and slid his copy of the police report back onto her desk. "Why would it *help* you?"

"I knew him his whole life, James. But not on a daily basis – right? You see people around. But how well do you really know them?"

"That is a question for the ages," he said, tolerantly.

"What I'm saying is, you don't really *need* to know them. Not if things go the way they usually go. You just know what you know. You never have the desire or the occasion to ask if there's anything you *ought* to know. But when a guy like this, at his age, and he's found in a parking lot on an Indian reserve – "

"In his pickup truck – "

"Right. In his pickup truck."

"It brings questions to mind."

"It does."

"And you knew him," Wingate said.

"Yes. I knew him."

He smiled at her and she recognized that glimmer of resignation so many of her co-workers already had. Nine months and he was already giving her that smile. "So what do you want to do, Skip?"

"I wish Jack Deacon could look at him and confirm for me that it was a wasp sting. And that it really was anaphylaxis."

"If you have any doubts, you'd better hurry. Isn't the funeral Thursday?"

"I know," she said and she scowled. "I wonder if Cathy's worried about why he was down there in the pickup. Eleven-thirty on a Saturday night. Who'd need a workman that time of night? We should find out if the souvenir shop sold filters."

Wingate got up in front of her desk and retrieved one set of the faxes. " Souvenir filters? Let me handle this, okay? I'll call Jack Deacon, get his opinion on the reserve hospital and their report."

"That's a good idea. Do that."

"Then I'll call this Officer Bellecourt and see if she thinks there could be any loose ends."

"Talk to Jack first."

"All right," he said. "Listen, I'm sorry, Hazel. I didn't know you knew him like that."

"I even babysat him a couple times. My dad drove me down to Kehoe Glenn and came back afterwards to pick me up."

"This was just a sad, tragic accident. But I'll . . . ," he said, holding the reports in the air.

"Thank you, James."

The rest of the day passed with no news and minimal disruption. Had Hazel known it was going to be the last such day for some time, she would have made an effort to enjoy it more. But it was hard to enjoy anything, and a dark cloud sagged over her. There were still reports to read, though, there was never any peace, not even on a Monday. She'd had to send Constable Eileen Bail down to the big warehouse clothing store to take a description of a young male shoplifter from the store manager; she had to personally look into reports that primary school kids were smoking cigarettes in the alleyway behind the Beverly Cinema; and she still had to compose an excitement-inducing text for the Port Dundas Annual Main Street BBQ, an event the OPS paid for every Labour Day as a public relations activity. Those who didn't like it called it a *stunt*, and it was a stunt, but most people liked it. Sometimes Hazel thought people asked for too little. The person who'd always loved it was Ray Greene. Frankly, sometimes she wished they'd do something different.

Henry. Henry Wiest was dead. Hazel was pretty confident nothing would come of her thoroughness, but she consoled herself with the thought that Henry would have appreciated it.

The next morning, Jack's voice floated up from the speakerphone in Hazel's office. Wingate took notes. It turned out Deacon had not seen the autopsy report. He'd met Dr. Brett and discussed the case with him, and he'd relayed what he knew to Cathy. But, he said, he hadn't wanted to assume privileges. So Wingate had faxed the autopsy along with Bellecourt's report to him and arranged for Wiest's medical records to be copied down to him in Mayfair as well. "Well, it's interesting," he was saying, "I've got the report and then I learned there were a couple of photographs as well. They didn't send you those, now did they?"

"No."

"Well, I decided to call this Bellecourt, and she said there were some pics of the body and the sting wound and she emailed them to me."

"You can do that, huh?"

"Yes, Hazel. Anyway, it's clear he was stung by *something*. Actually, twice. A wasp will do that. He was stung once on the face and once on the forehead, but it was hidden by his hairline."

"So there's at least one thing they missed," Hazel said, leaning over.

"Not really. The tox screen is clear."

"He was forty-six, Jack."

"It's sad, but it doesn't create doubt about the cause of death for me. There's quite a bit of pale edema around the facial wound in one of the pictures. It *looks* like a sting. His prostaglandins and the leukotrines were through the roof, and that's consistent with anaphylaxis, and pre-existing atherosclerosis *is* a risk factor in anaphylactic deaths."

"English, Jack," said Hazel.

"Thickening of the arteries," he said. "Mr. Wiest probably should have been on a statin since, judging by his medical records, he had hypertension. And, finally Hazel, the bloodwork from the reserve shows elevated levels of the enzyme that gets released when there's damage to heart muscle. An anaphylactic reaction can cause a heart attack, Hazel, that's what I'm saying."

"Okay."

"This satisfy you?"

"I suppose. Does it satisfy you?'

"Well, you asked me for an *opinion*, Hazel, not a finding. I'm satisfied with my opinion."

"Huh," she said, and the tone of her voice made Wingate tilt his head at her. "Actually," she said to Deacon, "one other thing occurs to me. How common is it to be stung by a wasp at night? Aren't they usually tucked up tight in their beds at the hour Henry was stung?"

"I don't know. I could look into that."

"Will you?"

"Sure."

Wingate leaned forward and disconnected. Hazel had been taking notes during the call and she continued to write after Deacon's voice was cut off.

"So?"

She held a finger up. After a moment, she turned her notebook to him and he saw what she'd written there under a number of point-form notations:

Probable heart attack
Wasp sting at night?

"Jack just said he agreed with the reserve's autopsy."

"No, he didn't," said Hazel. "He said his *opinion* was that it was accurate."

"And you don't agree?"

"I want to be sure."

"Okay, listen. I won't get between you and your hunch anymore, but I don't think the grieving widow is going to take too kindly to your second thoughts while she's getting ready to bury her husband."

"He's being cremated. And I wish I didn't have them. Second thoughts."

"You want to have a reason to doubt. That's what you're like. My advice is, as I was just about to leave for my first ever vacation as a Westmuir resident, to let it be."

"When are you leaving?"

"Thursday."

"Going to get to know the charms of our scenic county?"

"Will be completely unreachable."

"What're you going to do, though?" she asked, a little absently. She was adding something to her list.

"Just some reading. Reading, slowing down, and relaxing."

He left. She looked over the thing she'd written at the

bottom of her list. Under *Wasp sting at night?* she'd added, *Why the hell was he down there?* "Were you buying something?" she said out loud, as if the dead man were in the room with her. "Were you meeting someone? Is that why you parked in the back?"

She held the list up and then let it droop away in her hands. *What if you were still wild, Henry?*

She buzzed her assistant. "Melanie? Can you find me the number of Eagle Smoke and Souvenir on RR26?"

] 3 [

Tuesday, August 9, early afternoon

When Hazel walked up the steps of 72 Church Road for the second time in as many days, Cathy Wiest was already standing in the doorway, looking at her with an expression halfway between exhaustion and alarm. She was in a long apron dotted with soap suds and she was wearing rubber gloves. She held up her forearms like a surgeon waiting for a patient.

"I hope I'm not interrupting anything," Hazel said.

"Nothing important."

"Don't let me stop you from doing your work. I just wanted to come by and see how you were doing."

"Are you coming in? I'm dripping on the carpet."

Hazel stepped awkwardly into the house and removed her cap. "I won't stay." Cathy Wiest was walking back toward the kitchen and Hazel followed. "I just thought I'd come by – "

"You said that." Cathy was standing with her back to her now, at the sink. There was a tower of dishes to her right, on the countertop, and she was lowering them two at a time into soapy water.

"Looks like I've caught you at a bad moment."

"Not at all," Cathy said. "You can make yourself useful if you want." She held a towel out. Hazel took it from her. Standing beside her now, Hazel saw a curtain rod standing in the sink as well as several pairs of sunglasses.

"You are cleaning *a lot* of things."

"I'm going through the house and washing everything in it. The laundry is done, including the curtains, and I did the walls this morning." She passed Hazel a plate. "Are you trying to decide if I'm nuts?"

"No," she said, perhaps a bit too fast. "It's therapy."

"Obviously." She passed Hazel a pair of dice. She stared at them for a moment and then dried them and put them in the cutlery bin on the drying rack. "So get to the point, Hazel. You already know how I am. All the doorknobs in the house are soaking in a bucket of bleach in the mudroom. That's how I am."

"I'm sorry, Cathy."

"Are you here to make me *more* miserable?"

"No. I'm not," she said confidently. "I'm just wondering about a couple of things, a couple of loose ends."

"Loose ends." A stapler.

"You put a stapler in hot water?"

"There's no staples in it. Just dry it thoroughly." She watched the detective dry the stapler.

Hazel took a breath. "Did Henry mention to you where he was going to be Saturday night?"

"He was at the store until six. Then he said he had to pick up a shipment of filters. They come in huge boxes: it's easier to go to Mayfield to get them than it is to have them shipped all the way up here."

"The reserve is really out of the way if he was coming home with them."

"Maybe he had a call. Or he took the 26 and stopped to buy some water."

She heard Cathy stringing the scene together as she spoke. "No one saw him in the store," she said. "I called down about an hour ago to see if he went in. He didn't."

Cathy Wiest turned her hip against the countertop. "What are *you* saying he was doing down there?"

"I'm asking you because I don't know. You said he didn't smoke."

"So what? They did the autopsy, Hazel. I can't ask him why he went down there now, can I?"

"What about the casino?"

"I have no idea. He never went there when I've known him."

"But he did, you mean? He used to go?"

"Like I say, not while I've known him. Knew . . ." Cathy pulled the apron up over her head and walked into the hallway. Hazel followed her. Cathy was digging a pack of cigarettes out of a drawer in the hall table.

"I overheard Uncle Ed talking about a brief period of wild youth," Hazel said.

"You don't know about that?"

"Not in any detail."

"It was a hundred years ago, Hazel. He had a little gambling problem at one point. As far as I understand. And he took some money from the store a couple of times. I wasn't here, I just . . . oh, for Christ's sake – "

"Cathy, what is it?"

She'd turned away and clamped her hand over her mouth.

"Cathy?"

"Wait here." She went up the stairs behind them, leaving Hazel in a state of anticipation and confusion. She listened to the footfalls cross overhead and then back, and Cathy came down the stairs with one of those little manila envelopes banks give people their cash withdrawals in. It was bulging. She handed it to Hazel.

It was full of hundreds. Hazel said, "Ah."

"There's fifty-five of them."

"And Henry didn't normally carry around this kind of cash?"

"No."

Hazel hefted the heavy little packet in her hand. "Cathy . . ."

The woman's hand shook as she brought the cigarette to her mouth. "You're just going to wear me down, aren't you?"

"I want to redo the autopsy."

"Christ."

"Don't you need to know? You didn't have to show me the cash, Cathy." She tossed the envelope onto the hall table. "You must have doubts of your own."

"Don't you have to keep that?"

"It doesn't mean anything yet."

Cathy opened the drawer in the table again and took a second cigarette. She tossed the cash in and closed the drawer. "Do I have to do anything?"

"No. But I thought I'd get your permission anyway."

"You can just reorder the autopsy by yourself?"

"I have to ask a coroner, but it's fairly straightforward."

"Then why come to me? Why even tell me? Do you want my blessing or something?"

Hazel looked at a vase of flowers on the hall table. "I guess so."

"Just do what you have to do," Cathy said angrily.

Hazel went to the door and left it open as she descended the steps into the garden. It smelled like warm grass in the day's heat. Cathy Wiest called to her, and Hazel turned around in the riot of flowers. Cathy's face was burning. "How will I know when all of this is going to be over?" she said.

"The investigation?"

"No, Hazel." She spread her arms. "*This*."

] 4 [

Evening

Hazel was almost used to the renewed pleasure of eating dinner at her own table, going to sleep in her own bed, in her own house, under her own star-filled window. The time spent recuperating in her ex's basement had been almost as difficult as the back pain that had caused her to seek his aid. Now the back pain that had plagued her for years was mostly gone. With its absence, and the fact that she hadn't had a Percocet since the end of May, she felt renewed. Women her age weren't supposed to have renaissances, but here she was having one. Maybe the timing of Ray Greene's return to Port Dundas was supposed to be part of this rebirth of hers? Maybe she was *meant* to get out now. Actually retire. Get a hobby. Take care of her mother.

Hobby, she thought, and she laughed meanly under her breath.

She and her mother had settled back into what passed for their domestic reality quite quickly, and after escaping from an invalid's prison at her ex's house, Hazel began to find it much easier being with her mother. At first she chalked it up to relief at being out of Andrew and Glynnis's basement, but then she realized it was something else. Her mother was finally slowing down. The recent deaths of a couple of her close friends and some health troubles of her own were weighing on her. Which, Hazel thought, shouldn't come as a surprise. Emily would be eighty-eight in three weeks. Her time was coming. But it was still hard to believe that this locomotive of a woman was finally slowing down. She still needled Hazel endlessly, but Hazel was beginning to think her heart wasn't in it.

"I will kill anyone who tries to throw me a birthday party this year," she grumbled one night to Hazel over a dinner of grilled cheese sandwiches. "Or a cake with *any number* of candles on it. I don't want my wattle catching fire."

"Why don't I just make you dinner at home?"

"*You're* going to cook for me? A special dinner?"

"I can do more than grilled cheese or hangar steak, Mother. I cooked for my husband . . . on and off . . . for thirty-six years."

"Your infrequency of cooking probably prolonged your marriage. We could order in if you'd rather."

"I don't *rather*, but it's your call."

Hazel could tell that her mother didn't actually have a preference. She wasn't sure her mother cared about much these days, and although Emily was making an attempt to seem her old self, it wasn't particularly convincing. It wasn't even a year since a murder spree had come to its climax under this very roof. A mild-mannered psychotic named Simon Mallick had been crossing the country killing the terminally ill, seemingly at their invitation. He got all the way to *this* house and the mild-manneredness had worn off him by then: he staved in the head of one of Emily's oldest friends, Clara Winchester. It was no wonder Emily hadn't looked particularly well since they'd come back to this house. But really, Hazel had to admit to herself, her mother looked even worse than a woman who'd been through what she'd been through.

Emily was sleeping in front of the television when Hazel got in from Kehoe Glenn at six o'clock on Tuesday night. The kitchen was dark: nothing had been readied for supper. She decided to let her mother sleep and she cracked four eggs into a bowl and mixed them with a dash of cream and nutmeg. She fried onions and mushrooms in butter and then poured the egg mixture in. The smell of onions woke her mother and Emily shuffled into the kitchen looking bleary. "Did you turn off the TV?" she asked.

"It's past six, you know. You were asleep."

"No I wasn't."

"I just got in, Mum. You were snoring."

Emily sat down at the kitchen table, hovering over a chair before dropping into it. "I didn't hear you come in."

Hazel dished the meal out onto two small plates and put some bread in the toaster. Her mother refused a slice and picked at the eggs. "I think maybe we should go see Dr. Pass, Mum. You're flat, you know? Maybe he can suggest some vitamins."

"There's nothing wrong with me that can't be fixed by a facelift and a bottle of whiskey."

"I'm serious." Hazel slid half her mother's supper off onto her own plate, like she used to with the girls. The toast popped up and she dropped two dry pieces into the basket on the table. "Finish what's on your plate and you can be done."

"Don't talk to me like I'm an invalid," Emily said, and she pushed the meal away.

Hazel took both of their plates to the sink and washed them. Perhaps her grief over what had happened here was the reason for her lethargy, but Hazel suspected it was deeper than that. Her colour was wrong. "Listen," she said, "we don't have to stay here, you know. I can sell the place, we could get an apartment in town. This place is too big for us, anyway."

"You think I should be in a home."

"I don't."

Emily *humphed* and picked at a piece of toast in the basket. “Maybe we should both be in a home.”

“Our own home, Mum. Whether it’s here or somewhere else, but I don’t think either of us has to be alone. God knows if the home for spry annoyances would take you now, anyway. With the spring going out of your step and all.”

“I’ll grant you that my step is more spongy than springy these days, Hazel. But so will yours be when you’re eighty-seven. Just promise me the day before you want to put me in a home you’ll leave me alone in the house for an hour.”

“So you can gravely, but not mortally, wound yourself with a firearm you won’t be able to lift all the way to your head, Mother? Don’t worry, I’ll shoot you first if it comes to that.”

Finally, her mother smiled. “You were always such a romantic when you were a girl, Hazel. You so rarely show that side of yourself these days.”

The following morning, as soon as she walked into the station house, Wingate flagged her down. “Jack Deacon’s on the phone. All excited about stinging insects.”

“Excellent,” she said. “Ask Melanie to patch him through to the thingy.” She hung her coat on its hook. “Aren’t you leaving today?” The phone rang a moment later and she punched the speaker button.

“Thursday,” Wingate said.

"Thursday?" Deacon repeated in the speaker.

"James is taking his first vacation since arriving in Westmuir. Nine months without so much as a long weekend."

"I don't like to relax," James said.

"There's more than one way to die," said Deacon.

Hazel got to the point. "What d'you have for me, Doctor?"

"Well, it turns out there are nocturnal wasps, Detective Inspector. But they don't live in North America."

"I see."

"*However*, there's no saying what might happen to someone who steps on a nest in the dark. Sundown's almost at ten right now, and wasps do burrow. He could have disturbed something."

"And then been stung only twice? And on the face?"

"Anything is possible. This is nature we're talking about."

Hazel sighed. "All right. I was hoping for more, but never mind." She stole a glance at Wingate, who was squinting with one eye. "We better get Harvey Tilberg."

"You want to redo the autopsy."

"Who the hell is Tilberg?" Wingate said.

"Coroner."

Deacon spoke over them both. "He's going to want a reason, Hazel."

"According to the reservation canvass, nobody saw Henry in the smoke shop. It wasn't a service call, and he parked far away from the doors. He's not even an occasional smoker; he's got no business at all on the reserve. And he had a gambling problem once."

"What?" Wingate yelped.

"A long time ago. But he stole money at that point. And, well, yesterday, Cathy showed me an envelope of cash. It wasn't a *sickening* amount, but it was still fifty-five hundred."

Wingate closed his right eye. The force of her will and her peculiar way of building evidence for a case was something to see. He understood why she'd driven Ray Greene crazy. And in the end you had to agree with her! There was no way you were going to make your own logic as internally consistent as hers. Supposedly this was "instinct." He'd never really seen it. Too bad she wielded it like a mallet.

"So you think this is foul play?" came Jack's voice, finally.

"Committed by whom?" said Wingate.

"A jealous husband. An angry creditor. Someone who felt they were getting the short end of a stick."

"Armed with what? An angry bee? What's the weapon?"

"That's *our* job, Jack."

Wingate was facing partially away from her as she continued to negotiate the reinvestigation of Henry Wiest's body. After a few more exchanges, Deacon acquiesced to whatever Tilberg deemed necessary. It was never good karma to have to redo another doctor's postmortem, but he would serve as requested. She pressed the button on the star-shaped console, and the doctor was cut off. She felt Wingate's eyes on her.

"Something is wrong," she said.

"Are you sure you're not looking for a last hurrah or something?"

"I never had a first hurrah, James. Are *you* totally satisfied?"

"Well, what we know is that the band police, a respected institution, with well-trained officers, wrote a thorough report that covered all the bases. We know a wasp sting is not only possible but likely; we know there are no witnesses, there were no signs of a struggle, no contraband in Wiest's car, no drugs or alcohol in his system, forty-five dollars in his wallet . . ."

She was smiling, listening to him. "I know."

"But? Would you be doing this if you hadn't known him?"

"I would have wondered about it, sure. But I might not have felt so strongly about ruling out foul play as I do in this case. I know there's a chink in your armour, James. You can live with this."

"I'm going to be on vacation, so it won't matter."

"That's right. So go. Don't let me make you any crazier."

"Unless you're right."

"No, you go. I have all the resources I need. You need to recharge, James! Let yourself go for a week. You look a little drawn these days."

"I am going, don't worry. Just don't cut me out of the loop if one starts forming."

"You think this is the right thing to do, don't you?"

"I'm on vacation."

"You *are* the loop, James," she called to him as he exited her office.

] 5 [

Wednesday, August 10, late morning

The following morning, Howard Spere showed up with a boyishly excited look on his face. He'd been dispatched as the intermediary between her office and the coroner's, and now he was here with the papers. The label from a packet of grape jelly was stuck to the side of his suit jacket – Welch's. She imagined him furtively trying to flick it from his fingertips to the floor in whatever diner he'd had breakfast in this morning, eyes out for the waitress. He was hanging on her doorknob, dangling a sheet of paper pinched between thumb and forefinger. "Did someone order a body?"

"You find this a cheerful business, Howard? I thought you knew Henry Wiest."

"I did. In fact, I knew him well. He would have been pleased to know we were being thorough."

"That's what I thought. But would he have been pleased to know we now doubt the cause of his death?"

"Do we?" he asked.

"That's why you're bringing me those papers this morning." She held her hand out for them. He passed them to her and she found the line her name had to go on and signed it there.

"What I meant – "

"I know what you mean, Howard. He deserves the truth."

Spere left with the papers and she settled down to go through Tuesday's reports. Maybe something unrelated would catch her eye and lead to a brilliant deduction, like it did in the movies. Kojak chomping on almonds and realizing the murderer had used cyanide. There were only three reports and there wasn't a single interesting thing in any of them. A keyed car in Port Dundas, a stolen bike in Kehoe Glenn, a fight over a girl in a bar in Hoxley. Maybe Henry was murdered by a jealous husband who happened to have a thing for bikes. And hated Buicks.

She signed off on the files and closed them up. She'd seen a lot of dead people in her years. She'd seen things she would never be able to forget, including things she never wanted to talk about again. You had to have the talent to depersonalize when dealing with all the awful things that could happen or be done to a human body. But you could never separate yourself enough. Your body still responded, still felt a refractory pain. You could not witness the kind of dead she saw in her work and not want to help them if you could.

She went down to the funeral home in Kehoe Glenn with Spere and stood away from the drawers as they got Henry off of his metal bed and onto a gurney. She stared at a calendar on the wall of the cold room while she listened to the sound of plastic and zippers. There were three boys jumping off a dock in the picture. An innocent summer scene.

The body went to Mayfair. She got the call to come down in the early evening. Spere met her by the staff door beside Emergency, where they waited for ten minutes, watching a man sleeping on a gurney. He wore an oxygen mask. It looked soothing to have oxygen pumped into you, but that man did not look like he was having a pleasant experience. At least Henry was already dead. A secretary they'd never seen before led them down into the autopsy room. "What happened to Marianne?" Hazel asked.

"She went back to school."

The new girl didn't look like she could be older than twenty. She sashayed down the hall in front of them, and Hazel traded a look with Spere. "We didn't come here to end up in the cardiac wing, Howard."

The girl left them at the door to Autopsy and the two of them went in. Deacon was still in his scrubs. They could see Henry Wiest lying on his back on the metal table. Deacon pulled his mask down. "I think you'll find this interesting," he said, offering a hand that neither of them shook. He led them back to the table.

Hazel tried not to look at Henry's face, but she couldn't ignore the Y-shaped incision in his chest, which Deacon had reopened. The top of the man's head was missing.

"So," said Deacon, "they left everything in the cavity – "

"Like when you buy a chicken," Spere said, and they both spared him a momentary glance.

"And?" said Hazel.

"And it was a heart attack. For sure."

She exhaled, and it was relief, but Deacon wasn't done.

"But it wasn't a wasp sting that did it to him."

He beckoned them to lean down to look close up at Henry's face. He'd been stung once high on the cheek and once under the hairline. Deacon lay a gloved fingertip just below where they could see the sting mark on his cheek. It was a black dot, as black as if it had been made with a lead pencil.

Hazel leaned down closer and Spere nestled in beside her. "What kind of wasp leaves a black mark?" he said.

"Watch this," said Deacon. He had a one-centimetre pin in his hand. "I got this off of the bulletin board in the staff room." He leaned down, and with a gloved thumb and forefinger at the edges of the mark, he gently stretched the skin. The black dot expanded and they could see a thin, bloodless tunnel about half a millimetre wide descending into the dead man's cheek. Deacon held the pin above the hole, his pinky against the top of Wiest's eye socket to steady himself, and then he let it go. It dropped with no resistance into the wound almost all the way to its head, like a blade into a sheath. Then he withdrew the pin and held it under the light. It was completely clean.

"What the hell is going on?" Hazel said.

"Well, I have a theory," said Deacon, "I already resected the 'sting' on his forehead, but I thought I'd wait for you to do the second." He set the pin aside and picked up a scalpel from the tray beside the autopsy table. He set the tip of the blade above the wound and drew it down through the centre of it, splitting the skin neatly in two directly through the black mark. There was no blood at all. Hazel turned away, feeling her skin fizzing. "There you go," she heard Deacon say.

She turned back and looked at the edge of the cut. He'd separated the incision with his fingers. "Can I swab this?" Spere asked.

"Go right ahead, but I can already tell you what it is."

Hazel looked into the wound. The channel Deacon had split in half was about the pin's length and its edges were as black as the exterior of the wound. "It's a burn," she said quietly.

"Got it in one," said the pathologist.

"From what?"

Spere was running a Q-tip upwards from inside Henry Wiest's cheek to the skin. He sealed it in an evidence bag.

Deacon removed his hands from the man's skin. "You know what can cause a massive infarction, pathological signs of anaphylaxis, and a burn mark?"

"I gather a pin from a hospital bulletin board isn't the answer."

"No, it isn't." Deacon turned to Detective Spere. "Howard?"

Spere was lost in thought for a moment, a rare state for him, Hazel thought. Then he said, "He was electrocuted."

She stood in Deacon's office with his phone against her ear. She'd been on hold for a full minute. Finally, the friendly voice returned. "Queesik Bay Police Service."

"Who's your acting chief?" she asked brusquely.

"Do you mean shift chief or the commander?"

"Whoever's top dog down there at this very moment."

"That's Commander LeJeune."

"Put me through to him, please."

She waited a moment. "LeJeune here." It was a woman's voice.

"This is Detective Inspector Hazel Micallef calling from the Port Dundas OPS. I need to have a face-to-face with you and one of your constables, Lydia Bellecourt."

"What is this in reference to, Detective Inspector?"

"An investigation of yours."

"Well, I'm just heading out for the day, but I can see you first thing. Say, eight-thirty, if that's not too early."

"It's too late. I'm already in Mayfair. I'll be there in ten minutes."

] 6 [

Keeping well within the cover of the forest, Larysa passed two days in hunger. And yet they were the best days she'd passed in recent memory. She'd been keeping the sun to her right during the mornings and letting it glide down to her left in the afternoons and evenings. Just before dusk on both days, the orange light poured through the trees sideways, just as it had when she'd been a child and her parents had let her wander in the woods near their house. Larysa knew that the sun's light took mere minutes to reach the earth, while the light from stars could take centuries. But she liked to imagine, as she kept to the cooler, darker parts of the forest, that this pre-dusk light was the exact same that had shone on her as a girl.

It was almost Tuesday morning now. There had been no human sounds since she left Queesik, only the sounds of birds singing and squirrels scolding. Being cautious was her only option now, the only thing that was keeping her alive. By now, Bochko would be on her trail, but with any luck, he had no idea exactly where she was headed. Knowing him though, she wouldn't be surprised if he could smell her from a hundred kilometres away.

By the late morning, the forest had begun to thin out, and she was close to where the towns of the Lake District started. She walked the shoreline of a small lake that fell to scrub and marsh around its western edge, and she felt exposed. But standing in the open, she saw that she was very close to Kehoe Glenn. That was where Henry had lived. In the distance, she saw where the highway divided and one part of it swung down over a little bridge – that swoopy feeling in her stomach every time they drove over it – and went under an archway with the name of the town on it. If she waited until nightfall, she could cross the highway and track up and around the town. But nightfall was twelve hours away and she didn't think she had time to wait. She'd have to make some moves out in the open.

In two and a half days, she'd eaten nothing but berries and wild onions and chewed on burdock leaves. She'd been sick a couple of times, but her strength had got her this far, and it would get her the rest of the way.

When dusk began to fall, she chanced it over to the town-side of the highway and vanished into the trees below it. She hoped she hadn't attracted any attention. She was wearing a blue T-shirt under a ratty black sweater and a pair of grey sweatpants that were too big for her, with the word CANADA in black letters down the right pantleg. Perhaps she looked like a local.

She followed the lights of the town laterally and then emerged onto a quiet, sidestreet intersection. There was a corner store there and on the other side of the road a car dealership. Everything would be easier if she had a car, but she had no idea how to steal one, and a theft would draw attention. However, outside the corner store, a bike was leaning up against a lamppost, and she saw the opportunity to get two things she needed at once. She went in, walking casually and looking down. There was a kid standing at the front counter getting the shop owner to count out candies from a bucket into a paper bag. He was taking the candies out one by one with a small pair of plastic tongs. She was quick about it: she took a bottle of water quietly out of the fridge and pushed it down the front of her pants. Then she took a pack of cookies off the shelf and stuck it up under her shirt. Then she idled in front of the magazine rack for a moment while the kid got his order tallied up on the cash register and slipped a map of the county, with all of its major towns shown in little inserts: Dublin, Kehoe Glenn, Kehoe River, Mulhouse Springs, Port Dundas, Hoxley, Hillschurch, Fort Leonard. When the kid was going for his money and she figured they'd both be distracted, she strolled out of the store, silently wheeled the kid's bike away from the post, and then hopped on it and rode away down a cross-street as fast as she could. If there was any shouting about it, she was too far away to hear.

She rode the bike into a little gully where a stream would have been running in the spring. According to the street guide of Kehoe Glenn, she was close now to the address she'd seen on the man's driver's licence. She rode along the edge of the gully.

When she got to what she thought was the house, she crept silently around the front and confirmed it was number 72. Then she returned to the ravine. She wanted darkness to fall before she tried to go in; she wanted the house empty. It wasn't empty now. There was a face in the back window, looking down, doing something. She presumed it was the lady of the house. She was talking to someone else in the room, a person Larysa couldn't see.

She waited until nightfall, but the lights in the house stayed on until the very early hours of the morning, and when Larysa next saw the woman, there was no doubt she was alone, and that she had not slept. Perhaps she would never sleep again. Dawn gave way to daytime, and Larysa finished the stolen cookies by midday. Her water was almost gone. She tried not to fall asleep – the woman would *have* to leave at some point – but she dozed anyway. When she woke, the woman was still in the house.

By the time the sun had vanished for a fourth time in the west – Wednesday night – the emptiness of her stomach and the awareness that staying in one place was dangerous convinced her she had to act. She left the bike in the trees and crept up the edge of the lawn and along the red-bricked side of the house around to the corner. From here, she could see the road. She sidled along the front of the house to the door and knocked lightly. She'd carefully kept the two parts of her weapon in different pockets in the front of her pants, but now she snapped the cartridge onto the muzzle and held the device against her leg. She'd picked up a rock the size of her fist in the ravine as back-up. It was in her left hand.

Someone was approaching the door and when it opened, Larysa was looking at an exhausted, sallow face. There was confusion in the woman's eyes. "Can I help you?" she asked.

"I am lost," said Larysa.

The woman opened the door more fully and Larysa brought the weapon up and fired it. Two long, thin darts flew out of its mouth on the ends of two wires and penetrated the woman's blouse. She threw her head back and stiffened. A sound as long and thin as the wires rose from the woman's lips. Then, just as suddenly, the power left her, and she crashed in a heap in the front hallway. Larysa pushed the woman's insensate body backwards into the house and closed the door. It had been open for all of ten seconds.

] 7 [

Wednesday, August 10, evening

The Queesik Bay Police Service (QBPS) served the Queesik reserve as well as six communities between Mayfair and Fort Leonard. The band force was actually larger than Port Dundas's, despite having a smaller catchment. They were well funded and their jurisdiction was absolute: anybody who committed a crime within band territory would be arrested and charged according to the QBPS's own statutes. It was mind-boggling to Hazel how much independence band police had. But one thing was incontrovertible: petty crime was as rampant on the reserves as it was anywhere, but major crimes were much lower, and reoffending was rare. Sometimes when the subject of band police came up at the detachment, she couldn't tell if the resentment she heard was because Indian police were better funded and had better resources or because they closed more cases.

"Will you look at this?" she muttered to herself. She was sitting in the public area in front of the intake desk at the Queesik Bay Police Service in a comfortable plastic chair with excellent back support. It was an open-concept headquarters: intake was a curving desk with two elevated chairs behind it, each one containing a uniformed officer either taking calls or dealing with the public. Both officers were young men in crisp light-blue uniforms.

The station house stood on its own beside the concentration of buildings at the heart of the reserve. There was also a hotel, a large convenience store, the social services office, a hospital, a garage, and the casino. She knew that a minor network of roads snaked off the two-lane blacktop that cut through the middle of the reserve, and that more than ten thousand people lived here. There was a community centre and a skating rink, and the Triple-A team that played in that arena a couple of times a week in the winter provided the best live sport in the county. None of the buildings were more than twenty-five years old, and from what Hazel could tell, the HQ had been built within the decade. Inside, it bustled with activity: behind intake the whole operation was visible within a generous atrium. Thick orange light poured down into it as the sun set behind the building. There were officers seated in ergonomic chairs at semi-circular desks on which sat new computers. She noticed a few officers walking around with electronic tablets in their hands, which they tapped on with plastic styluses.

She waited ten minutes and then was shown into Commander LeJeune's office. It was a compact room behind a glass partition, with a native woodcarving on the desk and a drum hanging on the wall. There was another officer present: this was Reserve Constable Lydia Bellecourt. Both she and LeJeune stood when Hazel entered and she shook their hands in turn. Bellecourt was a very tall, young Ojibway with astonishingly long and sleek black hair constrained beneath her cap. LeJeune gestured for them to sit, and then she handed both Bellecourt and her guest file folders on which the tabs read, "07/08/2005: Wiest, H. P. WM, DOB 06/11/1959."

"I know RC Bellecourt already faxed a copy of this up to your Detective Wingate, but I thought we might all need a clean copy. What with the urgency of your visit."

"That's . . . thoughtful of you, thank you," said Hazel, finding it hard to strike the exasperated tone she'd planned on deploying. "I do have to say, however, that although I admire the procedural efficiency, I was a little surprised that the autopsy was done on the reserve when the victim was a resident of Westmuir County."

"We had permission from the victim's wife, DI Micallef."

"But what about us? What about the OPS? We didn't deserve a heads-up?"

"All of the reports were faxed to your detachment as soon as they were completed. I'm afraid paperwork can take a long time. We try to be thorough."

"Well, all I know is that a man is found dead on reserve property and before the body is even cold, you've done your autopsy and let people wander back and forth over the scene. There's no evidence collection, no pictures of the site, and no witness statements. You have a pretty little police station, but I'm not sure you know what you're doing in it."

"Oh dear, you're quite upset, Detective Inspector," said Commander LeJeune. "But let me reassure you, we followed all the applicable protocols in Mr. Wiest's death. His next of kin was notified and consented to the autopsy in our jurisdiction. Normally it's a matter of some urgency, as you know."

"There's a proper hospital fifteen minutes away that could have done that and it would have been in the right jurisdiction to determine whether the death looked suspicious."

LeJeune had folded her hands over the report. "We *have* a proper hospital. One, in fact, better equipped than Mayfair General. In any case, there was no evidence of foul play, no defensive wounds, no material witnesses to his death, and no suspicious matter near the site. Therefore, there was nothing to photograph – except for the dead man's body, which we *did* do, please check page three of your documentation – and no reason to canvass beyond the smoke shop. And no one in the smoke shop saw or heard anything suspicious."

"I beg your pardon," said Hazel, working up to the desired tone, "but when a healthy man of forty-six dies in the parking lot of a native smoke stand – especially if he's a nonsmoker – there's a reason to canvass *right there*. Or do you discover bodies in the parking lots of your reserve so often that it's normal to you?"

The commander paused before answering. "When people die of natural causes in *your* town, Detective Inspector, do you start rounding up the usual suspects?"

She'd decided for the time being to leave out what Deacon had discovered. "Your whole investigation presumes an awful lot, Commander."

Constable Bellecourt stepped in. "Detective Inspector, there was nothing at the scene to suggest anything more than a tragic, but accidental, loss of life. I did take names when I was on the scene and I was ready to do follow-up, but the autopsy confirmed that he'd died of a heart attack brought on by an anaphylactic reaction."

"Well, maybe you needed to dig a little deeper," she said, brandishing her copy of the police report. "Henry Wiest lived in Kehoe Glenn. He was a well-known businessman in the area, owned a hardware store, and had, literally, hundreds of personal relationships through his store. No enemies, no troubles, in perfect health." She was going to keep the information about the old gambling problem and that little packet of cash to herself for the time being. "Yet he collapses and dies in a parking lot down the road from here when he has no reason to be there. Do *you* think the Eagle Smoke and Souvenir Shop would have called Henry Wiest down from Kehoe Glenn to change a lightbulb?"

"Maybe he did smoke, Detective. Maybe he didn't want anyone to know."

"Then why not stop at the first shack outside of Mayfair on his way back home? There'd have to be a dozen places to turn off on Highway 41 for cigarettes before entering the reserve, and there are four other smoke shacks before the Eagle. Maybe they were selling something special or unique."

"Like what?"

"You would know that better than me, Commander."

LeJeune appeared to be looking at her in a pitying fashion. "Am I . . . missing something here, Detective?"

"No," said Hazel flatly. "I just want to be sure you're completely confident that your investigation was thorough."

"I'm beginning to understand you think differently."

Hazel opened her portfolio and took out a copy of Deacon's autopsy and passed it to the commander. LeJeune began reading it slowly. After a moment, she muttered, "Goodness" and passed it to Bellecourt. She put her finger on what Hazel presumed was the salient detail.

"Oh gosh," said RC Bellecourt.

"So my next question is, where would a person in

Queesik Bay come across a Taser? Or something like it?"

"I doubt that's what made these marks on Mr. Wiest," said Bellecourt.

"Well, unless you have electronic wasps here, it had to be something that could pierce a person's skin and give them a lethal shock."

"Tasers aren't lethal, Detective Inspector."

"I know they're not supposed to be. But fifty thousand volts is an unpredictable amount of electricity, don't you think?"

"Do you not have Tasers on your force?" LeJeune asked.

Hazel shifted in her seat. "We don't need them."

"Everyone needs Tasers. And they don't kill people unless you bash someone over the head with one. And it's not volts that kill, anyway. It's amps. Current, you know? How many Taser deaths were reported in North America last year, Lydia?"

"There were none, Commander."

"Detective Inspector Micallef thinks it's possible Henry Wiest was killed by a Taser."

"I must admit," said Bellecourt, "I do think it very unlikely. A Taser barb stays in the victim. It shoots out what are little more than two miniature jumper cables. They really get in there and they can leave a significant wound. These 'sting' wounds in Mr. Wiest weren't made by a Taser."

"I didn't think of that, Lydia," said LeJeune. "That's

excellent."

"Jesus Christ," said Hazel. "The point is, he was murdered. He was *electrocuted.*"

Commander LeJeune's eyes lit up. "Oh, thank you," she said.

"Thank you?"

LeJeune was accepting a tray of tea from one of her administrative assistants, and she put it on her desk and poured each of them a cup. "Try this," she said. "It's cranberry tea. It's excellent for a lot of things." This woman was so poised it was unholy. She reminded Hazel of Chip Willan, but where his stance was one of self-possessed malice, LeJeune was being genuinely professional. Her attention was still on someone standing in the doorway behind her. Hazel finally turned and caught another constable, this one a man of about twenty-eight, mouthing something to his commanding officer.

"What is going on here?" Hazel asked.

"I'm sorry," said LeJeune, waving the man away, "it's just that we're planning a small party for Constable Bellecourt here –"

"I'm getting married."

"Congratulations," Hazel muttered.

"We won't be disturbed again."

"It's fine, I understand."

"Let's get back to the matter. So, it *wasn't* an insect sting that killed Henry Wiest. And you need to reopen the case.

I understand that now. You will have our full cooperation."

"Thank you," said Hazel after a moment spent digesting the strange aura of honesty and warmth in the room. These people needed to be 40 per cent more cynical than they were. She turned to Bellecourt and tried to act gracious. "Honestly, my heartiest congratulations, Constable."

"Are you married, Detective Inspector?" Bellecourt asked.

"Not anymore," she said, and the glow in the constable's face guttered slightly. "Look, if you really want to help me, make me an introduction to your pathologist."

"Of course," said LeJeune. "I'll have Lydia tell Dr. Brett you're on your way over."

"And then I want to poke around a bit."

"Would you object to a chaperone?"

"You mean a carefully guided tour?"

"You may want to go into the casino," Bellecourt said.

"Do you think I should?" she asked. "What's it like in there?"

"Well, if you're going to poke around, you might as well have a look in there. Lots of people in the casino. But if I accompany you, I can smooth the way, you being in non-reserve uniform and all. Or are you going to go plainclothes?"

"I'll go see your doc first," Hazel said. "And sure, you can meet me at the casino in half an hour, Constable Bellecourt. I suppose I might as well have a gander."

"You could meet Lee," she said.

"Lee?"

"Her fiancé," said LeJeune.

"As long as I don't have to witness too much joy."

"Lee's the manager of the casino," LeJeune continued. "You'd probably want to make his acquaintance anyway. Maybe you can stand a few feet back, Constable, to cool your ardour."

That was agreeable to Bellecourt, and Commander LeJeune placed a call to the hospital and arranged Hazel's visit. She gave her a map of the reserve and circled the hospital. "It's a two-minute drive," she said.

"I'll walk it." Hazel took the map and rose and the other two women stood and watched her out. She felt eyes on her as she retraced her steps to the front of the detachment and left the building.

It was still more than twenty degrees outside and the sun hadn't set. It was Wednesday night, but cars were streaming into the front parking lots of the casino just down the road to her left.

The main road – which was called Queesik Bay Road locally but was officially RR26 – ran directly in front of the building and she turned right, following the map. The hospital was visible from where she was, a large, low building with a roadside post topped by a large H. Church Bay Road, the one that ran behind the casino, met RR26 just before it. She got to the hospital in ten minutes and got directions to the morgue from the information desk.

The man who met her, Dr. Brett, brought her into his office. He was a handsome man in his fifties with a short, red beard. Commander LeJeune had already faxed the Mayfair autopsy. "Looks like we screwed up, Detective," he said.

"Do you even know what a wasp sting looks like?"

Brett opened a file folder that was sitting at the edge of his desk. "Yes. It looks exactly like a hard, swollen, raised welt, white in the middle where the venom has been injected and ringed with red." He slipped out a couple of 8 x 10 photos and slid one of them across to her. He laid the tip of a pen on the image of Henry Wiest's cheek, where there was an angry red dot. "Here's an excellent representation of one."

Wiest's body had lost its lividity by the time Deacon had seen it on his slab, and it had looked completely different than what she was seeing in Brett's picture. Here, Wiest had been dead for less than ninety minutes. He still had colour; his flesh still looked alive. She realized, perhaps with some disappointment, that there had been no cover-up here. Any doctor, even a particularly talented and discerning one, probably would have concluded Wiest had died of anaphylaxis due to an insect sting. Probably a bee or a wasp. Any hope that this Dr. Brett was involved, somehow, was already vapour. "Fine," she said now. "I'm gathering that, knowing what you know now, you're not of the opinion that there was any way to arrive at Dr. Deacon's interpretation when you looked at the body?"

"Likely not."

"Then tell me this. Do you agree with Dr. Deacon's report?"

"Well," he said, "I've already made the mistake once of not seeing everything in front of me, Detective. I'd better not make it again. It certainly *sounds* reasonable, but I'd have to do my own autopsy over."

"And say you did, then. Keeping a completely open mind, what other possibilities would you be considering?"

"I wouldn't consider any other possibilities unless new evidence presented itself."

"Meaning?"

"Meaning that I would confirm Dr. Deacon's autopsy, with the understanding that if I made any other findings, they could have an effect on my interpretation."

"Is it likely that after a third autopsy, meaningful new discoveries could be made?"

"Anything is possible."

"But is it likely?"

Brett's tongue worked the space behind his upper lip. "You are trying to get me to say I agree with Dr. Deacon's findings without redoing my own autopsy, Detective Inspector. That's not cricket."

"But it *sounds* like Henry Wiest was electrocuted, yes?"

She saw a faint look of irritation cross the doctor's face. "Look, I was trained at the University of Toronto. I did my rotations at Mount Sinai Hospital and Sick Kids. I have a subspecialty in infectious diseases. I'm not a country bumpkin and I'm not even a native, but I'll tell you something: if you've come up here to catch us out, you'll be sorely disappointed. This is a *working* community, with experts, mostly Indian, at every level of the municipality. I didn't do further tests because I didn't think it was necessary, and almost every pathologist faced with a body that presented as Wiest's did would have stopped where I did, too."

"But. Given everything you know now, being a trained doctor and everything, it really does look like he was electrocuted. Wouldn't you say?"

"*Yes.*"

"Thank you, Dr. Brett."

] 8 [

The same night

Outside of the hospital, the August night was finally falling, and Hazel realized she'd been working for almost twelve hours.

She retraced her steps toward the casino and walked down the long driveway lined with bright flowers up to the front doors. RC Bellecourt was waiting for her. The constable offered her hand – everyone was so bloody proper here – and the two of them went inside. Instantly the remaining daylight was annulled. Smoked glass gave the casino an intimate nighttime feel, and as she approached the inner doors, she could also feel the soothing blast of air-conditioning from within. One of the casino's security guards was standing beside a podium and stepped out toward them as they reached the inner doors. "Is there anything wrong, Constable Bellecourt?" His uniform was too big on him.

"No," she said, "not at all. This is Detective Inspector Micallef, and she's just here to have a look-see."

The guard offered his hand. "Jesus," Hazel muttered as she shook it.

"Now, ma'am, I hope you won't be gambling while on duty! That would be against provincial laws."

"Oh, I wouldn't do that," Hazel said. "I just wanted to look around."

"Well," he said, "normally, you'd need a player's card to go in. It's a members-only casino, but anyone can be a member."

"Where's the fun in that?" she said. "If just *anyone* can be a member?"

The guard smiled warmly at her. "That's just the rules here, ma'am." He stepped aside and let them pass.

The moment they entered the casino proper, the dark silence of the foyer was cancelled by an eruption of sound and light. Electronic bells clanged, chips clacked against each other, voices rose. And although it was much cooler in here – as she began to walk between the banks of slot machines with Constable Bellecourt exactly two steps behind her – she also detected little ribbons of sour heat coming off the machines and the people who worked them. Overheating transistors and flop sweat. There was a seizure-inducing scintillation of light everywhere.

Bellecourt leaned into toward her and said into her ear, "Dr. Brett is a nice guy, huh?"

"A prince." She tried to put a bit more distance between them, but from the sounds of the constable's footfalls, she was keeping up.

It was a huge room, at least the size of a football field. It looked like it could hold five thousand people. As she walked toward the back, she saw, through a cut-out in one of the walls, that there was a little poker room with men in it gathered around tables. She turned away and walked toward the table games. Men and women sat or stood around these tables, throwing dice or placing bets on green felt. The occasional hoot of triumph broke through the low-level hum of disappointment. As if a sound were being played through individual speakers scattered throughout the area, she heard the same defeated groan go up in one place and then another. There was something . . . *damp* about the whole place, as if everything and everyone in it had been swabbed down with a moist, dirty cloth.

She paused at the craps table, which had raised sides and a playing field within it. She watched the impenetrable ritual, and the people participating in it watched her and Constable Bellecourt nervously. One man rolled the dice while others looked on and sometimes everyone cheered and sometimes a few people cheered and others emitted the defeated groan. And then sometimes, the three-man crew running the game would suddenly take all the chips and the baize would be left bare. She shook her head in wonder and walked toward where there had been a huge roar. This was a roulette table with people standing around one side of it three deep, and the croupier was shouting, "Twenty-three black! Big winner!"

Hazel leaned over the shoulders of the people at the rear of the crowd and saw the croupier putting a heavy Plexiglas cylinder on top of a pile of green chips. The croupier was bringing out a big pile of purple chips and stacking them at the back.

"Two-hundred straight up pays seven thousand," he said, and he pushed the purple chips onto 23.

"It's a lot of money," said Bellecourt, and Hazel involuntarily brought her shoulders up around her ears. "Unfortunately, it has the steepest edge in the house and people who get hooked on the game lose a lot of money." They stepped away from the action. Bellecourt was smiling. "I was wondering if you want to meet Lee now. I told him we were coming."

"Will I have to shake his hand?"

Bellecourt grinned. "No. But I might have to kiss him."

"Why don't you run off and get him."

"Well, he can come and meet us. I told him we were coming."

"I'll be fine here for a minute, don't worry."

Bellecourt dashed away, happy to be of service, and Hazel continued down the line of table games. She wished now she'd brought a picture of Wiest with her so she could show it around, but she was already drawing on the fact that one had to have a card to get into the casino. She'd start there with the manager and establish whether Wiest was even a member.

The amount of activity at the gambling tables was bewildering to her. She walked slowly through them, heading toward the gift shop, and at the bottom of the aisle, Bellecourt was waiting with an imposing man stuffed into a grey suit. She was holding hands with him, but when she saw Hazel, she disentangled herself.

"Lee, this is Detective Inspector Hazel Micallef."

Hazel offered her hand to him before he could stick his own out. She was getting the hang of this place. "Lee . . . ?"

"Travers," he said. He was a strong-looking, beautiful fellow, with a muscular neck. She placed his accent as Midwestern.

"You're not from here?"

"Ann Arbour," he said.

"Lee was in the casino management program at U of M. There was an opening up here, and luckily, he applied for it." She was gazing up at him hungrily. Hazel understood why Constable Bellecourt was so smitten with this wholesome Midwesterner. He looked like a movie star.

"Lydia tells me you're investigating the death of that guy they found in the parking lot up the road," he said.

"That would be true."

"I have to say it's shocking when something like that happens up here."

"Meaning murder isn't common on the reserve?"

"Murder? It was a murder?"

"Did you know Henry Wiest?"

"Maybe we should go to my office. We could talk there without all the clanging and banging."

"Two cops and the casino manager's bad for business, huh?"

"Take a look around you, Detective Inspector. Nothing distracts these people for long. I just thought we'd hear each other better."

"No, that's fine," she said, "I'm not planning on staying long."

"I've seen the man's picture now, but I didn't know him," Travers said.

"Can you tell me if he was a casino-goer?"

"I can tell you if he was a member of the casino."

"Well, that would be a start."

Travers unhooked a rope from its stand and went behind a row of tables where an entirely other kind of business was going on. Men in suits and women in long skirts populated this area, which was full of computers and drawers and security guards wandering back and forth. Travers was surprisingly spry for a big man, and he turned this way and that, putting a hand on one person's shoulder, then another's, passing a friendly word. It had to be a big job, keeping people this focused and motivated in an environment of odd extremes. He stopped at a console in the middle of the work area and typed on a keyboard. His fingers seemed too big to press the keys accurately. A moment later, he returned, shaking his head. "Nothing," he said. "Was he a sneaky type?"

"Sneaky?" she asked.

"It's not impossible to get a membership card made up in a false name. Or to come in with someone else's card."

"Why would a person do that?"

"Because they're *sneaky*," said Bellecourt, and she and Travers shared a little laugh.

"No. I don't think he was the sneaky type."

"Then he wasn't here," said Travers. "He wasn't a member."

"Okay, then," said Hazel. "Maybe the two of you could fill me in on a couple of other things, then."

They waited patiently, like children.

"Does this place foot the bill for the station house and the hospital?"

"Absolutely," said Travers. "And the skating rink, and the community centre."

"Isn't it a little hazardous having a casino right in the middle of the reserve?"

Bellecourt answered, smiling. "For who? Natives suffer from gambling addictions at about the same rate that non-natives do. But we keep an eye on the community and we try to identify problems before they get serious."

"So some of the profits here go into your addiction-counselling programs?"

"No," said Bellecourt. "The province pays for that. Part of the original arrangement."

Hazel was shaking her head. "I'm sorry if this comes out the wrong way, but that's a hell of a sweet deal."

"Well, it's certainly better than being landless and homeless, I agree."

She decided it was time to take her leave. "You've both been most helpful," she said. She exited through the cacophony to the rear doors and back into the fresh air.

The back parking area was much like the front: big lots with high light standards. In the intervening fifteen minutes, night had fallen and the lamps cast giant pools of warm light over the asphalt. She wondered how much light there had been in the back of Eagle Smoke and Souvenir. Because here, there were dark zones where the circles of light did not meet. Perhaps something untoward could happen in scraps of darkness that would not be seen by others. Clearly it was time to pay a visit on her own to the smoke shop. There was nothing in the QBPS report that mentioned the presence of surveillance cameras, but maybe there was some footage of *something*. If she owned a smoke shop on the main road in the middle of an Indian reserve, she'd have surveillance cameras. Hazel walked quickly toward the rear of the property and stood at the edge of the lot. There was no one parked this far away from the casino. Who would bother? Beyond her was a riot of trees and scrub, the same forest that surrounded everything down here, including the smoke shop's parking lot. Plenty of places for hives – no mystery why the cause of death had been so easy to settle on. She leaned her body in toward the trees and listened and thought, for a moment, she could hear a distant buzzing. Then, suddenly, she did, and it was coming from very close to her body. She startled back two huge steps and then slumped. It was her radio vibrating on her hip. She unhooked it. "Micallef," she barked.

"Hazel? It's James. Where are you?"

"I'm at the Five Nations Casino. Haven't you left yet?"

"I didn't get a chance. Something's happened to Cathy Wiest . . ."

] 9 [

It took her thirty minutes to get to the emergency clinic in Kehoe Glenn. Wingate was waiting for her when she arrived.

"Have you seen her? Is she okay?"

"She's okay," he said quickly. They went down a short hallway. "She's in a room now."

"So it *was* a Taser?"

"I don't know. The paramedic said she had two puncture wounds in her chest."

"Just punctures?"

"Like the ones on her husband."

"Oh man," Hazel said. "What the hell is going on here? Have you been able to talk to her?"

"Not yet. I've told you everything I know." He opened a door and Cathy Wiest was sitting up in a hospital bed with a white bandage wrapped around her skull.

Hazel turned in the doorway. "Everything?"

"Sorry," he said. "And she was hit over the head with a rock or something."

"Good lord." Hazel dragged a chair around to the side of the bed. "How are you feeling, Cathy?"

"Oh, my head is just killing me."

"She has to stay overnight for the concussion watch."

"What happened?" Hazel asked.

"I woke up in the bathroom. There was blood all over my blouse. And the door was closed . . ."

"You told the paramedics it was a girl who attacked you? Did you know her?"

"No."

"Do you think Henry knew her?"

"I guess he must have." Her voice was faint and querulous. "She killed him . . . didn't she? With that . . . gun."

"I don't know, Cathy. Tell me, did you see the gun?"

"No. It happened very quickly."

"Did wires shoot out of it? Did you see any wires?"

"I don't know. She was standing there and next thing, I woke up in the bathroom." Her eyes landed on Hazel's and they were empty and haunted now. "You knew something, didn't you? That's why you wanted a second autopsy."

"I didn't know anything, Cathy, honestly."

"Why didn't you warn me?"

"I just . . . I was doing my job. I didn't think I was right, but I had to look into it."

"Well, I guess you were right." Hazel put her hand in Cathy's. Cathy grasped it.

"Can you describe her?"

"She was dirty. Like she'd been crawling through fields."

"How old was she?"

"Young. Twenty. Twenty-two. She had an accent."

"What kind of accent?"

"I'm not sure. She didn't say very much. Maybe Swedish. Or German. Her eyes were like an animal's, like a raccoon in the street."

"Do you know how long you were in the bathroom?"

"Over an hour. I woke up, I don't know how long after she hit me, and she was still in the house . . . I heard her on the floor above. So I stayed where I was. She was throwing things around. And then she left and I stayed in the bathroom for another half-hour before I came out."

"Did you go upstairs?"

"I stayed in the kitchen."

Wingate had gone out and now he returned with a doctor in a white smock. "I'm Dr. Morton," he said. "How can I help you?"

"I want you to discharge Mrs. Wiest."

"Oh," he said. "She needs to stay under observation. She took quite a conk on her noggin."

"This woman is in danger of more than a concussion, Doctor. I'll keep her safe. But if the person who did this to her is still in the area, you could have a situation on your hands here."

"Couldn't you leave an officer with us? Or a couple?"

She thought about that for a moment. Then decided against it. "I don't think so."

Morton directed his attention to his patient. "Are you comfortable with this, Cathy?"

"Where am I going?" she asked Hazel.

"My house."

Cathy Wiest gave her doctor a searching look. He said it was up to her.

"You'll take Mrs. Wiest out to my house in Pember Lake and stay with her, please, Detective Constable Wingate?"

"Absolutely."

"Cathy, this is the key," she said, decoupling one-half of her keychain from the other. "My mother is there. You remember Mayor Micallef?"

"Yes."

"That's who it is, only she's even more difficult now. Just go on in with James and there's a guestroom on the second floor. Take a bath if you like, and try to rest. James'll wake you every couple of hours if you fall asleep to make sure you're okay."

"All right," said Cathy, and now that everything had been arranged and there was nothing else to do, the energy drained from her body and the remaining colour vanished from her face.

"And do I have permission to enter your house?" Hazel asked her.

"Oh. Yes, of course."

Dr. Morton left to process her discharge and Cathy got gingerly out of the bed. Wingate left again to give her some privacy while she dressed.

Hazel helped her get changed. "What did he do?" Cathy mumbled, as if to herself, and Hazel held the woman by the arm to allow her to get into her pants.

"We don't know anything yet, Cathy. Nothing. But we're going to work it out. I promise you." She got Cathy her shoes. "If I could get a sketch artist into the detachment in the next fifteen minutes or so . . ."

"I don't know how much I remember . . ."

"Do you want to try? Before James takes you to my place?"

She raised her eyes to Hazel. "Okay."

She got Cathy's keys and put her into the car with Wingate. She told him to put Melanie on the sketch artist and get him in quickly to get a rendering of the girl. Then she drove out to the Wiest house and parked on the street in front of it. Its windows were completely dark except for a glow emanating through the windows on either side of the front door. It sat, a dark silhouette under the half-moon, on its patch of land and seemed totally devoid of life.

Hazel tested both the front and back doors and they were locked. One of Cathy's keys worked in the back door, and Hazel went in quietly and listened. It sounded like the house was empty. She flipped a switch and the kitchen came to light.

The table was littered with tissues beside a vase of flowers. Hazel closed the outer door and stepped into the house. A bulb buzzed overhead in the otherwise silent room. The darkly coloured flowers – tulips – were closed tightly for the night. There were similar vases on tables throughout the main floor, a total of eight in all. So after she'd swabbed down the house, Cathy Wiest had decided to anoint and fumigate it. She must had every tulip in Westmuir County.

The kitchen was otherwise clean and there was nothing out of place on the rest of the main floor. The inexpensively furnished living room yielded nothing of interest. Their television must have been twenty years old: it had a power knob that you had to pull out and a dial with the UHF channels marked on it. This was a man who could easily have hooked up his own pirate cable or satellite but never had. The fireplace was more up-to-date than the electronics in the house. All of it spoke of a marriage where conversation was more important than sitcoms or sports: these were people who found each other interesting, for whom being distracted together was not nearly as desirable as simply being together. Hazel began to feel a note of grief creep into her thoughts as she continued to look around. To judge by the state of the house, and everything people said about Henry, this had been a happy place. It would never be one again.

She went to the bottom of the stairs quietly and turned on the light. The drawer from the hall table was pulled out and its contents scattered on the floor. She saw the bank packet leaning against the moulding beside the dining room entrance. There was still cash in it: she counted it out. Three thousand. Someone had taken twenty-five hundred and left the rest behind? So maybe it wasn't about money. Or maybe that was all the girl was owed by him. For what? Drugs? A sexual service? How wild was Henry Wiest? And who was this girl who took only half the money?

Now Hazel realized there was a sound here, hard to place – it was coming from behind one of the doors upstairs. She pushed the cash down into a pocket and climbed the stairs with her gun drawn. The noise was coming from behind a door in the hallway to her right. She stopped and controlled her breathing, holding tight to the newel post. It sounded like someone was flipping paper. But anyone who was in this house had already heard her walking through it, and that meant they intended to finish their business no matter what danger it put them in. Which meant, also, that they were going to be prepared to defend themselves. There was a metallic sound from behind the door: someone fiddling with a lock or sliding hanging file folders along their railings. She crept toward the closed door, gritting her teeth, then stood to the side of it, her heart squeezing anxiously. "Police!" she called, her firearm up close beside her cheek. "Open this door and come out hands in front! If you have a weapon, throw it out into the hallway before you!"

The sounds continued, more frantically now. She didn't know if there was a window in the room, but she suspected there was, and it occurred to her that it might be smarter to rush out of the house and wait on the lawn for whomever it was to jump down. But to judge from the sounds within, confusion reigned behind the door and Hazel judged that her moment had arrived. She turned her hip and kicked the door in. It smashed against the wall inside the darkened room and she heard a high-pitched cry and the sound of paper being torn. She stood in the doorway with her gun out in front of her. "Don't move! I *will* shoot!"

Now there was silence, and she could smell the scent of ammonia. She kept her gun out in front of herself, reached to the side of the door, along the wall, and flipped the light switch. A cloud of white feathers was settling on the floor in front of her. Standing on a pedestal at a height of four feet was a dumbstruck white cockatoo in a cage. It was huddling in the farthest corner looking like it was having a heart attack, its yellow comb plastered down tight to its skull. Hazel stood down and holstered her weapon. "Good god," she said, and the bird's black eyes leapt in its head in terrified misery. It spread its wings: a slow, helpless movement, and then closed them up against its body in an effort to get as small as possible. The paper at the bottom of its cage was torn into ragged strips.

"It's okay," said Hazel, breathing deliberately, slowing her heartbeat down. She began looking around the room with more focus now and saw that it had been turned upside down. Books and paper were scattered everywhere. "Just a little misunderstanding. I won't harm you, birdie." The creature opened its beak in a wide, tremulous movement, as if to squawk, but no sound came out. There was a puddle on the floor at the base of the pedestal and she noticed the bird had upended its little tin cup of water that normally hung from the bars. She approached the cage and gently unlatched the little door, speaking softly to the mutely squawking bird the whole time. She took the tin cup out, closed the cage, and retreated into the hall.

The bathroom was through the master bedroom, which was empty and silent with bare bedside tables beside the perfectly made bed. A couple of the drawers were standing open. She looked inside them briefly, but if anything was missing from them, she couldn't tell. She filled the bird's water from the sink. It was the least she could do. She stood and looked at herself in the mirror. Her pupils were tiny, and Hazel stood for a moment studying herself. Was her face thinner now than it had been before the summer? One of the side effects of Percocet addiction is edema and she'd gotten used to the sight of loose flesh in her cheeks and along her chinline. Now it was gone. It had been three and a half months since she'd had a painkiller and now she could see her face again. A simple physiological change, but it hit her like a revelation. Even more than the cessation of withdrawal symptoms and the return of normal, bearable pain, this spoke to her complete escape from addiction. She was looking in the mirror and seeing her actual self again.

But this wasn't the place for a revelation. She corrected her drift and opened the medicine cabinet door and looked in on the hair products and razors, and on the top shelf there was an array of orange pill bottles. One of the pill vials contained a whole whack of OxyContins. Someone'd had an enthusiastic GP. She looked at the label, but the pills had been transferred from some other bottle: the label on this one was for Tylenol 3. She imagined that Henry Wiest had been no stranger to pain. She was sure there were still at least thirty pills in the bottle, but it was impossible to know when they'd been poured in here. Even so, thirty didn't sound like a problem. She'd get a month's worth, easy, every time Pass wrote her a prescription for her back. There was also a tiny ziplock bag of pot behind a can of shaving cream. Four small buds inside, maybe an eighth. More people smoked pot casually than you could imagine and it was less suspicious than the Oxys. Westmuir was overrun with pot, increasingly potent varieties, too, but there was no violence over it and the most harm stoned people ever did was rewatch

Jim Carrey movies. If Henry Wiest had wanted pot, he wouldn't have had to go to Queesik for it, she was pretty sure of that. She looked at the other bottles. There was an unfinished prescription for erythromycin dating to 2002, another vial containing a few Valium, and a fourth bottle that was half-full of the antidepressant citalopram. The prescription was made out to Henry Wiest and the label specified that there were four refills remaining. She studied the vial. The prescription was current. She replaced the bottle and closed the cabinet.

Back in the bird's room, the cockatoo was still huddled in the corner of its cage. Hazel opened the door to the cage and replaced the water cup. The bird watched her with huge eyes.

This was the room that had been ransacked, although there were those drawers in the bedroom as well. The office had been torn apart. It was hard to imagine how to start to look for what might be missing from the room. The drawers were emptied out and tossed to the sides, whole shelves of books had been pulled down. Hazel crouched and started looking through the papers. These were innocuous files: car ownership papers, telephone bills, warranties. Old banking accounts with wads of elastic-bound cheques bulging out of them. What had the girl been looking for?

She returned to her cruiser and called in. "They had a bird," she said to Wingate.

"What?"

"There was a bird in a cage. In the office."

"And what else?"

"A big fucking mess. She was looking for something."

"Did she find it?"

"I have no idea."

] 10 [

Thursday, August 11, morning

Radio cars had been out all night sweeping the highways and rural roads of Westmuir, looking for the girl in the sketch artist's rendering. She had a high forehead and large, intelligent, light-blue eyes. An average mouth, rendered expressionless by the artist, lips closed, and a tapering, rounded chin. Her long brown hair had been parted in the middle, curving tightly against her skull and pulled back. If not for the state of the girl when Cathy Wiest saw her, she would probably have been quite beautiful. In the drawing, she looked eighteen to twenty, and when Hazel saw it, she remarked to herself how the girl looked confident, engaged, and withdrawn all at once. It was not an unusual face for a girl of her age;

Hazel imagined she would be able to slip in and out of the world at will. She was going to have to show herself if they were going to catch her.

Detachments in Fort Leonard and Telegraph Heights had been activated and a total of eighteen cars searched until sunrise for signs of a young woman armed with a Taser-like weapon. It had been bold to knock on a door, maybe she would do it again. But there were no sightings of her, and she did not reappear on any doorsteps that would bring her to their attention again.

They kept two cars at each detachment dedicated to the search and put out an APB with a description of the girl and the sketch that had been made of her.

The smoke shack was, so far, the only promising vector in the whole case. Hazel was sure hundreds of people – residents, tourists, workers, summertime renters – went in and out of it. But was it a connection to the girl?

She'd gotten home after midnight the previous night, and she found Wingate sitting on the couch, leaning his head against the wall. The one lamp that was on illuminated his hands in his lap. He woke when the door closed and reached for his cap on the cushion beside him. "I got her here by about ten-thirty. She's asleep now, I think."

"How often do I have to wake her up for the concussion checklist?"

"Every couple of hours or so."

"Poor thing. She can't even sleep. Anyway, thank you for keeping watch." She took off her jacket and tossed it over the back of the couch. "Did my mother make any trouble?"

"Didn't see her at all."

"I didn't think you would."

"Is she all right, Hazel?"

"She's eighty-seven. Eighty-eight this month."

She'd bade him goodnight and gone to make sure her mother was actually in the house. She was. There was a long, thin bump under her bedcovers.

Hazel woke Cathy, as instructed, about every ninety minutes during the night, but as of five in the morning, she fell asleep herself and didn't go into the woman's bedroom until eight. She shook Cathy on the shoulder then and, after looking her over, decided the woman could safely be left alone. She left a note for her mother pinned to the back of her door, and another for Cathy on the kitchen table, telling her there was an officer outside the house and that when she woke, this officer, Eileen Bail, would bring her into the detachment. There were more questions, but she wanted Cathy as rested as possible. As soon as she left the house, she called down to Bail, who was finishing a twelve-to-eight, and asked her to do a couple hours of overtime in her car, outside the house in Pember Lake. She waited ten minutes for the cruiser to arrive and told Bail to bring Cathy in when she was ready.

When she got to the station house, she brought Wingate

and Constable Roland Forbes into her office. Forbes was about to take his detective's exam. She thought it might be good for him to sit in. He dragged his own chair in and the two of them sat on the other side of Hazel's desk. "This is what I'm thinking. Someone called Henry down there, to the smoke shop in Queesik Bay. And when he got there, he encountered this girl and there was an altercation and she discharged this weapon at him."

"What's the chance it was a mugging or something like that?" asked Forbes.

"Why would she go to the house and attack the widow then?"

"I guess not. How did she know where he lived?"

"Well, that goes to the question of their relationship," Hazel said. "We don't know enough about it yet."

"Should we be visiting that smoke shop?" said Wingate.

"I think so. But I'm not sure I should be the one. I met with the police commander on the reserve yesterday and I don't know if I want to show my face down there right now."

"Why?"

"She seemed more like a kindergarten art teacher than a skip. And she's got an angle, only I don't know what it is. I'd like one of you to go down there and see what the place is like.

"You're out of here in three hours," she said to Wingate.

"You need me on this case," said Wingate.

"Forbes can do it. It's reconnaissance, you know? Fact-gathering. Just go."

"I haven't made detective yet," Forbes protested. "I don't know if the other officers – "

"Just go down and buy a pack of cigarettes, would you?"

"Okay," he said. "I can make some notes. I can write it up if you want."

"Go forth, Gumshoe."

When he left, Wingate said, "What are you thinking?"

"I just want him to buy a pack of cigarettes. Look around."

"*No*, Hazel. I mean with this case."

"We need to develop a blind spot to the murder and the murder weapon right now and focus on the reason Wiest was down there in the first place. I think it's fair to assume that Wiest somehow knew this girl, and we need to find out how. That might tell us where this girl is heading and what or who she's looking for. If she isn't already done."

"I don't want to make things any more complicated than they need to be, Hazel, but you should know Willan's office called."

"Oh. Excellent."

"They said they expect to be notified in the future when cross-jurisdictional resources are being used, such as police cars in a countywide hunt."

"Well, are they for amalgamation or not? Jesus."

"There was considerable overtime in Fort Leonard."

"So what. Isn't he impressed with there being a killer on the loose?"

"I think he wanted to be notified."

"What's the point of having moles if they don't report back to you?"

"I think it's about getting the right clearances for extra – "

"Oh, *fuck* the clearances!" she shouted, standing suddenly. "I mean, just, we almost had *two* bodies on our hands just now . . ."

"I know."

Her chair had shot out when she stood, and she reached behind herself to pull it back into place. She sat. There was a long silence in which her outburst seemed to bounce off the walls. "So, when are you heading out?" she asked him finally.

"Sorry?"

"Your vacation, James?"

"Oh." Silence. "After my shift."

"Okay. I'll keep in touch with you."

"Are you mad at me now?"

"No, I'm not."

"Willan's turning into everyone's problem, Hazel."

"I'm not mad."

There was more paperwork to catch up on, another whole pile of it, and Hazel started drawing the file folders down in front of herself and flipping them open. One report spoke of three kids stoned out of their gourds and jumping into the Kilmartin River from the bridge at the end of Main Street. Their names were noted here, names she recognized as the offspring of multi-generation Port Dundas families. Had her cohort been as problematic when she was a teenager? There'd been fast cars and drinking, to be sure, but she didn't recall them taking their very lives into their hands. In the 1950s there'd been no such things as drugs, not even soft drugs, but now there was something out there that could make kids so numb to risk that they'd jump into a fast-moving river at night. But all this was going to have to be back-burnered for now.

She called Dr. Pass when she was done with the surprising amount of petty crime that had unfolded in twenty-four hours in the locality. Hearing of Emily's lethargy, he'd told Hazel to bring her in. He'd get a rush on the tests he'd take and have an answer for them quickly. She felt relieved after speaking to him, but she knew whatever he found, it wasn't going to be as simple as a case of the flu. She could feel it.

Cartwright knocked on her door at eleven. "Cathy Wiest is here."

"Send her in, please."

Cathy entered, and her colour wasn't much better than it had been the night before, but her eyes showed she was capable of thinking straight, and that was all

Hazel needed. "Sit down, Cathy." She waited a moment, then asked Cartwright, who was standing in the doorway to see if she'd be needed, to get them both coffees. "Did you sleep?"

"On and off. I kept . . . waking up."

"Yes . . . sorry about that. And I'm sorry you've had such a terribly rough ride, Cathy. I'd do anything not to have you sitting in a police station so soon after your husband's death."

"Who was she?"

"We don't know yet. But it would seem from the state of your house that she was looking for something. Can you imagine what it might have been?"

"I have no idea."

The coffees arrived, with a plate of digestive cookies, and Cartwright left them on the desk and hurried out. Hazel pushed Cathy's coffee toward her. "I have some difficult questions to ask you, Cathy. I'm sorry."

"I understand."

"Let's just get the worst of it out of the way. Is it *possible*, do you think, that Henry was having an affair?"

"It would never have entered my mind before. Henry was . . ."

"I know."

"I'm supposed to say it's possible, right? If that girl killed him with that thing, how could anything *not* be possible. But not the Henry *I* knew. We've – we'd been together for twenty years." She was studying Hazel's reaction. "You're divorced, aren't you?"

This took her aback a little. "Yes."

"Would you have known if your husband was, if he'd been . . . I'm sorry. Maybe he was."

"It's all right, Cathy. He was. But I didn't know because I wasn't paying attention."

"Would you have known if you had been?"

She thought about it. It was pertinent. "I don't know. I think I would have noticed if he was out a lot and I didn't know where he was. Or if something about him had changed. Did Henry seem different to you at all lately?"

"My husband was the most even-tempered person I've ever known."

"Well, was he often out of the store? During the day? Did he have appointments at night?"

"Sometimes. He was called on a lot, like you know. But there was nothing ever the least bit suspicious about any of it, and half the time, I'd run into the person he'd helped in town, or they'd come into the café and sing his praises. He was always where he said he'd been."

"What about money, Cathy. How was he with money? Was there any trouble? I mean, in general?"

"I don't think so. We were fine. I had my own business to keep track of, and he dealt with his own, so I don't know the details, but the store was doing very well. I know that he did his own books. They're at the store if you want to look at them. There was no debt, we paid for almost everything with cash, although I know he claimed every last cent that came through the store. I have to admit, I had a creative accountant for the café, but nothing serious, and Henry always said your taxes were an investment. It wasn't worth the couple thousand a year it would cost him to have a bookkeeper. Henry was on the up-and-up. Unless he was the best liar on the planet and he was having everybody on . . ."

Hazel made a mental note to have someone go down to the hardware store and liberate the books. Was he buying something from this girl? For her? Would his accounts show anything untoward? There was that cash in the envelope, but fifty-five hundred dollars in cash wasn't an alarming amount of money. She wasn't going to comment on Cathy's last statement because anything was painful conjecture at this point, and she didn't need to go upsetting her unnecessarily. But of course it was possible Henry Wiest was not at all what he'd seemed. There were people like that and you never knew, or you found out in a shocking concentration of events that exposed a secret. After everything his widow had gone through, Hazel was praying fervently there wouldn't be any more surprises.

Cathy was waiting for something, and the silence was agitating her. "What are you thinking now?" she asked.

"Nothing concrete. It's just, we have to find out what brought him down to Queesik Bay."

For some reason, it was this statement that caused Cathy to drop her head into her hands and begin to weep. "Oh *god*!" she cried into her hands. "What did he do?" She looked up at Hazel and her brown hair flew back, revealing eyes silver with tears and shimmering like the sky before a lightning strike. "What on earth did he do? What kind of person was he, that he would have been mixed up with a girl, that he would have *had* something of hers! And she . . . she kills him *in a parking lot*?"

"Please, Cathy, please try to calm down. None of this has to mean that Henry did *anything*. This girl could have been crazy. It could have been a random encounter and she got your address off his driver's license."

Cathy stared at her.

"I'm just hoping there's something, some loose thread at the edge of your mind that might point somewhere."

"I told you," she said. "He had to pick up some filters. He left the house at ten at night. It was a little strange, but you knew Henry. If he had to go do something, he went and did it."

"Do you know who his friends are, Cathy?"

"Sure, some of them. Half of them were in the Business Improvement Association. They're normal guys."

"Okay," said Hazel, and she sighed. "Where do you want to be right now, Cathy? Is there someone you'd like to go to? You're welcome to stay on with me, as long as you wish, I'm not kicking you out."

"I can't be around people right now."

"Well, my mother will leave you alone, so do stay on if you want, okay?"

She nodded quickly, hiding her eyes. "Thank you."

"Constable Bail is your personal driver. If anything comes to mind . . ."

Emily was asleep on the couch when Hazel returned to Pember Lake for lunch. Cathy was in the guestroom on the second floor, resting, Hazel hoped. There were faces on the television nattering mutely. Her mother had lately taken to turning the sound off, but she seemed to like the presence of movement somewhere in the house, even when she was asleep, as if her mind lacked the energy to make its own dreams. Hazel switched the TV off and sat in a chair across from Emily. In sleep, her cheeks were sunken and her mouth gaped. There was no detectable personality to an unconscious person: her mother was a mere creature, not a woman with a history and a character, and Hazel was saddened by the sight of this insensate figure on her couch. This animal that was her mother was coming to the end of her time on earth. Hazel moved from the chair to sit beside her, and she took one of her mother's hands in her own and just held it. It was cool and light and made her think of the frightened bird in the Wiest house.

Police work had trained her to live in the present, but it wasn't good discipline for being with others, where you had to be more alert to the future and the time you had left with them. She knew it was natural to ignore how time was stealing the present from you, how it lent itself to the illusion that you'd be able to get to all those important conversations you were meant to have with children and parents and friends.

She let her mother sleep another ten minutes and even drifted off for a moment herself before snapping awake. She shook Emily gently and her mother opened her eyes and stared out into the room. "How are you feeling?" Hazel asked her.

"Tired," her mother said.

"You got my note?"

"What note?"

"The one I pinned to the back of your door."

"The one that said we have a guest who may or may not be at high risk of being murdered in my house? I got that one."

"She's in no danger. And neither are you. Consider it a good deed."

"I'm not going to be unkind or anything, Hazel. But if she's visited by a maniac, I'm running out the door."

Hazel understood the source of that sentiment and let it go. "We have an appointment with Gary Pass tomorrow morning," she said.

"There's nothing wrong with me."

"Let him decide that. It's been a while since you had a checkup anyway."

Emily stifled a yawn. "This house is too hot."

"It's not hot at all, Mum. It's very comfortable. Feel your own hand: it's cool."

She touched her hand absently. "My circulation was never very good. But this room is warm."

Hazel got off the couch and held her hand out to her mother, who took it and levered herself up. "Go for a walk, okay? Or go work in the garden a little. Get your heart pumping. You're not active enough these days and it's making you sluggish."

"You want me to get a job?"

"Just do something with your time."

] 11 [

Afternoon

Constable Roland Forbes, dressed in a pair of slacks, a windbreaker, and a homburg, drove in a leisurely fashion down RR26 – Queesik Bay Road – in the detachment's only unmarked police car, looking for Eagle Smoke and Souvenir. There were smoke shacks littering the side of the road the moment he turned off the 41a and onto the 26, but the one he was looking for was the largest and brightest of the lot. A neon sign announced its location two hundred metres before he saw it, and the building itself was like a western storefront, with a wooden porch and a wide, triangular gable above it. A wooden eagle with little white bulbs for eyes stuck out of the gable with the legend THE EAGLE above it in bright red neon. There was parking in front, as well as on the north side of the building, and there was a taxi stand with a single cab waiting in front of the store, under a lamppost. A small trailer by the roadway served as a drive-through for cigarettes. The store itself looked more like a saloon than a smoke shop, and although he was in civilian clothes, he entered with caution. His wife, Janice, had often told him that even in the nude, he looked like a cop.

Inside, the store was fairly busy. Directly in front of him was a section of clothing, mostly sweatshirts and T-shirts adorned with the crest of the Five Nations, and a couple of browsers (tourists? On a Thursday? Perhaps in the middle of August) being helped by an Eagle staff member. Deeper in the store was a rack of books on native life and local history, a candy counter, some magazines, and a series of shelves stacked with knick-knacks like you'd find in any Canadian airport: maple candy, little stuffed animals with Canadian flags, Mountie banks, and so on. Behind it were assorted leather goods and a glass case full of fine art made from bone and antler and local stone.

The cigarette part of the business occupied the entire south wall. Forbes had once smoked a pack a day, but he'd been quit of the habit for more than three years. Looking at cigarettes didn't bother him anymore, although corner stores had once given him a frisson. The brands were stacked in cartons, ends out, in little cubbyholes along the wall. The boxes mimicked the look of national brands. The red carton, which looked like it contained his brand,

DuMaurier, was called DKs. He remembered coming down here in the 1990s to get the cheap ones when he was short of cash. There was a row of glass counters in front of the cubbyholes, showcases of cigars, bongs, rolling papers, and pipes. Good to show the product, not so good if it walks out. A man was coming down along the counter, in front of the cubbyholes, letting the ring on his middle finger clack on the metal division between the glass counters. He was tall and moved with jerky movements, as if he suffered from the beginnings of some motor illness, or he was drunk. His skull was shiny and bald. A sew-on badge on his shirt read *Tate*, but Forbes wasn't sure if it was a vintage bowling shirt or a uniform. He wondered if he should have taken some notes already. "Can I help you?" the man asked.

He'd come down here with a general approach in mind. If there was anything illicit available in this place, he wanted the guy to know he was interested. People he personally knew had bought corn liquor, Viagra, painkillers, knock-off perfumes and electronics, native hunting licences, and a lot of other things on reserves. He knew that half the convenience store owners off the reserve came down and bought skids of smokes. They weren't allowed to sell these off the reserve, but many stores sold them under the counter anyway, for cash, and cops turned a blind eye because half the force smoked.

Forbes said, "Don't see what I'm looking for, yet."

"Well, what're you looking for?"

"I'll know it when I see it," he said.

"All right, I hope we got it then." The man walked away. Hard to call the interaction suspicious, he thought. Forbes lingered in the store, trying on some hats. Tate sold a man two cartons, and then the couple who'd been in the front of the store paid for a T-shirt and some magazines. They asked where the casino was, and Tate directed them six kilometres down Queesik Bay Road. "Can't miss it," he said. "Even more neon than us." They all laughed.

Forbes decided to try again. He picked up a pair of earrings. "What kind of gems are these?" he asked the man. The shop was empty now. Maybe he'd get Tate into a deeper kind of conversation.

"Gems, sir?"

"Are they real?"

Tate looked at the price tag. "For thirteen bucks?"

"Ah. I thought it said a hundred and thirty. Never mind then. Hey – you got any idea where I could get something a little more special than this? It's our anniversary, and I brought my wife to the casino for the weekend, but already she's lost a few hundred bucks. I thought someone local might know where I could get her something to cheer her up?"

"I don't suppose she likes cigars, does she? We have some very high-quality Cubans here." He moved down the counter to where the cigars were.

"Well, no, she doesn't smoke at all. But maybe you're going in the right direction."

A door at the back of the shop opened quickly and a man stepped inside. "Earl?" The counterman looked over at him but said nothing. "Ronnie says he needs a fill before – "

"Hold on, for god's sake," said Tate. He apologized to Forbes and strode down the length of the counter to the other man. Although he lowered his voice, Forbes heard him swear at the other man, asking him if Ronnie had told him to come here. The man mumbled something and Tate dug into his pocket and slapped down some keys. The man picked the keys up and scurried off with his head lowered.

Tate returned to Forbes. "Sorry. I'm surrounded by idiots."

"No worries," said Forbes.

Tate looked down into the glass cabinet once more before remembering that his customer had told him he didn't want a cigar. "I'm not sure what you're looking for, sir. Maybe if you just tell me what it is . . . ?"

"Well, I guess I would have seen it if you had it. Someone just told me I could – anyway. Never mind. It's all good."

The counterman was following him down the counter as Forbes made his way toward the door.

"Who sent you here to look for this mysterious *thing*, if you don't mind me asking."

"A total misunderstanding," Forbes said. "You know, I'll just take a pack of cigarettes. Those blue and white ones."

"ID, please," said the man behind the counter.

"Really? I'm flattered."

"We have to ask everyone who buys cigarettes. By-laws."

"Oh," said Forbes, and he got his wallet out. His badge was in the same pocket, but he left it there and flipped open to his driver's licence. Earl or Tate looked at his name and then looked down onto a monitor that was embedded in the countertop beside the row of glass cases.

"Packs or cartons, Mr. Forbes?"

"Just a pack," he said. He paid cash for it. When he crossed back into Westmuir, he pulled over for a coffee and tossed the cigarettes into a garbage can. The entire exercise had been a waste.

Hazel returned to work around one and looked for Wingate, but Constable Eileen Bail buttonholed her in the doorway of her office and bodied her back down the hall. "Jordie Dunn is here."

"Who?"

"Lives three streets over from the Wiest house in Kehoe Glenn. Housepainter, used to work with Wiest on odd jobs or subcontracts, been on the bowling team forever. Says he wants to talk to the detective in charge only."

"You think he knows something?"

"All I can tell you is he's nervous as hell. But like I say, his lips are zipped."

"All right," she said, and she clapped Bail on the shoulder. "I'll try to find out what he knows, I guess."

"You're going to interview him alone?"

"No." Her mind was elsewhere still. "Are you ready?"

"Just waiting for you, Skip."

"Excellent."

They entered the room and Dunn looked up at her anxiously through wire-rim glasses that magnified his eyes very slightly, to disconcerting effect. He was a short, wiry man with nervous hands, and he was hunched over the table in a peacoat, looking like he didn't want to register on anyone's consciousness. "Good afternoon, Mr. Dunn. I'm Detective Inspector Hazel Micallef. You've met Constable Bail, I gather."

"Yes."

"Well, what's on your mind, Mr. Dunn? How can we help you?"

"I wanted to ask you if you thought – if I could ask you a question?"

"Sure."

"Was Henry . . . killed by a bee or not?"

She didn't answer for a moment, just pulled the chair out on the other side of the table and made herself comfortable. "Why would you ask that, Mr. Dunn?"

"I just, you know, sometimes I go out and destroy nests for people. I didn't think bees stung at eleven o'clock at night."

"So what do you think happened?"

Dunn cracked his neck. "I'm saying I don't know."

She opened her notebook and wrote the date. "You two were good friends, weren't you? You knew Henry pretty well."

"I knew him," Dunn said. "We bowled, sometimes we worked together, but we didn't talk on the phone or nothing."

"So not so well?"

The man didn't reply.

Bail said, "Mr. Dunn?"

"Do you think that Henry was murdered?" Dunn asked. "Just tell me that."

"I don't know. But it's possible."

"Goddamnit. I knew no fucking bee stung him."

"Just because you know bees? Or something you know about Henry?"

"Nothing. I don't know *anything*, okay?"

"Do you have any idea what he was doing on the Queesik reserve?"

"I didn't know Henry's business. I'm just here because I liked him, you know? And I had a feeling . . ."

She let him go inward for a moment, then she asked, "Do you have business on the reserve?"

"Me?"

"No, I'm asking the table."

"Sorry. I feel shaky," he said.

"Why?"

"Someone *I* know was murdered!" He turned then, very suddenly, and vomited across the corner of the table and onto the floor. Bail had to leap back a foot or two.

"Whoa, whoa," Hazel said, and she reached over to touch his wrist. "Constable – will you get us – " Bail dashed from the room. "Just calm yourself down, Mr. Dunn." He raised and lowered his shoulders slowly, trying to control himself.

"His poor wife."

"You know Cathy?"

"Everyone knows Cathy."

"Did you know them as a couple?"

"A little." He raised himself up when he saw Bail re-entering with a roll of paper towel and another glass of water. He accepted the water and drank, cleaning out his mouth. "Sometimes I worked for him."

"Do you think it's possible they were unhappy?"

"How would I know?"

"Did you ever see Henry with another woman, a woman you didn't recognize?"

"Why? No."

"What about money. Did he ever need money?"

"Henry?"

"Okay, do you think anyone would want to harm him?"

The man's colour had changed and he was holding his chest. "I think I'm going to be sick again." Hazel got up quickly and grabbed the garbage can from the corner of the room. Dunn snatched it from her.

"I'll get someone to drive you home," she said. She put her hand on his back. "Spend a few minutes calming down before you go. This is my card." She handed it to him and beckoned Eileen to come out. In the hallway, Hazel said, "I want to let him stew a minute. Something more than the behaviour of bees is bothering him." But after a minute or so, he emerged, looking a bit better and ready to leave. "Oh," said Hazel, "I was just going to ask you . . . Cathy told me Henry was going on a call Saturday night. Do you know if he was on a call?"

"I haven't spoken to Henry in" – he thought for a moment – "three weeks? I have no idea what he was doing."

She thanked him and sent him off again. Had he just lied to her? It was another detail in a case that was becoming miasmic in only three days. Forbes was coming in as she was leaving the interview room. "Hey – what'd you find down there?" she asked him.

"Nothing. Nothing at all. The guy sold me some cigarettes."

"Damn it. That was Jordie Dunn. You know him?"

"I think so."

"He threw up."

"Why'd you call him in?"

"I didn't. He came in of his own accord," she said. "He wanted to know if Henry had been murdered."

Forbes made a face. "Did he know Henry was murdered?"

"No. He thought what he'd read in the paper was

far-fetched. He seemed to know something about bees."

"Maybe you should put him on the investigation."

Hazel laughed. Yes, she was probably going to need all the help she could get.

Wingate drove to the cabin on Gannon Lake and unpacked his things. The cabin was one of five that faced the water and trees on a quiet little patch of land. He'd been told two of the other cabins hadn't been filled for the week, so he had the place almost to himself.

He'd bought some groceries on the way up, and he put them in the fridge, aware of his footsteps padding around on the wood floor. Smoked trout, milk, pasta, pecorino, roasted red peppers, plum tomatoes, oranges, butter, a loaf of wholegrain bread, carrots and cucumber, a bottle of red wine, and a head of iceberg lettuce. Enough for the weekend. His plans were to do the minimum amount of physical movement. Beds and chairs only, plus books. He'd brought a couple of detective novels as well as some crummy American celebrity magazines. He also had some sample detective sergeant exams in his bag. (*How varied my inner life is*, he thought.) It was early to be living in hope, but he'd been a detective constable for almost three years. He was thirty-one years old. If all this change he'd gone through since David's death was to be for something, he had to keep moving. He hadn't arrived at a mental space where he was ready to love again, but he sure as hell felt like working.

It had been a little awkward leaving in the midst of an investigation, but if anything happened – and he dreaded and anticipated something happening in about equal measure – he knew he'd hear from Hazel. Maybe, if he was lucky, there wouldn't be a break in the case until next Wednesday. Five days of R&R would be enough, if he could get that.

He hadn't had a break since he arrived in Port Dundas in November of last year. It had been a busy year since, perhaps busier than any he'd experienced in Toronto. It was as if the whole county was undergoing a sea change. You could smell it: the first hints of cold threaded in the fall air, that told you summer was really over, that winter was on its way. It was in the impending changes at the station, with Ray Greene coming back, with whispers of what amalgamation was going to bring. He'd heard rumours that the station was going to be moved to another location. He had to presume it would still be in Port Dundas, but who knew what this commissioner was capable of? The way Hazel talked about Chip Willan, he sounded like a bull in a china shop. Who knew what the future held anymore?

He chopped a bit of lettuce into a bowl, added tomato, cucumber, and some of the smoked trout, and headed out to the lakeshore with one of the magazines. It promised to tell of the tribulations of a Hollywood couple who were having trouble conceiving. The husband was widely understood to be gay, so the story was just part of the ongoing folderol about his viability as a leading man and international sex symbol. Probably the wife was gay too. It had long ago stopped galling him, this masquerade in which the truth was known by everyone who had considered it. He imagined most of the people who were the subjects of this kind of attention were already half insane from believing their own stories.

He took his cell down to the lake.

] 12 [

Friday, August 12, morning

The following morning, Hazel made tea for herself and her mother. Cathy remained asleep in the guestroom, but Hazel had opened the door a crack to ensure the woman was actually there, and she was. Emily had already forgotten that she had her appointment with Dr. Pass in an hour. When Hazel reminded her of it, she made a sour face.

"I used to pinch that man's cheek. Grace Pass says he wet his bed until he was ten – she thought I'd know what to do about it."

"Well, you *were* the mayor."

"I told her to wait until January and put him on an ice floe. And you trust him to prod me with his tools?"

"He's your doctor, Mother. You're supposed to be in his office at nine. So none of your games."

"I'll play whatever games I want to."

"I think you're depressed."

"I get disgusted, distracted, and dead-tired; I do not get depressed. That's you, my dear. My generation never had time to pity itself: we had work to do."

She drove her mother, more or less in silence, to Gary Pass's office, although Hazel turned the radio on halfway there to cut through her mother's fuming. Emily reached over and turned it off. Gary had recently moved his office farther down Pearl Street, to take advantage of the extension of "Mall Row," due to happen some time in 2006. It seemed that developers were taking a gamble on the growth rate in Westmuir, and they were placing a lot of their bets on Port Dundas. In 1995, you couldn't find a grocery store north of Mayfair larger than two hundred square metres, now you shopped in football fields. Down on Pearl there was a giant Canadian Tire that had replaced the little one on Main Street in 2001, a big discount clothing chain, and a bunch of big chain eateries. The seventy-seat That's a Spicy Meatball! was giving Fraternelli's Osteria a run for its money. Everyone called this progress, but no one could say whose progress it was.

Gary Pass's new office was still half in boxes, and his receptionist apologized to them and took them directly into the doctor's private office, where they waited for him to appear. Emily sat stone-faced, looking at pictures of Gary's kids on the walls. Finally, he entered and tried to give both of them hugs, but he had to accept a handshake from Hazel's mother. "So," he said, taking his seat behind his desk, "what's going on?"

"My daughter thinks I'm an old woman," Emily said. "She thinks you have a pill for that."

"We just might," said Pass, smiling a little too warmly. It made Emily sit far back in her chair, like a truculent teenager.

"She's lethargic," said Hazel. "She has no appetite, she falls asleep in the middle of the day in front of the television, and her colour is bad. She thinks it's normal."

"Do you think it's normal, Your Honour?"

"Don't be sarcastic with me, Gary, unless you want to hear some stories about how much your mother worried about your toileting when you were a boy."

The smile faltered, just a little. "I got over that. What can I help *you* with?"

"I eat, I sleep, I celebrate the million little things that make old age such a joy. I'm a little more tired than I used to be. I don't sleep as well at night."

"She's fried all day long," Hazel said.

Pass held a hand up. "Listen, it's time for a checkup *anyway*. Let's do our normal bloodwork, listen to your heart, take your pressure, check your eyes, and so on. If there's anything amiss, it'll turn up. Okay?"

Hazel looked at her mother, who was still staring at Pass, or perhaps through him. "Is that okay, Mum?"

"When I was elected mayor of this town for the first time, you were drinking from a sippy cup," Emily said quietly. "Now you want to listen to my heart."

Hazel and Pass waited for where this thought was going to lead her, but that was it. Pass stood up and squared a couple of file folders with a clack on his desk. "Well, then, why don't we move into one of the exam rooms, and we can get started."

It was eleven in the morning when Roland Forbes arrived back on Queesik Bay Road. Hazel had wanted him to go back right away the afternoon before, but he convinced her he'd been sufficiently noticed by Earl/Tate to warrant just a bit of discretion on their parts. *Good instincts, Gumshoe.* Needing to be around for an extended period of time in broad daylight was going to take a light touch, though. For one thing, he couldn't go back down in the unmarked, in case someone had really taken notice of him. He borrowed Hazel's personal car, instead, a Mazda 3 with eighty thousand kilometres on it. It was a 2003: she'd put all that mileage on her car driving the ten kilometres back and forth from Pember Lake to Port Dundas. It looked like a woman's car, too, a category he thought included all Datsuns and Mazdas.

The main road on the reserve ran within a kilometre of the shoreline of Queesik Bay. The closer the road came to the lake, the more likely someone would be parked there in order to access the water to fish or swim. This was what he'd have to do – locate a lookout on the Eagle in a bend in the road close enough to the water to disguise why he was there. He'd brought a pair of high-powered binoculars, and when he was installed on the shoulder beside a marshy tract of land, he lowered the two rear passenger seats and lay between them on his stomach. With the glasses steadied against the rear window, he was able to see the comings and goings through the front door of the Eagle, although the activity inside was hidden.

Janice had made him a special lunch for his "first stakeout," a cloth lunchbox that zipped shut and contained a rare roast beef sandwich on a baguette, two large red apples, a Thermos of coffee, a big bottle of water, and some whole grain crackers with a hunk of cheddar in cling wrap. He was to text her every hour, or whenever something exciting happened. He stared hard through the binoculars and watched a number of people enter and exit Eagle Smoke and Souvenir. He texted Janice: *Stakeout under way*. An hour later, he texted, *Numerous cigarette and souvenir purchases have been duly noted.* At one o'clock in the afternoon, he forgot to text, and she wrote to him asking what was happening. He wrote back, *Bored silly*.

He'd worked out categories and taxonomies by the middle of the afternoon. General categories were *On foot* and *By vehicle*, and *By vehicle* was subdivided into *Car* and *Taxi*. There were categories for *Alone* and *Not alone*. Some people came out with bags, some not. There was no way of knowing if the bagless people had made purchases or not, but a person buying only a pack of cigarettes wouldn't have a bag.

No one who went in alone came out with anyone. No one who went in with someone left without that person. People who came in taxis left in taxis. Sometimes a person who came on foot left in a taxi. That was the only variation. By three in the afternoon, he was out of food and water and more or less out of patience. He called Hazel. She answered curtly and wouldn't talk to him for more than a few seconds. He hung up and stared out the rear window. Real romantic, a stakeout. He made a checkmark under *On foot* as a man entered the shop from the road.

Hazel dropped her mother off at home. Emily said, "Off to visit the undertaker now?" as she closed the door to the house, but she'd ignored the sniping. The whole time she'd been in Pass's office, the facts of the case were piling up in the hopper of her mind. There was a point when likenesses and dissonances began to coalesce in a case. She didn't have all the hints, all the resonations in place, but there was too much lining up. Not enough for an image to form, but enough to sense one.

Now she was thinking again that it had to do with money. A precise amount. The girl had taken precisely what she'd been owed. But then she'd also torn the office apart looking for something else. The money had been right there in the front hall, in a drawer. Unless that was where she'd looked last. She didn't seem to lack confidence, this girl. Stunning the wife, conking her in the head and ransacking the place wasn't exactly subtle. And why had she left Cathy alive? Had this girl *intended* to kill Henry?

Finally, could there be a connection to the casino? What if Henry had gone back to a forgotten vice and somehow gotten entangled with this girl? When she got back to the station house, she had Cartwright track down a wallet-sized picture of Henry Wiest. She tucked it into her breast pocket, along with a photocopy of the police sketch of the thoughtful-looking young woman.

] 13 [

Afternoon

Hazel Micallef parked her unmarked as close as she could get to the casino's doors so the walk from the car to the entrance would be as short as possible. She went in unmolested and her luck held out. One of the three guards was the man who'd admitted her with Constable Bellecourt two nights ago. "Back for more?" he asked.

"Got a quick meeting with Lee."

"Awesome. I'll let him know you're coming."

"Oh, don't bother. I have to use the, uh, first and I'll just go to the office. I know where it is."

"Is this police business?" he asked.

She wasn't sure how to answer that. Maybe it was better that she was just here as a civilian, albeit a civilian in uniform. "No," she said.

"Well then, without Constable Bellecourt accompanying you, you'll need a member's card. It's a technicality, sorry. You can get one over there at Member Services. Line up on the right."

"Member card, huh?"

"Sorry," he repeated. "Policy."

She stared at him, to no effect, and she went and stood in the line between two other prospective new "members," fuming, and then slid her driver's licence across the desk to a woman with a blank look on her face. She gazed at the card and typed Hazel's particulars in. She pointed over her own shoulder mysteriously, and when Hazel looked at where she was pointing, a flash went off. "Come back in ten minutes," she said.

"Ten minutes? What about my licence?"

"We just do a quick check. Then you get it back. A lot of fake IDs come through here, unfortunately."

To her left, at a porthole in a wall covered in Plexiglas, a man came up and gave his name, and another woman gave him his new membership card and his licence back through a little opening. At least they were thorough, Hazel thought.

For ten minutes, she stood in the vestibule and watched people come and go from the interior of the casino. On one of the walls there were pictures of people holding big cardboard cheques. These people were jackpot winners. She understood that some people had a system for winning jackpots, but they required patience and a big bankroll. Not all of the winners looked happy. Imagine the problem you had if forty thousand dollars wasn't enough to solve it.

After ten minutes, she got in line on the left to pick up her card. A woman in front of her in line collected her driver's licence and her new membership to the casino, an exciting-looking black card with a display of fireworks on the front. Hazel gave her name and got the two cards in return. She pocketed her licence.

The guard showed her how to run the card through the reader. "What, really, is the point of this?" Hazel asked.

"Self-exclusion."

"Self-exclusion?"

"Problem-gamblers exclude themselves from the casino. If they try to run their card through, they get caught and we toss 'em."

"Really."

"Good luck, ma'am," the guard said.

"Yeah. Thanks."

He opened the door for her and she plunged into the air-conditioned scintillance and stood before a bank of slot machines. She headed into them, like a deer into cover, and walked with her head down as she tried to figure out the best path to get to the poker room. She'd decided to head there first, as it was out of the way of the main floor, and from what little she knew about poker, people who played it liked to talk. Maybe she'd hear something. Show around a picture or two and listen. Poker was popular. It was on every other channel, guys with stubble squinting. Maybe someone had seen Henry Wiest in here. Tying him to the casino – without a member's card – would be a very useful bit of information.

The laneway between the machines led directly to the back of the casino. The word POKER was painted over an archway. She walked casually to a cut-out in the wall beside the entry. There was a man in a good suit typing on a keyboard. He saw her approach.

"Officer?"

It wouldn't do to correct him, so she let it stand. "Sorry to bother you . . . Calvin . . . I'm just down from Fort Leonard and I'm looking for this man." She slid the picture across the top of the cut-out. "Unfortunately, this is in regard of a next of kin. I was told I could find him here most afternoons."

"Oh gosh, of course," said the man, and he studied the picture for a moment. Then he passed it among some of the other bosses in the room behind him. Hazel looked around herself subtly, making like she was sopping up the atmosphere as she waited for the photo to make the rounds. There was no one looking at her. Calvin returned with another man, a man in a better suit. No nametag. Absolutely a native. Paydirt?

"I'm head of the poker room, ma'am. I'm here eight hours a day, six days a week. If the man in this picture was a regular, he came in in a dress. But I think I would have noticed that, too."

"Maybe he's a recent regular?"

He beckoned her around to the entrance and then impatiently waved her over the threshold. He pointed at a player. "Today's his third time here. This guy" – he pointed at another table – "was a regular for three years, quit for a year, and this is his first month back. Three guys at the back there, on table six, are playing in this poker room for the first time. I clock everyone in, Officer, and I never forget a face."

"Okay. Point taken. What about other parts of the casino? Maybe you've seen him elsewhere in here."

The man's expression changed slightly. She would have called this new expression *shut down*. "Did he play poker or not?" he said, not entirely unfriendly.

"I thought he did."

"Perhaps your information is incorrect?"

"I suppose it could be."

"Then I've answered your questions."

"Yes, you have."

She turned smartly and left. A little checkmark got inscribed in her mind. But what was it marking? She believed that that man had never seen Henry Wiest in his life. She decided to try the table games. In the open. But what then? Flash images at patrons? That didn't seem like a good strategy if she wanted to get the most bang for her buck.

She followed the wall along the side of the bar and went back into the forest of slot machines, moving casually. At the other end of the casino was the high-stakes room, tucked into a corner. Looked good. She crossed quickly into the elegant-looking room. The carpeting was thicker here, and woven with a rich Indian-culture motif of leaping salmon and bears standing proudly on their back legs. There were only a couple of tables each of blackjack, roulette, baccarat, craps. The cognoscenti didn't sniff at Four-Card Poker or Crazy Twenty-One. They preferred, it seemed, to blow their cash on the classic gambling games.

There weren't too many people here. The roulette was popular, and so was blackjack, but it seemed that throwing the dice was too much work for the rich. Three employees were standing around it, yakking. Baccarat was another universe, with people shouting and making checkmarks on cards. The blackjack tables were like covens of witches: crony old women, mostly Asian, hunched over their holdings. It didn't seem like a place to ask too many questions.

The croupiers at the craps table, however, were bored out of their skulls, and they brightened perceptibly when she approached. "Hello, gentlemen."

A man holding a long rake-type stick said, "Don't arrest us, Ossifer! It's the roulette game gots all the illegal booze!" There were three of them there, and one of the men laughed, but the one on the stool behind the table was having none of it.

"Don't talk like that, Lane. She's an officer of the law. OPS."

"It's okay, boys," she said, backing off comically. "I'm just here on a next-of-kin job. Travers knows I'm here."

"What does Travers know you're here for . . . DI Micallef?" he said, reading her nametag.

"I'm looking for this guy." She handed the picture to the man on the stool. The boss. "Name of Henry Wiest. I understand he plays here sometimes and I'm trying to track him down."

"What'd he do?"

"It's nothing he did," she said. "There's been a death in the family and no one can find him."

"Maybe he's the death in the family," said the rake.

"Lane? Jesus. Ma'am, Detective Inspector, you're free to look around, but this is, you know, this is a service industry and how'd it look if you were some kind of process server looking to serve this guy, your Henry, with a letter from a judge?"

"I never thought of that," said the rake.

"You see?" said the stool. The third man was just watching.

"Yeah, I see," said Hazel, and she took the picture back, thanking them with some kind of a bow and feeling a little stupid. She walked past the roulette table, and she was darned if the croupier didn't give her the hairy eyeball. She was beginning to feel unwelcome.

This feeling only intensified when Commander LeJeune

met her at the edge of the room. She was smiling. "I *heard* you were lurking. What else did we miss?"

"Well, I'm a member now," she said, and she flashed her casino ID at the commander. "I can come and go as I please."

"To the casino."

"So, what are you all, like, hiding in a zebra costume and following me around?"

"Percy, from the poker room, gave me a call. He thinks on his feet, that Percival."

"Do you take me out in chains now and parade me before your people?"

LeJeune frowned at that. "That would be slightly less-than-playful banter there, Detective Inspector. What's got you so mad?"

"Just all the paleface stuff, the fact that an officer of the law, in the same province, incidentally, that you're living in, gets a cross-eyed look from every Indian in the place."

"Oh come on, Detective. You're free to do as you please. *Mi casa*, and so on. And who called you paleface? Did someone actually call you *paleface*?" She laughed heartily.

"I never said anyone called me anything. Don't try to paint me into that corner, LeJeune."

"Oh, calm down. What are you looking for anyway?"

"I didn't find it." She wanted to get out of here, now. There was a small knot of people in attendance around them, not sure if they were listening in on something interesting or not. "If I *had* found something, you'd know."

"Well, good."

LeJeune's even-tempered approach was grating on her nerves. She weighed the value of being conciliatory against trying to piss her off. She decided to compromise. "I presume you accept now that Henry Wiest was murdered."

"I don't accept anything."

"What would you say if I told you we'd had more . . . *activity* since Henry's death?"

"Well, I would need to know what you meant by that."

"Cathy Wiest was attacked. In her own home. Shot with a Taser-like weapon, just like Henry was."

For the first time, LeJeune's expression changed. "By whom?"

"I'm going to take the Fifth on that, Commander. Until we know more. All I can tell you is that our investigation points to *here*."

"It does, does it?"

"What would you have us do? Your own autopsy was wrong and you all seemed satisfied with your own conclusions. But the Wiests are *my* responsibility and after you gave signs of moving on, I thought it wise to run our investigation in the background. I think you would have done the same thing."

"I shudder to think of the consequences of that," said LeJeune. "But fine. You made your choices."

"We did. And when we learn something, we'll let you know."

"Why do I feel I'm being invited to my own party, now?"

"I haven't invited you to anything," Hazel said, and that did it. LeJeune's facade of total Zen collapsed and she narrowed her eyes at the detective inspector. "We did the footwork, Commander. If you want in on this investigation, it's under my authority."

"Cowboys and Indians?"

"Whatever you want to call it."

Now the smile was back. "I'm not sure what I would call this. How about you do your thing, but you check in with me any time you step on reserve land?"

Hazel had no intention of letting LeJeune know anything about her movements. "Absolutely," she said.

Outside, continuing the conversation with LeJeune in her mind, she forgot she'd brought the unmarked and it took her five minutes to find it in the parking lot. She was giving LeJeune a piece of her mind, and the commander was really feeling the heat, holding her hands up, apologizing. *You may be under the illusion that everything is always as it seems, but out here in the REAL world, we know it rarely is.* LeJeune looked horrified, and then the phone on Hazel's hip rang. "WHAT!" she shouted into it.

"Skip?"

"Who is this?"

"It's Roland . . . I'm sitting in your car on Queesik Bay Road? Drinking cold coffee out of a cracked Thermos."

"Sorry, Roland."

"Where are you?"

"Walking to my car about six kilometres away from you."

"You're on the reserve?"

"I am. But I can't talk. Has anything come up?"

"Not really."

"Keep up the good work," she said. She hung up on him and called Constable Costamides. Hazel had sent her down to the Wiest store that afternoon. "What's the news?"

"I don't think I found anything. His manager, Janis Hoogstraat, was in the store and she said Henry had taken the account books home."

"Was that normal?"

"Actually, she sounded surprised when she couldn't find them. Then she remembered he'd taken them home."

Hazel thought about the ransacked office. "I'll see you back at HQ," she said.

] 14 [

Evening

She had an idea where those ledgers were. They were, or had been, somewhere in the mess of Henry Wiest's destroyed office. But could the girl with the stun gun have been looking for *ledgers*? Who would Taser a stranger in her own home and then tear the place apart looking for paperwork? No, the girl's presence in the house had nothing to do with ledgers or cheques. Maybe Henry had brought his accounts home in order to hide an unusual transaction, like those hundreds in that envelope.

Was the girl a dealer? Maybe she'd dismissed the weed in the medicine cabinet too quickly. Was it possible what she saw there was for personal use, but the rest of it was going out the door? And he'd hooked up with a charming urchin at the casino. God, that felt like a long shot. But you could always filter the proceeds of a minor operation like that through a small business.

She still had Cathy's keys and she let herself into the house, hoping that if she heard the bird, it wouldn't terrify her this time, or vice versa. "Helll-ooo, birdie . . . it's Hazel. Don't be scared, birdie . . ."

There were no sounds from the office, and she pushed the door open to find the birdcage was gone. For the second time in this house, she removed her sidearm. So someone had been here between the attack and now and taken the bird. Or it was on the lam.

She was beginning to feel exhausted.

She set aside the mystery of the cockatoo and stepped into the destroyed room. A ledger. That's what she was looking for now, one of those big, hard-covered books with black tape down the spine. Something like that, or else one of those cerlox thingies. She found a yellow file folder that said *Cafe* on its label. She righted the desk chair and sat in it. These were bank statements from the café. Hazel settled in and began to read. She'd never had any idea how much it cost to run a restaurant, or if it was hard to make a living from one. Judging from the statements, it was possible to make money, but there was a lot of overhead, too. It looked like Cathy took in about six thousand dollars a month over her costs. Not a fortune but enough to live on. Some months, it appeared as if she was doing better, but the bottom line didn't change much: on months where she made more money, she also had more expenses. This was to be expected: if you sold more coconut cream pie, you had to buy more coconuts.

She stopped and listened for a moment. Every creak in this house was making her heart race. None of the other papers pertaining to the café seemed to point anywhere. She kept flipping through stapled, paper-clipped, perforated, and folded paper that had been strewn everywhere. A folder full of stale-dated income tax forms. These she flipped through as well, to get an idea of the household's income. For the last five years, it seemed that Cathy was bringing down just about what Hazel thought she would be: ninety thousand, some years closer to a hundred. Running a restaurant was a tough business, but Cathy's had been around for ten years now and she knew how to do it. Henry's returns were here as well, and the store contributed the lion's share of the household income and there was a lot of it. The Wiest name had been good for eighty years. Generations of families had shopped there. It looked like Henry was bringing in over a quarter of a million every year. That was his profit, after supplies, personnel, and other costs. He owned the building. That was an excellent living; it would have kept them both in style and she didn't have to work. But she did, and they lived modestly, and as far as she could tell, they respected, but did not admire, money. Henry had already endowed a countywide hockey trophy. It was top prize in each division of girls' hockey in the region. It was called The Wiest Westmuir Trophy.

There was nothing in this room and there was no way of knowing if there had been anything of interest when the girl went through it.

Hazel went down the hallway to the bedroom and flipped the lights. No other forms of life. The two open dresser drawers were the ones she'd spied last time, both pulled all the way out, the top one concealing the lower. A bloom of clothing burst from the top drawer. She went through the top two drawers, found nothing, and closed them. The bottom one was closed. Hazel opened it and lying almost centred on top of a folded Hudson's Bay blanket was a ledger book. She grabbed it greedily.

She opened the ledger. It was hard to make out what all the cheques might be for; there were so many company names that could have been his suppliers. She ran her finger up the columns, scanning the recent entries. She flipped pages back and forth, comparing dates, checking monthlies, looking for easy patterns. There were many. But just two weeks ago, there had been a cheque made out to cash for ten thousand dollars. July 31, five days before his body had shown up in the Eagle's rear parking lot. Cashable by anyone, but it looked as if he'd cashed the cheque himself. He hadn't wanted to categorize the expense; probably thought he would be able to cancel the debit out and explain it away if his accountant – or the government – ever asked. So what was the ten thousand for? He seemed to have spent forty-five hundred. And then the girl had helped herself to twenty-five hundred. Was this about money or not? What was this bloody girl looking for?

Roland Forbes was starving. It was five o'clock in the afternoon. But he'd be home in time for supper: he'd seen something a few hours back, and then he'd seen it again. Now he was sure. He pushed himself up to his knees and stretched his stiffened back. Sometimes police work was almost comical: you committed to actions that made you look and feel ridiculous. But then, sometimes you got to have this feeling of a job well done. Milled out of the dailiness and normality of the world sometimes you could make out patterns and resonances. He sat behind the wheel moving his head around on his neck in little circles and looked at his tick marks again.

The people who arrived at the Eagle alone, on foot, or in vehicles of their own, were both men and women.

The people who arrived alone on foot or in vehicles of their own and who left with bags were both men and women. Of the men and women who had arrived on foot, and who clearly made purchases, some left in taxis. Some did not.

The people who arrived alone on foot and who left *without* bags were men and women.

Of these men and women, some took taxis. Some of those taxis turned left onto Queesik Bay Road and some turned right, in the direction of Dublin, the edge of the reserve's territory, and Westmuir County as well.

And two men and one woman had arrived in their own cars, gone into the smoke shop, left without bags, and then got into taxis, leaving their cars behind. And all of those taxis had turned right.

2

Saturday, August 13, and Sunday, August 14

] 15 [

She rode the bike under the moon, north out of town, and kept to the smaller roads, just in case. She no longer had the electric gun on her. She'd used the last cartridge on the woman, and there was no hope of getting any more. They had been effective.

It would be easier now with the cash. She'd grabbed some clothing out of the drawers in the bedroom – a blue hoodie, a couple of pairs of socks, and a pair of pants – and when she stopped at a gas station, past midnight, she imagined she looked like any other person out at night. Still, she kept her face hidden within the hoodie, as she bought another map, a bar of soap, and a chocolate bar. She ate the chocolate ravenously as she continued on the bike and felt the sugar swelling in her veins, driving her on. She hadn't felt this alive in a long time.

All along the roads here were quaint signs pointing down lanes to cottages. Little wooden fish or buoys with names painted on them. She went down one, the road turning to gravel, and rode the bicycle all the way to the bottom, where a line of cottages was spread out along the reedy shoreline of a lake. Some of the cottages were lit – these she avoided and carefully walked the bike between two that were quiet and dark. She leaned the bike against one of them and shucked her clothes in the dark before walking down to the water's edge, naked, with the bar of soap in her hand.

The water was cool but not cold; it was getting close to the middle of August now. She'd seen the date on a newspaper: yesterday had been Wednesday, August 10, 2005. Now the lakes would be keeping some of the daytime's warmth in the nighttime. She gratefully slid in waist-deep and dunked herself. When had she last felt this kind of peace? She washed herself from head to toe and even used the soap to wash her hair. It wasn't shampoo, but it would do.

She swam out in the calm, past the ends of the few docks where watercraft were moored. There was plenty of evidence of children here in the form of bathing rings and blow-up toys. She had the feeling that she'd stumbled on to a little community, the kind of place where you could leave your kids for a few minutes and you knew someone would be watching them. You wouldn't even have to ask.

When she'd been a child, her parents sometimes had rented a place like this, usually once a summer, where her father could get away from his desk job in the city. Sometimes they'd go with their neighbours – Anton and his wife, Theodora, and their son, Nicolas, whom she had liked. They'd splash around in the water and make elaborate meals at one or the other's cabin, and then the adults would stay up clinking glasses and telling stories. Larysa thought back on those days, and remembered herself at ten, and twelve, and fourteen, thinking about a boy her age, just one wall away, one wall separating them. She'd been a romantic girl, imagining her wedding, the look on her father's face. Of course she'd marry Nicolas. There was no question of that. She wondered where he was now. Last she'd heard, he'd moved away to school. She'd stayed at home while she studied for her masters in human physiology, and rarely thought of him anymore.

She floated on her back beneath the clear, star-filled sky and the moonlight glinted off the parts of her that stayed above the water: her toes, the tops of her thighs, the little mound of belly, the tops of her breasts. A prickling of pubic hair floated on the surface of the water like tiny fronds. Her body had changed later than most. Her mother had reassured her that the same thing had happened to her when she was a girl, and it took sixteen years for Larysa's body to wake up and change. Now she liked what she saw: she was slender, but not thin, with good legs and breasts, and even her face had changed in the last three years: all the teenaged roundness was now gone. There was an angularity to her face, something longer and more adult had settled into her features. She felt she had a face that had to be taken seriously, a face that would look all right if she smoked with it. But she was training to be a nurse, so smoking was out. At least smoking tobacco was. She was still a kid, after all. No more. She'd never be able to think of herself as young girl again.

When she got out of the water, the air set her skin ablaze with cold and she felt every hair stand on end. She rushed back between the cottages where she'd left the bike and used the sweatshirt to towel off. When she was dry enough, she dressed and huddled, bent over for warmth, against the wall. It was too late now to get anywhere else, and she had to sleep. It would have been possible to use some of Henry's money to get a motel room, but she was too tired to carry on for the night. Instead, she waited, bundled up in her clothing, until she was sure no one had seen her, and then she broke into one of the cottages she was certain was empty, quietly cutting the screen out of a back door with the knife Henry had given her. Then she used it to pry the plate off the base of the door handle and unscrew the mechanism. She was in luck: in a place like this, people didn't worry too much about the security of their doors. She wheeled the bike into the cottage.

Inside it was silent and the air was stale and cool. She was certain that no one was living here right now. She moved through the rooms in the dark and only switched on a light over the bathroom sink. It was enough to see by in the rest of the cottage. It was clear that no one had stayed here recently, and perhaps that meant she could spend a couple of days here, recovering. The fridge was empty, and the beds were unmade, but by the glow of diffused light, she was able to find some bedding, which she threw on the couch. She lay down and closed her eyes, but her mind was still revving from everything she'd done and been through in the last few days, and she could not sleep. By now, she realized, Henry's wife would have gone to the police and her existence would be confirmed. She could have killed Henry's wife. What would another have mattered? They'd be looking for her now. They knew what she looked like.

She couldn't sleep. She got off the couch and looked at her drawn, thin face in the mirror. Too thin. Her hair was straggly. If the police had a likeness of her, this hair would give her away. She got her knife out and took a hank of hair in her fist. She leaned over the bathroom sink and hacked it off. Her hand came free again and again with sheaves of light brown hair. She stared at them in her palm and thought with wonder that the tips of the hairs in her hand had probably emerged from her scalp at a time in her life when there had been no trouble at all except getting her essays in on time. These dead cells had been alive briefly in their follicle and then, like a shadow expressing the passage of time, they had been pushed out. They'd had one of the old movie channels in the living room in Bochko's house. In one of them, a woman said, "Here I was born, and here I died." That was what the body did, measuring out its hours and days in hair and nails. Rings around your years.

Larysa dropped the hair into the sink and took another handful of it up.

When she was done, it looked pretty ragged, but it was different. She didn't look at all as she had before, and that was what mattered.

She woke to a smart rapping on the door. She'd fallen asleep. It was late morning now – perhaps even early afternoon – and someone knew she was in there. She called out, "Just a second!" and threw on her pants and pulled the hoodie down over herself. She put the knife into the pocket in her sweats.

It was a woman standing at the door, a giant thing holding a zippered portfolio the size of a laptop against her chest. Larysa opened the door, hoping she could somehow skate through whatever this was going to be and then go on to plan the rest of her day.

The woman offered a cheery "Hullo!" and stepped into the cottage, looking around. She saw the bedsheets on the couch and turned and frowned at Larysa. "Why didn't you sleep in the bedroom?" She made an angry face. "Are the beds not made? I told the girl to make the beds."

"No, no," said Larysa. "She made the bed. I thought bed was too soft."

"Nonsense," said the woman. "They're Posturepedics. They're new, too." She walked into the kitchen and pulled out a chair. "I'm just here to give you your receipt. I wasn't expecting you until tomorrow morning – didn't you have the place from tomorrow?"

"Oh, well, I get off early and I thought I come up – "

"How'd you get in?" said the lady now, her head just slightly tilted.

"Back door."

She was still for a moment. "You French Canadian or something?"

Larysa hesitated. "Yes. From Quebec."

"I can tell from your accent. Subtle, but I can pick up those kinds of things. Nothing gets past Rita. *Nest pah?*" Larysa laughed. It came out sounding a little strangled. "And you rode your bike in from the train in Port Dundas? Rather desperate to start your vacation!"

They shared a laugh now, the landlady's rough burble covering Larysa's anxiousness. She'd become talented of late in the game of playing along, and luckily the landlady had never met the woman she thought Larysa was.

"Hubby's coming up with your daughter?"

"Ah, she has school early tomorrow, and they come up after."

"Funny, you said in your email that she had already finished her summer school," the woman said, looking up.

"I mean, *ballet* school."

"Ah, of course. Who has school on a Saturday in the middle of summer, anyway?"

The lady tore a thin white piece of paper out of a receipt book and handed it to Larysa. "Well, that makes it official. You'll get the damage deposit back by mail once we've checked everything." She stepped forward to give Larysa the paper slip and took the opportunity to look around. "Did you bring *anything* with you?"

"My husband is bring everything we need."

"Milk? Butter?" Larysa shook her head. "Well, this is silly. Do you have money, at least?"

"Of course."

"Well, give me ten minutes and I'll drive you into town. Ridiculous sitting in the dark without so much as a cup of tea and a piece of toast."

"Oh, don't worry about it," she said, waving the woman away in as friendly a fashion as she could muster. But she was going to have to get out of here right now. No more resting, which was unfortunate, because her energy was still building. She needed more time to plan, but the landlady was insisting on being helpful.

"Splash some water on your face and meet me outside in five minutes, young lady. What's your name, again?"

"Kitty," she said, and she went to get ready to be seen in the world.

The town was called Compton Mills. She remembered seeing the name on the map. Gilchrist wasn't far away. When the landlady was deep in the frozen-foods aisle, Larysa told her she was going to use the washroom, and she walked back out to the parking lot. It was the kind of place where people just left their car keys in the ignition, or tucked up under the visor. It was a pity because back at the cottages the children from other cabins had already filed out, laughing and fighting, and the water would be full of them. Just an hour among children would have done wonders for her, and she could have had the cottage for the whole day. But she had to get going now. She had not been careful enough. There would be too many people looking for her now.

] 16 [

Saturday, August 13, morning

He called her at home at 5 a.m. He'd been awake since before dawn. "James?" she said when she heard his voice on the other end of the line. "Is everything okay?"

"I couldn't sleep. Thinking about the case."

"Nothing is happening, James. You're on vacation, remember?"

"I'm not so good at it. How's your mother?"

"Imperfect."

"What did Forbes discover?"

She squeezed her eyes together; she wasn't quite awake. Her body could manage to stay asleep until six most mornings; five was still too early. "Something about the taxicabs down there."

"What about them?"

"Like I said, Detective, I'll be in touch if there's anything you need to know about. Right now, your orders are to tan and drink, okay? And stay out of my way."

"I'll have my phone with me," he said.

Hazel made it to the station house by eight, around shift change. There were cars coming in and out of the rear lot of the detachment, more than usual for a Saturday morning. As she got out of the cruiser, she flashed on the image of Wiest's pickup parked well behind Eagle Smoke and Souvenir and wondered if he'd been one of the special passengers. Then she wondered if possibly everything that they had seen at the Eagle was unrelated to what had happened to Henry Wiest. What if this girl was pregnant, what if this had to do with paternity, and they were meeting to settle something? How well had he known this girl? Another wild guess to file away.

She was at the back door of the station house, and she could see three officers standing with their back to her at the end of the hallway through the door's windows. They were looking into the pen. Something was going on.

She entered and heard a strong, low voice coming from the pen. She took her cap off and held it at her side as she walked down the hall. A scrabbling sound caught her attention from inside the photocopy room halfway down the hall and she saw the Wiest bird sitting on its branch inside its cage beside the paper cutter. She had time enough to say, *What the fuck is . . .* to herself before she came to the end of the hallway and Melanie Cartwright stepped directly in front of her. "Hi."

"Uh, hi. What's happening?"

"Willan is happening."

Hazel's expression turned dark. "Is he here?"

"Not exactly."

She strode down the hall toward the pen, and when she turned the corner and came into the big, open area, she saw Ray Greene sitting on the edge of a desk and many of her officers standing around listening, some with looks of bewilderment on their faces. Greene saw some of the staff look past him, and he turned and there was Hazel standing at the back of the pen. His hands, which had been busy in the air as he spoke, froze and settled in his lap.

"Detective Inspector," he said.

"Mr. Greene." He winced slightly at the lack of protocol and got up to offer his hand. She took it and shook perfunctorily. "My punishment?"

"If you choose to look at it that way."

"I choose."

He turned his attention back to the rest of the pen and said, "That'll be it for now, everyone. We'll be sorting out various details in the weeks to come, but you've got nothing to worry about. In fact, as I said, you'll be getting *more* resources, not fewer. You'll have what you need."

He pushed off the desk and walked past Hazel into the hallway she'd come down.

"Let's go to your office," he said.

She followed him. "You want me to clean it out now?"

"Look, Hazel, you've got your hands full. With one body and an attack on someone else, this is a big case now. Commissioner Willan thought you could use me."

"*I* could use *you*?"

He waved his hands around at the mess on her desk. "I can make do in the pen for the time being."

"Are you looking forward to being a mall cop, Ray? Because that's what Willan is dreaming of. A big shiny Cops 'R' Us for the whole county."

"Chip Willan is going to bring OPS Central into the twenty-first century, Hazel. You should come along."

"Are all the kids doing it?"

He shook his head and decided to sit behind her desk. He was done trying the soft landing. "Why don't you just do the rest of your script, Hazel? Then we'll do mine, and then you can call me some names, and this'll be over and done with."

"Do you think I'm the villain in my script, too?"

He sat up straighter and leaned over the desk. "I have no *idea* who you are right now. It would be interesting to know that. It might help me to understand what, exactly, has been going on up here for the last week or so."

"I'll save it for the judge, Ray. In the meantime, Willan's up to his shoulder in your fundament and he's dying to work your mouth, so talk."

She noted the faint, upward curving of his lips.

"Fine. You've got two attacks, some kind of insane woman armed with a stun gun, you've got Roland Forbes buying cigarettes again, and a detective on vacation in the midst of a huge case. Have I left anything out?"

"Looks like you have your sources."

"I thought you might have some details to add to my outline.

"Nope," she said. "See you later." She made to leave, but he spoke, in a firm tone, to her back.

"You're free to go when I'm completely debriefed."

"You're debriefed," she said. "Girl kills man, cop pretends to smoke."

"Is that what your report says?"

For the first time, she locked eyes with him. This man had been her colleague and then her deputy. A good man, a solid detective. But never much of an imagination, and, she even thought it then, a little long in the tooth. This was what Willan was replacing the dinosaurs with. And *she* was supposed to report to *it*.

"You'll have my report when it's done, Detec – what do I call you, anyway?"

"Hazel . . ."

"What's your rank, Ray?" He didn't answer her. Superintendent, probably. She pushed her tongue hard against her upper teeth. "Will I get a memo?"

"We're getting six new bodies in here, Hazel. More

resources. At least one more detective, and our own forensics guy."

"You mean someone's losing six bodies."

"Port Dundas will be the hub for all of Central."

"Well, good for Port Dundas, then. See you later." She went to the door. "Did your script end this way?"

"Sort of."

"No, it didn't." She was already halfway out. "I didn't call you an asshole."

] 17 [

It was best to stay to the sideroads. It was a strange feeling to drive; she hadn't been behind the wheel of a car for more than two years. The feeling of freedom was incredible. She could just point the thing south and be gone. But she had a job to finish, and she was intent on seeing it done now.

When she got to Gilchrist, she drove the car down a gravel road and parked it in what appeared to be an unused garage back from the road a ways. The garage door was stuck in an open position and a rusted boat launch took up a third of the space. She was able to wedge the car in alongside. From beyond the falling-down little building, the car was in shadow. It didn't matter now, though, if anyone found it: she was mere kilometres from her destination, and once she finished her business there, she'd be gone. No one would be able to trace the car to her, even if they did find it.

This was the backcountry. No more cottagers this deep in: two hundred lakes of varying sizes seemed to be enough. That's about how many she counted within a two-hour drive of that big city on the map: Toronto. She'd been there once for a couple of days, and she thought now of the pleasure of going back there. There was nothing keeping her here after this. And if Terry didn't have what she wanted, Sugar would. Mr. Sugar would have it for sure. She had to leave him for last, to be safe – he was pretty close to where she'd started – and she'd figured him for it all along. But Terry, just in case. Maybe it was Terry. She'd always thought that he had no idea what he was actually involved in, he was that dumb. He was soft and dumb and he'd take whatever he was offered. And he didn't seem like a guy with much money, anyway. It was probably a waste of time. Still, it could be him. If it was, then she'd be able to stay away from Mr. Sugar altogether. That would be a good thing.

She recognized Terry's driveway, it was the one with the wooden cowboy silhouette whose arms spun in a breeze. It had taken her less than half an hour to walk here from where she'd stashed the car. She knocked on his door.

"Hi, Terry," she said.

He cast his eyes out wildly beyond her, looking for something he didn't find. "What are you doing here?"

"I come to say hello."

He held his teeth together tightly. "I'm not alone, f'r chrissake."

"No matter! Invite me in."

A woman's voice came from the hallway. "Terry? Who is it?" She arrived beside him. This would have to be the wife. "Hello there!"

"Hello, madam," said Larysa. "I'm Kitty."

"Kitty, what a lovely name. Come in. Are you one of Terry's students? I mean, *Mr. Brennan's*? Isn't that so hard to say? Come in."

Terry stood aside and she entered the house and walked through the little front hall to what Terry had told her was called an "atrium" the last time she'd been here, more than a month ago. "A very beautiful house," she said.

"Thank you," said Mrs. Brennan. Soon she would say, "Call me *Bridgit*," or whatever, and then they would be on a first-name basis. Mrs. Brennan came around her and led the way into her kitchen. "I don't meet a lot of Terry's students. You must be in grade twelve?"

She laughed. "Oh, I'm older. Mr. Brennan is tutoring me. I call him Terry, too."

Mrs. Brennan's smile did not skip a beat. "Ah, that's right. Terry mentioned he might have to work late on and off because of you! But I didn't realize he'd started."

"I make time during the day," said Terry lightly. "During lunch I fit in half an hour, and Kitty stops by my office."

"How excellent. Sit. Come and sit." She dropped the two of them off at the kitchen table. Then Larysa saw her make a face. Her eyes and mouth sucked up into the middle of her features and she was saying, "*Ooo, ooo!*" – what on earth was she doing? But then she saw it was a baby. A baby on the counter in its little rocker chair. She hadn't known that Terry was a father. A baby with a baby. She stared at him while his wife fussed over his offspring. It looked like all of the muscles in his face had gone slack.

Terry Brennan mouthed, *What the fuck?*

Mrs. Brennan put on the kettle. Now Larysa saw the fat pink fist writhing above the edge of the chair. "How old is baby?" she asked.

"Five months. A total tiger. Terry can barely lift him." Larysa walked around the table to the counter. Terry's eyes widened. The baby was roiling in his little bouncy chair, all arms and legs and belly and diaper. He was naked except for his diaper. He looked like a raw chicken wrapped in a hand towel.

"Look at him go."

"He's fulla rocket fuel!" said Mrs. Brennan. She was a pretty woman. Young, probably mid-thirties. How long had she been in the picture? And what did she see in dumb, slow Terry? Larysa smiled to herself. The only thing anyone *could* see in Terry. He was malleable. And she'd given him a *son*. "You hungry, Kitty? I can always make you a quick toastie."

Larysa laughed. "What is a toastie?"

"Bread, cheese, toaster oven. Or bread, tuna, cheese, toaster oven. What is your accent?"

"From Paris," Larysa said.

"I thought you sounded French."

"Sometime people say I talk like Eastern European, but people with good taste always know I am French."

"*Je parle un peut!*" Mrs. Brennan said.

"Oh, very nice," Larysa said. "You are a very good French speaker!"

"*Merci.*" The kettle boiled, and Mrs. Brennan turned her attention to it. Larysa looked back down on the baby. Just beyond the upper rim of the bouncy chair, she saw Terry sitting utterly still in his chair, his eyes on her, his mouth frozen in a half-made expression. "So what does Terry tutor you in?"

"Law," said Larysa.

"Law?" said Mrs. Brennan. "Since when do you teach law, Terry?"

"Law of *averages*," said Larysa.

"Oh, *math*! That's not law."

"Law of *jungle*."

"Oh, ho," said Mrs. Brennan now, but there was finally something there, Larysa heard it, the first inkling in the woman's voice. She moved away from the preparation area and back toward her baby.

"I like a cheese toastie," Larysa said. Mrs. Brennan leaned over and smelled the baby.

"Oh my, what a rude little baby!" she cried. "Filling his diaper in front of a guest!" The baby had smelled neutral, even nice. But Mrs. Brennan scooped him up and took him out of the room. The instant she was gone, Brennan sprung to his feet and had her forearm twisted up in his fist.

"What the heck are you doing here? How'd you even get here?"

She wrenched her arm away from him. "Tell her come back, Terry. Baby can stay in the other room. But she should be here for this, no?"

"I don't know what you want, but whatever it is, it can be dealt with the next time I see you."

"Sure. You think you ever see me again after today? You're *very* not smart, Terry." She showed him the folded hunting knife. "Tell her come in, or I put this into your eye right now and cut it out. Then I go find the baby. Cut baby *up*."

"Hey, Colleen! Come back in here."

"I'm just settling the baby!"

"The baby better wait."

Colleen crept back into the room. "Whatever this is, I don't need to be any part of it."

"It's nothing," said Terry. "She just wants a refund because I'm not, I guess I'm not the best tutor for her specialty. How much is the refund, Kitty?"

Then Colleen saw the folding knife in Larysa's hand. She took a moment to categorize it and put her hand over her mouth.

"She's going to hurt little Stephen!"

"No, she's *not*," said Terry Brennan.

His wife stood there on one side of the kitchen counter, trapped in her terror. Larysa said, "Terry have something which belongs to me."

"Absolutely," he said. "Just remind me again what the figure is?"

"Oh, Terry," Larysa said, laughing brightly. Of course he didn't have it. But she wasn't done. She was here now. She said, "Are you sure? Don't you pick up something of mine?"

"Ah! Ha ha!" Terry Brennan said, urgently remembering something that wasn't there. "That! Of course, I forgot I had that. Now where did I put it?"

The blade came out with a metallic *whack* and instantly she had the point at the side of his neck. Mrs. Brennan shrieked very briefly, like a gun going off. Larysa grabbed a handful of hair from the back of Terry's head and pushed the tip of the knife in, bending his throat back. He swallowed. A little dot of blood appeared under the point. "Go and bend down on the counter. I am moving you there. Careful."

"I have whatever you need," he said.

"Terry?" said the wife quietly. "Who is she?"

"She's from the special needs group, Colleen. It's gonna be okay. I know her. Right, Kitty? We're going to talk about this."

"Yes, absolutely we talk," she said. Brennan was braced against the countertop, his arms at his sides, and she held the knife against the softness under his chin. "Tell Colleen Brennan what it is you have."

"Please, Kitty."

"Tell her what it is. Then you take me to it, and this is over. I go."

"Terry, you can tell me," Mrs. Brennan said, her voice wet and anguished. "It doesn't matter what you've done. Just tell her what she wants to know and we'll deal with the rest of it."

"Your wife is beautiful," said Larysa, "she has good thought. You should listen to her."

The baby began squalling in another room.

"Stay," Larysa said when Mrs. Brennan twitched. "He is almost ready for tell you."

The eye that faced her, in the side of Terry Brennan's head, roved wildly, like a spooked horse, and he said, "I'll tell her about it all, Kitty, I'll confess it. But I still don't know what it is you think I have . . ."

"I know," she said, "I know you don't have it."

"Good."

"And I know you will tell her everything."

"I will! I will!"

"Tell me what, Terry?" said the wife, and Larysa pulled him up off the counter, and then, her hand still on his shoulder, she extended him backwards and drove the knife deep into the middle of his back. This was a knife for quartering game. Brennan collapsed like someone had cut his strings, gasping air inwards the whole way down. She turned to his wife, who was as motionless as a photograph.

"How do you know if a man is telling you the truth?" Larysa asked her.

Colleen Brennan's stunned eyes ticked over to the stranger. "What?" she said.

Terry Brennan was quivering against the back of the counter. "How do you know when a man tells the truth!" she shouted.

"No, no, no – " the wife gibbered, and Larysa put the tip of the knife into her husband's throat and pulled it across.

"Answer is: you don't."

] 18 [

Mid-afternoon

Hazel sent a text to Wingate – she figured a text might buy him a few more minutes of vacation than a call would – and put her phone back in her pocket as she went through the door to the sound of wailing. It was almost too raw to be human, and she realized it was a baby. The man's wife was sitting at the kitchen table, trying to calm the infant, but there'd been too much sudden activity all around him and there would be no settling the baby down.

Mrs. Brennan rocked him in her arms, but she was silent, her eyes focused on something in another room. Spere's SOCO team was already there when Hazel arrived, and it was ranging throughout the house, collecting samples, taking photographs, bagging items, dusting, swabbing, logging. When she came into the kitchen, Mrs. Brennan looked up at her briefly, confused. A PC from Fort Leonard had arrived before she or Spere's crew had gotten here, a woman whose nametag said Quinn. The movements of the SOCO officers were ghostly in the background.

The girl had been here. This was all Hazel knew. But she had a name now: Kitty. The man had called her Kitty. She'd appeared at the house around three in the afternoon and half an hour later, she was gone, and Terry Brennan had been medevacked to Toronto Western for emergency surgery. But no one thought he'd make it.

The baby had settled a little now, his snuffles coming spasmodically, and Mrs. Brennan was whispering to him and stroking his head.

"Mrs. Brennan?" Hazel said softly. "Do you think we can talk now?"

"I thought she was going to . . . kill Stephen."

"How do you think your husband knew this Kitty?" Mrs. Brennan looked up, startled. Hazel put a hand on her knee. "Colleen? It's okay. There's no need to be afraid."

"When is the hospital going to call?"

"Soon. They're doing what they can. Was Terry involved in anything unusual you know of?" she asked, moving deftly over her omissions. "Or was he absent from the home a lot for unexplained reasons?"

"No . . . no. Terry taught math at Gilchrist Middle. She said she was a student of his. That he tutored her."

"Do you think that's true?"

"No," she said quietly, wonderingly.

"Mrs. Brennan, did he ever go to Queesik Bay? You know, the reserve? It has a casino on it?"

The woman was clearly still thinking of something else, and her eyes drifted over to one of Spere's SOCO crew, who was dabbing at a countertop beside her with a cotton-tipped swab. He examined the end of the swab and put the whole thing into a ziplock bag.

"Mrs. Brennan?"

"I don't know. I didn't keep tabs on him. Maybe I should have kept tabs on him." The baby's mood had changed and now he was grabbing at the necklace that hung down between Mrs. Brennan's breasts. She smiled at him with a worried expression. "Can someone call the hospital?"

His pulse, she'd been told when she called, had been thready at the crime scene, his vitals almost non-existent. Spere's team was packing up. "She didn't go upstairs, is that right?" Spere asked the stunned wife.

"No, no. I think they were in the kitchen the whole time."

"All right, then," he said. When he walked past Hazel, she smelled hot mustard on his breath.

"I think he's getting hungry," Mrs. Brennan said, and for a moment, Hazel had thought she meant Howard. "Can I feed him?"

"Of course," said Hazel, and she watched the woman going through the motions of putting the baby into his bouncy chair on the countertop. She opened her freezer door and took out a couple of colourful frozen pucks off a cookie sheet, one green, one tan-coloured.

"I make his food," she said to no one in particular. "It's better for him."

She put the little pucks into a bowl and stuck the bowl in the microwave. Hazel's phone buzzed on her hip but only once and then it stopped. When Colleen's back was turned to get the food, she quickly unhooked it to see if she'd missed a call. But it was a text message from Wingate: *IS HE ALIVE?* . . . She put the phone away. Janice Brennan was staring at her. "Was that the hospital?"

"No . . . no, something else. I'm sure they're doing everything they can." She moved to the other side of the counter, dismissing PC Quinn with a look, and Mrs. Brennan began to feed the squirming child. "Colleen . . . you said the girl wanted something from your husband. Did she say what it was?"

"No. Terry said he didn't have it and the girl said she knew he didn't have it, but then . . . then she – " She mechanically slotted the spoon into the baby's open mouth, slipping in little loads of what Hazel thought was probably peas and chicken. She remembered briefly the pleasure of sating a baby's hunger, how easy it was to know what they needed. "You think Terry was in trouble?"

"What kind of trouble?"

"Did he have debts? Did he have any . . . habits that were unusual?"

"I don't know. I don't think so." The woman was keeping her mind focused on the baby, but she was in shock. She held the spoon too far from the baby, and he, in turn, was watching her very closely. Finally, she put the spoon in his mouth.

Hazel asked her: "Can you think of *any* reason a strange girl would come into your house and – "

Suddenly, the other woman dropped the baby's bowl and spoon onto the countertop and gripped its edge, as if to stop herself from spinning out into space. The baby caught its breath, his hands shooting up in front of him, motionless. Then he opened his mouth and an unholy, piercing scream came out of him.

"I don't know! I don't fucking know any fucking thing at all! Okay?" She breathed willfully, trying to regain control. The baby had lapsed into the silent part of a deep, terrified infant squall, the silence that presages the heartsick-making wail that follows. They both waited it out, and Mrs. Brennan took the baby out of his chair and held him. "I don't want to know who my husband is right now. If he's a low-life, lying, cheating, sleazeball, it can wait. I just want to know what's happening to him."

"All right," said Hazel, holding up her hands in surrender. "I'm going to call the hospital in one minute. I, I was told the ambulance chopper will be putting down" – she looked at her watch in a sort of vaudeville gesture – "right about now. I can call down in, five minutes. But anything that might help us get a jump, Mrs. Brennan, for instance, do you have any idea – *any idea at all* – what might have connected your husband to this Kitty? Even a hunch?"

"Well, I guess he was screwing her, wasn't he? And she showed up looking to see how much her silence was worth to him. He was going to tell me . . . but then she . . ." Mrs. Brennan trailed off. "She cut him anyway."

Not money, Hazel thought again. And whatever it was, the girl was still hunting it. Her phone buzzed again. Just once. She asked to use the bathroom, and once the door was closed behind her, she unhooked it and looked at the screen. It read, *Patient DOA*. She looked at herself in the mirror. It was fixed to the wall. She forwarded the text to Wingate.

On her way out, she pulled Quinn aside and quietly told her to check the contents of the Brennans' medicine cabinet.

Back in her cruiser, she phoned Forbes. The young fellow was cottoning to the job. He'd rented a car for today's stakeout, to keep his identifiability low, and simply drove back and forth along Queesik Bay Road every twenty minutes or so, stopping here and there, at different distances from the Eagle, and noting his impressions. He told her there was increasing activity as the day went on: a lot of people buzzing around, a lot of traffic. It was now a week since Henry Wiest had told his wife he was going out to pick up some filters in Mayfair and had parked there, many kilometres from where anyone would have expected him to be, and been murdered. The case had put on flesh over the intervening week, and with the stolen vehicle and Brennan's death, she felt that certain energies were gathering. The girl, this Kitty, had come out into the open. What did it mean? Was she done? Maybe, Hazel thought disconsolately, the case was already over.

What had happened in Queesik Bay a week ago had happened among a swarm of tourists coming through the region, as they did every weekend of the summer. Perhaps Henry or Kitty had used the cover of the crowds to conduct whatever business had been between them. If so, maybe the investigation could use the same cover to discreetly track one of those taxicabs. The traffic in the countryside on a mid-August weekend could be good camouflage for an unmarked to follow a taxicab. She called Wingate to ask him what he thought of that. He said it sounded risky. "But worth it?" she asked.

"It could be. As long as you're discreet."

"I'm the soul – "

"Don't even try. Just have an escape route in case anyone starts acting suspicious, okay?"

"Don't worry about me."

"I'll have the cell."

She called Forbes in and drove her own car, the Mazda, directly to Mayfair and then tracked back up through the reserve toward the centre of the settlement. She passed the casino on her right and carried on until she reached the Eagle about six kilometres away, toward the Westmuir County town of Dublin.

When she got to the smoke shop, she parked her car exactly where Henry Wiest had, to test the universe, but also to see if the appearance of a car in that area was a signal to anyone. She stayed inside five minutes, looking alternately through the windshield into the woods and backwards in the rear-view. Her car, stopped where it was, appeared to spark no one's interest at all, so she backed up and parked halfway between the road and the woods. She was more or less to the side of the shop now. The taxi stand was in front of the store, but both taxis were out on errands. The stand, with a lamppost beside it so it would be visible at night, was in an oil-slicked patch of gravel behind a low brick wall that enclosed an oval of grass and flowers.

She hadn't seen any cameras around the back of the building, but there was one on an overhang that covered the long porch in the front of the shop. It had a view of the parking area she was coming out of, and she saw, as she came around the front, there was another camera above the door and pointing toward the road. None of this had been on RC Bellecourt's report. It would have been useful to see those tapes. Why hadn't they been collected? There were so many oversights in the reserve's investigation that it made her furious.

She drove out to the position Forbes had taken when he'd started his surveillance on the smoke shop. It was a good spot, shielded from the road by trees, but with a clear line of sight to the Eagle. She continued to watch people file in and out of the store. It was coming up on five o'clock in the afternoon now, and she realized she could have a long wait in front of her. She had half a Tim's club sandwich on the seat beside her, having been unable to stop herself from consuming the first half an hour earlier. With any luck, she'd see the sign she was waiting for before she got too hungry and then she'd be really grateful for it when she got to it. Fifteen minutes later, she'd eaten the other half of the sandwich and she was still hungry.

Her instinct every time she reached this juncture, when the temperature of an investigation went up beyond her comfort zone, when she knew time was flowing through her hands like water dashed from a bucket, was to *push*. Something seemingly immovable would have to be moved. And she had always been like this; she shared this trait with her mother, this inability to wait and see, to let things develop. She wanted to drive back to Eagle Smoke and Souvenir and lean on this Earl/Tate guy. *Just come out with it. A guy died in your parking lot a week ago. Something's going on here. Or not. But you're going to convince me one way or the other tonight*. She saw herself gripping the front of his shirt and yanking him forward over the countertop. This aggression was a good trait to have in her line of work. But if she braced the man who seemed to be in charge in there, she might never find out who Kitty was. And she wanted to know who Kitty was.

At six in the evening, just when she was getting so hungry that she almost left, she saw a man in a quilted, shiny black windbreaker get out of his car and walk into the Eagle. Two minutes later, he left the shop and walked directly to the one taxi that was waiting at the stand. There was something about the way the man walked that struck her. She got her binoculars out to look closer. When the man got into the back seat, he passed something small and shiny to the driver, and the driver looked at it, handed it back, and made a right-hand turn out of the driveway. To the north.

She let the cab get a good three hundred metres down RR26, and then she pulled out of her hiding place and got in behind it.

] 19 [

Early evening

Hazel adjusted her speed to keep a comfortable gap between herself and the taxi. She could just make out a head in the back seat, a wiry nest of black hair. The passenger's hand kept coming up in front of him and it took Hazel a while to realize he was pushing his glasses up on his nose. A nervous gesture.

She was tempted to pass the cab and look, but by then it was turning off the reserve road and toward Highway 41a. The 41a was one of the county's prettiest drives: it curved east-west along the north shore of Queesik Bay on its way to Westmuir's main artery, the 41. But before the cab got to the 41, it turned north again and followed Sideroad 1, which was a road laid down by a surveyor some hundred years ago. This sideroad, and many like it, did nothing more than divide fields into long tracts.

Sideroad 1 was straight and flat, although she was sure the curvature of the earth made it impossible to see farther than a few kilometres ahead. The taxi was driving at a leisurely pace between the deep green of the corn and soy fields, crossing the roads that ran east-west up through there, the "lines" on which the old farmhouses and homesteads had been built with the fields in front and behind. She stayed more than a kilometre behind and watched them pass: Seventeenth Line, Sixteenth Line. At the Ninth Line, the cab turned right again, heading east. This was an epic drive and she made herself fall farther back, to the point where she could no longer see the tires of the taxi. She watched it moving off east along the Ninth Line, and she reached the road herself and made the turn. In the distance, she was sure she saw another car, coming up another sideroad. Then she realized it was stationary, sitting in profile, below the Ninth Line. A long, black Mercedes. She kept up. The cab was still a few kilometres ahead of her. Before it reached the sideroad with the Mercedes parked on it, the black car pulled out and drove in front of the taxi by about fifteen hundred metres. Hazel lengthened her distance again. She passed the sideroad where the car had been waiting and, up ahead, saw it turn down another one, leading the taxi down another sideroad. The fields were lush and high here, mature soy undulating like the surface of a green sea. Less than a hundred metres below the Ninth Line, a stand of trees extended irregularly into the field behind. Judging from the narrowing serpentine of trunks, the copse occupied a dried-up creek that no one had ever cleared. It was a vertical burst of green above the swaying heads of soy. That's where they were going. Into trees? She decided to watch the rest from a distance; she made the next left-hand turn and stopped the car. Anyone looking behind at her would conclude she was driving away on a road to the north and dismiss her as a danger. The soy wasn't high enough to hide her, but she felt that her presence pointing the other direction wouldn't disturb the scene. She got out of the car and stayed low as she came around the back of it. She stilled the binoculars against the bumper.

The black Mercedes had stopped near the trees and the taxi was driving past it a couple of car lengths. Then it stopped and discharged its fare, who got out on the left side of the cab, his back to Hazel. He stepped forward, but she already knew who he was. The man went to the side of the road and stepped down off the shoulder. She could only see him from the waist up. He was walking toward the trees. Then he vanished into them. Nothing happened. Both the cab and the Mercedes remained where they were. Then, a moment later, a man and a woman emerged from the woods. They walked calmly up to the road and got into the taxicab. The black car made a three-point turn and came back out to the Ninth Line. The taxi followed behind it. There was someone with long hair driving the Mercedes.

He was wearing a ballcap. Hazel got back into her car and drove up to the Tenth Line. She dialled Wingate's cell.

"Where are you?"

"I'm driving west along the Tenth Line. You're not going to believe who I just saw."

Constable Forbes was standing at the front counter of the detachment when a man he recognized came into the station house.

"Aren't you supposed to be on vacation?" he asked.

"I'm refreshed."

Forbes looked at his watch. "You've been gone for forty-eight hours. I thought you were taking the week off."

Wingate lifted the counter flap and walked through. "Is she back yet?"

"She is."

"You come along, okay?"

He knocked on Hazel's door, and entered on "Come!" and Hazel looked up. She'd been tapping on her keyboard. "I just talked to you."

"I know. I can't look at the water anymore. What are we doing?"

"I'm looking up an address on the MTO site."

"Guys?" said Forbes. "Whose address?"

"I just followed one of the taxicabs, Roland, one of the cabs *you* brought to my attention. It drove into the fields above Queesik Bay and let a man out in the middle of nowhere, beside a little grove of trees. You know how the forest pops up here and there in those fields?"

"Yes."

"The cab let Jordie Dunn out. And Dunn walked into the trees and vanished."

"Well, he lives in Kehoe Glenn, doesn't he?"

She put her finger against her screen and began writing. "Right at the entrance to town." She looked up at them.

"Should we inform Superintendent Greene?" Forbes asked.

"Do whatever you need to do," she replied. "I'm out of here."

"We'll wait for news," said Wingate. "You better go."

Jordie Dunn lived in one of the two-storey apartment buildings at the entrance to Kehoe Glenn, cheap living quarters for locals, the Lorris Arms. After his nervous appearance at the station house, she'd asked around about him and discovered he was an irregularly employed handyman with no family. His connection to Wiest was as he'd said: he sometimes came along on a job or Wiest tossed him a little gig. She understood that his specialty was wiring and plumbing. Dunn had also declared bankruptcy in 2002. As far as she knew, he'd been living in the Lorris Arms since 1999, which was when he'd moved into the environs. She didn't know where he'd come from, and an inquiry to the Ministry of Transport hadn't come up with any addresses before Kehoe Glenn.

On her way down, Wingate had called to say they would tell Greene that they were still collecting information. News about Dunn could wait another hour or two, until she'd had a chance to talk to him. Once she got Dunn back to the station house, Greene could sit in on the update. She pulled off the road that led under the gateway at Kehoe Glenn and went around the back of the Lorris Arms. She had no idea what kind of car Dunn would be driving. It was possible, if he'd made a purchase in those trees, that he was already home. She parked and walked casually to the front of the building. His name was on the directory inside the vestibule and she buzzed his apartment. There was no answer. She buzzed again and still nothing. She went back out to the front and looked across the road. There was a dingy little coffee shop with dusty-looking windows, but there were people inside and she'd be able to see the front door of the Lorris Arms, so she crossed and ordered a coffee. It was poured for her out of a carafe with coffee she was sure had been brewed the day before. It stank of rubber. She sat with it in the window and stared across the road, lifting the mug to her lips but not drinking from it.

The mug was still full an hour later, but it was cold, and Dunn had not entered his building. Her mind was travelling, gazing out over the quiet entrance to Kehoe Glenn. They had a little bit of AC in this place, but not enough to allow her to forget how hot this August was turning out to be. You could often count on a cold front in the county in August, something that finally smoothed the edge of July. July was always hot, but now August was hot, too.

It's your old hag body, she said to herself, *that no longer readily ventilates itself. The summer hasn't changed.*

But a lot of things had, actually. Driving down to the Indian reserve this week, her attention had finally been drawn to something she knew didn't belong in the landscape, and this last time – passing it earlier – she'd really looked at it going by in her window. The town of Dublin, which you saw if you came directly into the reserve from the north, was one of the county's prettiest little hamlets, and she hadn't paid attention to the sign because the first time she'd passed it, she'd thought it was a billboard.

But it wasn't. It was news. Some comfy housing corporation was about to dump a ready-made suburb here, right outside of Dublin, if not right on its edge. The sign, she had now confirmed, made the town itself sound like a selling point, it was "unspoiled country rustic." Dublin was also going to be lucky enough to share itself with not just Tournament Acres, as this monstrosity proposed calling itself, but the golf course that would also be built here. Which, as luck would have it, would have its own hotel. On the grounds of the hotel would be the world's biggest outdoor wave pool.

Why not an atom smasher for the old folks? It was

disgusting to think of, here, off the main highway – protected, you'd have thought – from these marauding people who wanted to live in Disneylands for their money to play in. It was *forty* minutes from Port Dundas, and Port Dundas had a *waterfall*. It made her throat tighten to think of it. The cutline at the bottom of the sign had read, "It's always your turn in Tournament Acres."

So they were going to gobble up Dublin. The summers were getting hotter and the small towns of Westmuir County were now officially bait for cityfolk.

She was staring at Jordie Dunn as the word *bait* drifted through her mind. He was walking up the front steps of the Lorris Arms. She stood so suddenly she almost spilled the cold coffee. He was inside now. She waited two minutes and then she crossed the road stiffly, unconsciously keeping her arms from swinging as she did, as if displacing that much air could warn him of her intent.

She got into the little, locked foyer, just as a woman was coming out of the stairway. Hazel waited for her to open the door and she simply slipped inside and went down the hall to 1F, Dunn's apartment, and knocked. There were sounds from within: a chair scraping back, followed by silence. Second thoughts. Who did he think was at the door? She called through, identifying herself, and when more silence came, she announced she knew he was inside. Then the door opened and he was standing there, looking sheepish.

"Yes?"

"Hi, Jordie. Can I come in?"

"I was just about to – " he said, but she put her fingertips on his door and pushed it open.

"Thanks," she said.

She stepped him backwards and he retreated into the musty apartment. Little particles of dust were catching light in the few shafts of illumination that pierced the gloom. She walked in slowly, watching Dunn's eyes and breaking her gaze long enough to look to her left and right. She stood a few feet in front of the still-open door, aware that her fingertips were tingling.

"How're you doing, Jordie?"

"Okay, I guess."

"You just getting in from church?"

"From?"

"Never mind. Why don't you pour us a couple glasses of water, Jordie, and you can tell me the price of soybeans."

He looked behind her to the hallway, still exposed in the open door, and she closed it. His kitchen was as dark as the rest of the apartment, although the sink and the countertop were spotless, as if he never ate there. It seemed a distinct possibility: she couldn't imagine Jordie Dunn so much as boiling an egg.

He opened a cupboard and took out a waterglass. There were three inside, and a couple of plates. The spigot coughed to life and spat out little gobs of water. He passed the glass to her and she left it on the tabletop untouched.

He remained by the sink. "Not thirsty?"

"No," he said.

He watched her sit at his kitchen table and she marked the effort it was taking him to remain still. "Jordie, why did you want to know if Henry Wiest had been murdered?"

"It was eleven o'clock at night."

"And at the edge of a wooded area. Would that be strange?"

"Depends."

"You're not afraid of insect bites, are you, Mr. Dunn?"

He seemed to slip through the air to the kitchen table, where he silently pulled out a chair and sat in it. "Take me in," he said.

"Don't worry. I intend to."

"Now. Take me in now."

"What's in those fields, Jordie? What's in that grove of trees?"

He pushed his seat back and asked her if she was done with her glass. She handed it to him and he poured the water she hadn't touched into the sink. There was a hurried shape to all his actions, like there was a countdown running only he could hear. "Let's go," he said. He grabbed his jacket off a hook on the wall and held the door open for her. He went out the back door of the building and she led him around to the front, where she'd parked her car. "Sit in the passenger seat," she said, opening the door for him and standing aside. He put his hand on the top of the door and a warm ribbon of liquid lashed against her blouse and her neck right before she heard the shot. The weight of his body knocked the door forward and pushed her to the ground. She went low, squaring herself behind the door, and listened to Dunn slide down on the other side. She could only see his legs below the door; he was braced against its inside, hacking blood onto the asphalt. His knees shook violently.

"Give me something, Jordie!" she hissed. "What's going on in that field?"

"He was trying to help her," he rasped, and she heard the back of his skull slap against the inside of the door.

] 20 [

Two hours passed before she was cleared to leave the Lorris Arms. She watched Spere's team work on the car and the body, and, in Dunn's apartment, she answered Ray Greene's questions. She told him who Dunn was, about his earlier visit to the station house, his status as a person of only a little interest before she saw him in that grove off of the Ninth Line. Greene was writing it all down. "Twenty-four hours I've been on the job, Hazel. Twenty-four hours, and I'm writing your name in a book."

"Willan must be drinking bubbly. Am I directing traffic in Telegraph Heights until the end of time now?"

"Because you got shot at in the line of duty? He's not that malicious." Unawares, he was sitting in the same chair she'd been in three minutes before Dunn's death. She remained standing. "I have three bodies now, Hazel. That's all the commissioner knows. For now. But the rest of this happens under me. And if there's a single deviation from the line of command, I'll end your career. You might work this case brilliantly, Hazel, but if there's a single rogue element in it beyond this point, you're done. I'll put you up for dismissal."

"You'd love that, wouldn't you?"

"You *actually* think I'd be rejoicing right now if your career had just ended the way Jordie Dunn's did? We used to be friends, Hazel. I've never once wanted something bad to happen to you. But I'm running a police department now and our friendship, whatever it is or was, has no bearing on anything. Because now you work for me; your well-being is my beat. I have to protect you. From the risks you face on the job. From Willan. And from yourself."

She stared at him for a three-count. Then she said, "We have to get my mother and Cathy Wiest out of my house."

"They've already been picked up. After that?"

"We go where Dunn went this morning."

"Can you do this without getting yourself or anyone else killed?"

"I don't know."

"Maybe this'll help you get started." He held his fist out. There was something in his hand: a little ziplock bag. He dropped it into her palm. "It was in one of Dunn's pockets."

She held it up. There was a green, twenty-five-dollar casino chip in the bag. It had the image of a little bird on it, and the word SPARROW'S.

"Does it mean anything to you?" he asked.

"Not yet," she replied. "Was there anything else?"

"Just his keys and his wallet. Fifteen dollars, a driver's licence belonging to a man named Caleb Merton, and two credit cards."

"Who's Caleb Merton?"

"I have no idea. But the ID had Dunn's picture on it. It looks legit, but it must be fake. Unless it's his real name."

Bail drove Hazel back to the station house. Her mother and Cathy Wiest were already there. Her mother looked displeased, but her expression melted when she saw Jordie Dunn's blood all over Hazel's pants. She was wearing a patrolman's jacket over a borrowed shirt now – forensics had taken her blouse as evidence – but she was still in her own pants. The SOCO's best guess put the shooter on the rooftop of the building across from the apartments. The shot came from four to six hundred metres away. No one had seen anyone mount the roof, nor had anyone been seen coming down from it. Someone with confidence and a rifle had gotten in and out without being detected. There were two shells on the gravel roof: one for each of the two shots. Hazel had the casings in an evidence bag, and after making sure her mother and Cathy were being looked after, she tossed the bag to Wingate.

"They're thirty-ought-sixes," he said, looking at them. "That's deer calibre."

"Why leave the shells behind?"

"Everyone shoots these," he said. "They're in a hundred different hunting rifles. They don't mean anything if the shooter was in a hurry, which I imagine he was." Wingate studied the casings. She lay the bag with the casino chip on top of them.

"Whoever did the shooting probably didn't want this left behind."

He turned the chip over and studied both sides. "Where's it from?"

"It was in Dunn's pocket."

"Sparrow's? Is there a casino anywhere in North America with this name?"

"I don't know. Maybe there's a tiny one in those trees."

Wingate turned the ziplock bag with the casings over in his hand.

"Dunn told me something," she said. "He told me Henry was trying to help her."

"The girl?"

"Kitty."

"What do you think?"

"I think someone's going to have to go for a walk in the woods," she said. "But I don't know how we're going to get there without being noticed."

"Someone's going to have to go in one of those cabs."

"You think so?"

"I think I know how, too."

"How?"

"I'll use the password."

"Password?" She squinted painfully at him. "What password are you talking about?"

"Something I saw in Roland's report from Tuesday. I'm going to need some money, though."

"What's the password, James?"

"You say Wiest wrote himself a cheque for ten thousand dollars?"

"I don't have ten thousand bucks, James. Will you tell me what your plan is?"

He handed the ziplock bag back. "I'm going to tell Greene first," he said.

After a pause, she asked him, "Will you at least tell me the password?"

"Ronnie," he replied.

] 21 [

Sunday

By noon on Sunday Ray Greene had signed off on a room at the Partridge Inlet Lodge and Wingate drove there in a rental Greene had also approved. A smart little new 2005 Mini Cooper. The wind blew it around on the 41. The BBQ fund had thirty-four hundred dollars in it, which Greene had given to him in a deposit envelope in cash. He had to sign a receipt for it. Hazel had looked on, a bemused expression etched on her features.

They'd decided to supply him with a false ID, like the ones that had turned up on Wiest and Dunn. He'd be "Pete Lupertans." Forbes had reminded them that Earl Tate, the counterman, had asked to see ID in order to sell cigarettes to him. No one had given it a second thought until after the names Doug-Ray Finch and Caleb Merton had arrived, attached to men who did not actually go by those names. After Brennan's death in hospital, they'd found another fake ID with the name *Kenneth S. Brehaut* on it. Wiest's and Dunn's IDs had been Ontario driver's licences, but Brennan's had been a health card. None of the names checked out in any of the provincial databases. Someone had generated them out of distinct first- and last-name combinations, so that person had access to some databases the general public would not. The IDs were identifying customers of whatever was in that coppice in the fields.

Wingate waited in line and got his Pete Lupertans casino card and then spent some time wandering through the casino, waiting for dusk to come. They were off-loading buses of senior citizens when he got there, and when he left, ninety minutes later, having seen nothing at all of interest, there was a lineup of retirees waiting to be bussed back to their suburban independent-living facilities. Some crimes were so plain, no one even noticed them.

He got back to the lodge at six in the evening. There'd be time to get a room-service meal before Hazel came down in her Mazda and worked point from one of the railway service lanes. Forbes had made dozens of observations from inside his car during the week, many of which were pointless, including wind direction. But Wingate admired the constable for his gumption and his initiative. And because he'd been thorough, they knew that although there were two taxis working the shop, only one of them took the car-abandoning passengers north. The driver of that car was named Thurlow; the other was called Feldman. It had been easy to look them up from the licence plates of the cabs.

He ate a salad, a piece of blueberry pie, and drank a coffee for dinner, waiting in his room. What was wrong with dedicating oneself in this way? For the greater good? How could someone in his position ever take a vacation when evil was so industrious?

Darkness would give him more cover than a pair of glasses and a ballcap would. The most important part of a disguise was that it didn't look like cover. Just something subtle. People look like each other all the time. A skillfully applied black moustache and a good quality hat were all he needed. Even to himself, he only looked like someone he'd once met. He had his cellphone on him, but it was on vibrate.

He walked into the Eagle at nine o'clock, confirming first that Feldman's cab was waiting at its post. He kept his distance from the counter, browsing the magazine rack. He'd gotten a decent look at the cabbie behind the wheel as he walked in. The man's head was lowered to a newspaper. This was Thurlow. He looked to be a white man in his fifties, with a circle of bare scalp surrounded by a fringe of hair. One arm hung out of his window with a cigarette dangling from the fingers. Inside the shop, Wingate thumbed through a car-buyer's guide. He waited five minutes, and then his phone rang on schedule and he picked it up and said hello.

"In place?" came Hazel's voice.

"Yes."

"We'll be on with you the whole time. We're tracking you as you go, so if anything goes wrong, ask for a cigarette in a clear voice and we'll be there as soon as we can."

He was out of the store. He walked directly to the cab, pretending to talk to someone on the other end, and got into the back seat. "I told you, Ronnie, I'm coming right now." He performed this line with real, contained anger. "You just wait there for me!" He passed his casino ID to the driver without comment. The driver held it in his lap and looked at it. "Fine. Just wait for me. I didn't come all this way to have you do it without me." He held his hand over the phone and spoke to the driver. "Let's go, Clemons."

"What?"

"Aren't you Clemons?" He talked into the phone. "No, I'm not talking to you, you fucking idiot."

The driver had turned around to look at Wingate. "Sir?"

"Hold on a second," he said into the dead phone. "This guy looks as confused as you are. Are you Clemons?"

"No," said the driver. "Who are you?"

He snatched the ID back. "I showed you who I am. Where the hell is Clemons?"

"Honestly, sir, I don't know."

"Well, whoever you are, let's get going."

"Where?"

Wingate glared at him. He said into the phone. "I'll be there in less than ten minutes. Don't start without me." He said to the driver: "You know where I'm going."

"I don't."

"What's your name?"

"Thurlow."

"Well, Thurlow," he said, digging into his pocket, "this is where." He tossed him the Sparrow's chip. Thurlow studied it. His discomfort was evident.

"I'm sorry, but I can't, uh – "

"Where is Feldman, then? I know Feldman will take me there."

"I'm sorry, sir, I don't know where Feldman is."

"But you know 'im." He stared at Thurlow in the mirror. "Fine," he said. He pretended to dial again. He put the phone against his ear. "Put Ronnie on again," he said. Thurlow was watching in the rear-view mirror. "Who's Thurlow?" he asked and then listened to Hazel breathing on the other end of the line. "Well, you fucking talk to him or you're going to have to hire another ferryman. Uh-huh. Fine. You want me to come in my own car?" He noticed Thurlow had his hand on the gearshift. "Hold on. You can tell him." He held the phone out to Thurlow. "You want to talk to Ronnie?"

"No, it's okay."

"Well then, drive. Before I lose my composure. I was supposed to be there fifteen minutes ago."

"Fine, okay," said Thurlow, and he pulled out of his spot. Wingate watched the door of the Eagle as Thurlow made his right-hand turn onto RR26. No one emerged from the building.

"Good," Hazel said to him on her end. "Just pretend to make a couple more phone calls. Talk to a few more people." She and Forbes were listening to Wingate's progress from a speakerphone in the community policing office in Dublin. They'd made it their headquarters. There were only two people here from nine in the morning to five at night, and only six days a week. Someone had to come down and open the door for her. They'd set up and tested the phone, tested the tracking signal, a signal that was being emitted by a device the size of a matchbook under the insole of one of Wingate's shoes. There were eight hours of battery life in the phone, and the high-test trace was good to about seven metres underground. They were lucky, too: there was a tower in Dublin. The relay was only eight kilometres from the field. "Be nice to someone now," she said.

In her ear, Wingate said, "I'll be back in the morning, sweetheart. You know Daddy sometimes has to travel for business. That's right. Kiss Daddy goodnight now."

Obviously he was someone higher up, a VIP no one had ever told Thurlow about. The cabbie drove slightly faster than he needed to: he was frightened of his passenger now, and he had excuses to fall back on if he got into any trouble. No one wanted to talk to Ronnie if they didn't have to, and this busy guy had come all this way for a reason. Best let someone else deal with him. Wingate was willing these thoughts into Thurlow's skull. They made the turn onto Ninth Line and the sound of gravel pinging off the chassis filled Wingate's head with images of tiny bullets flying around the car. There would be a black Mercedes waiting by the side of the road about six klicks in; Thurlow radioed ahead with the single word *incoming*, and then Wingate saw the Mercedes leave the shoulder about five hundred metres in front of them and lead the way to the little grove. Wingate saw that there was only one person in the car. His head rose about two inches above the headrest, suggesting the driver of the Mercedes was tall, over six foot. The car turned right and then Thurlow pulled up beside it. He said into his radio, *Just a drop*, and he turned around to Wingate. "This is it."

"I know this is it." He dug into his pocket for the American twenty they'd decided would be the tip, something unexpected to keep Thurlow inside the illusion that Lupertans was some kind of fat cat or out-of-town boss. Wingate handed it over to him and the man thanked him.

"Good luck," he said.

"I don't rely on luck, Mr. Thurlow. Now keep your mouth shut. Only Ronnie knows I'm here."

"Okay, sir," said the driver, and Wingate stepped out of the cab.

] 22 [

James Wingate walked into the trees. He put the phone against his ear and whispered, "You there?" and heard her faint reply from the other end:

"We're here."

He slipped the open phone into his pocket so she could continue to listen to his progress. Immediately he stepped into the shade, and he saw that the copse had more trees in it than appeared from the road. Three metres in, it swallowed him whole. A scrap of old deciduous forest, untouched because once a river had flowed here and people had used it and they had not cleared the land. Instead, they brought the boulders they dug up in their fields and put them here, among the trees and in the riverbed. Eventually, the river had disappeared. You could see the history of the place in it.

Apart from trees and boulders, there was nothing here, though. He walked in deeper. Behind him, he heard

Thurlow's car pulling away, and his skin horripilated. Sticks and last year's leaves cracked and tore under his feet and he imagined that the sounds were booming out to the ears of whoever was going to find him here and, perhaps, put an end to his meddling.

There was no one here. He saw no structures at all.

Wingate stood in the midst of it and turned in a slow circle. He looked up and saw only the trunks of trees, pouring upwards into a dimming sky.

He walked to where the grove thinned out a little and followed the old riverbed. There was a concentration of larger boulders in the river there, and he stopped and studied them. There was a space behind a particularly large stone, and he clambered across a couple rocks to look. Detritus was strewn beyond, including discarded wood and some chickenwire, and in the midst of it, he made out a large plate of rusted steel sitting on what appeared to be a concrete platform of some kind. As his brain adjusted to what was important in that welter of refuse, he also saw that there was a shiny black box about two centimetres wide and ten centimetres long, on the concrete, below the plate and protected by a Plexiglas shield. A card reader.

He scrambled down and looked at it. This was what the IDs were for. You checked in at the Eagle, you showed your casino ID to Thurlow, you ran it through this reader. Then you went in. He ran the card.

It didn't work. He tried it again. Then a male voice came from an unseen speaker. "Not working?"

"Nope."

"First time?"

"First time," Wingate said. "Am I supposed to run it through left to right or right to left?"

"I don't think it matters. Are you facing it the right way?"

"Yeah."

"Hold on."

The voice snapped off. Then there was a deep, metallic sound, *chunk*, and the metal plate popped up an inch. He got his fingers in under it and pulled it open. It was a heavy door on a pair of arcing metal hinges. It drew right up and revealed a set of concrete steps going down at a slant into the darkness. They'd been constructed against bedrock, these steps, and as he descended them, the space above his head got higher until he was standing in what seemed to be an underground cave of some kind. A light came on and Wingate looked up to see a series of lights in little steel baskets hanging from wires that had been tacked to the stone above. The light showed the cave narrowed again almost immediately, becoming a tunnel that led away from the chamber he stood in.

He was walking in a dead riverbed. There was a small channel carved in the stone at his feet in which a rill of water carried along: the remainder and reminder of the old river. This was the continuation of the passage it had carved into the fields and the bedrock over millennia before it was diverted and claimed.

As he went down, the door above him closed on its own, making a soft clicking noise followed by a mechanical sound when it was fully shut. The lights stayed on. The wires stringing them made shallow, drooping arcs between the bulbs. He hadn't seen a camera on the way down, and couldn't see any here, so he got the phone out.

"I'm in a riverbed," he whispered. "Fifteen feet underground. An empty riverbed, like a cave."

"We've got you on the screen here, James," Hazel answered. "We see you. Leave the phone on, but put it away and focus." He slipped it into his pants pocket.

The riverbed stretched out for about sixty metres in a meandering southerly direction before turning sharply to the west. Apart from the narrow cut of water in the ground, the walls and floors of the bed were dry. It smelled of the cold and the damp, though, and he was beginning to wonder what kind of casino, no matter how secret, would go to this trouble to hide itself. He needed to keep his mental compass points straight under here so he'd know, approximately, where the empty river was leading in context of the upper world. He came to the turn, made it, walked another thirty metres west, and then the bed began to curve again. It was impossible to know how many degrees off of due west he was turning, as the slow curve delivered him eventually to another door. But now he wasn't sure if the door opened to the east or the north. It was an elaborate entrance.

Why had they made this operation so vulnerable to detection? A taxi driving into a field to disgorge a passenger under the watchful eye of someone in a Mercedes wasn't exactly black ops. But he'd slipped in under whatever radar they had, and judging from the interlocking hoops a person had to jump through to get here, they knew if you were a legit customer. If you weren't, there was probably a hole for people just like you. A chill went through him. He was already adapting Hazel's methods: jump in the water – or the river – and look for a life preserver afterwards, if you needed one. And now it was too late to shake off her influence: he was in. He'd walked about two hundred metres. In deep. As he reached the door, he turned and looked over his shoulder, and saw the riverbed rising behind him. He'd also gone down. How far though, he wasn't sure.

The door had no handle. He stood in front of it, and after a wait that felt slightly too long to be safe, another metallic unlocking sound came from within, and the door opened. He went through it. Now he was in a manmade construction, a vestibule with a second door and a thick, Plexiglas window covered on the other side by a grey vinyl blind set in the wall to his right, with a tray like a teller's underneath. He felt heat at last, and a male voice asked him to put any weapons he was carrying in the tray. He'd get a tag for them, and he could reclaim them when he was leaving.

"Do I buy my chips here?" Wingate asked. They had decided back at the station house that the casino chip spoke authoritatively to what the activity was in here, and it was best, they thought, for him to go in appearing to know what he was doing. The voice behind the Plexiglas told him he could buy at the tables. *Good*, thought Wingate, *one surmise established*. "I don't have anything you need to take," he said, and the window slid shut. The second door buzzed open, and he went through.

And then he was in another world, a huge stone room with an imperfectly installed wooden floor and the river, now having found a second wind, meandering through the middle of it in a channel almost a metre wide. There were heating elements, like the kinds you found in the stands at amateur hockey games, hanging down and heating the frowsy space. The stream vanished beneath a particle-board wall that was at the back of the "room." So it *was* a casino. He was amazed. He'd never seen anything like it.

No one looked up when he walked in to the bright, high-ceilinged room in front of him except for a woman occupying a concierge's desk just in front of the door, on the other side of a very small, curving tile surface someone had cemented down onto the stonebed. "Hello," she said, holding her hand out. He shook it. Odd. "So this is your first visit?"

"Yes."

"Welcome, then. Food and drink is on the house. You can sit down and buy in at any of the tables."

"Thanks very much," he said. He handed her a Canadian twenty. She gave him a little, surprised bow.

"Welcome," said a man, coming toward him and extending his hand. "I'm Ronald Plaskett. I'm the manager."

"Pete Lupertans," Wingate said.

"Wonderful. Nice to meet you, Pete. Now, you got your card?"

"Yep."

"Who tuned you in?"

"I know Feldman from way back."

"Feldman should be getting a bigger cut, I tell you. So just show that card for chips, for food, for drink. Enjoy yourself. Roulette is tonight at midnight."

He patted Wingate on the arm and then continued on to talk with the woman at the desk. Mr. Lupertans was going to save some of his more specific queries for the dealers and croupiers.

He walked forward into the cavelike room and he worked against the tide of fear that was beginning to rise in him. He was here now, and anything could happen. He'd not been patted down, as he'd expected to be, but even if he had brought a weapon, there was no saying he wouldn't be patted down later. Being armed in this position was an open invitation to Murphy's Law. He had only his wits.

Some of the men here had a day's worth of stubble. There were tired-looking servers bringing coffee and sandwiches. One of the men – he had a tattoo on his neck of a pair of dice – drank a beer from the bottle. There was only one woman here and she was playing blackjack. She had a large pile of chips in front of her. Her eyes were unnaturally bright.

Now that he'd confirmed what was going on here, the next step was to do what a person like the one he was playing would do. And he guessed Pete Lupertans was here to have a good time and play.

He began to stroll through. There were two blackjack tables, one baccarat table, and one poker table. He now counted eleven men and one woman. There were five men at the poker table. He elected to be around as few people as possible at first, and he joined the woman and another man at a blackjack table. He got his money out. "What's the buy-in?"

"Whatever you say it is."

He stole a glance at the chips on the table. People didn't have too much in front of them, he saw with some relief. Five hundred would look about right. He peeled off bills.

The dealer counted them out smartly. "Five hundred in."

Plaskett looked over at the baize. "Go, Harry."

"Green?" said Harry.

Twenty-fives. "Yeah, green."

Harry pushed over a stack of twenty. “Five hundred out,” he called.

Wingate followed the lead of the other two players, putting out a single chip, and receiving his cards.

He knew enough not to ask for a card if he didn’t need one. He stuck against all threes, fours, fives, and sixes. He won a hand, and then he won another, and the other player won a bunch of hands and then he had seven hundred or so dollars in chips. A waitress came around with a tray. “Drinks or food?”

“I’ll have you,” said the man beside him.

“I’m not for sale, Ed. You want a bourbon, though?”

“Sure,” he said. He nudged Wingate. “She’s not on the menu.”

“I heard that. Can I have a beer?”

“Yep,” said the waitress. “You?” she asked the woman.

“Nothing,” said the woman.

The waitress retreated and Wingate used the opportunity to bond with a fellow drinker. “Pete,” he said, offering his hand in tight quarters.

“Ed,” said the man, shaking. “You gonna play the roulette tonight?”

“Should I?”

“I can’t tell you that, pal. It’s a matter of taste.”

The cards were going around. The roulette was a matter of taste. He let some time pass. Then he asked the man, “They got anything stronger than bourbon here?”

"What are you looking for?"

"You know. Maybe something that'll keep me going all night."

"Play the roulette. You won't be sorry."

It was just after nine in the evening. If Hazel could still hear him, she'd know that he was down for the roulette. The casino was a front for something else. Plaskett and his associates weren't against making some scratch with it, but there was another game.

He went up and down for the next two hours, shooting the shit with Ed and drinking a couple of beers. The woman was a good player. She knew how to leverage her bets. But when midnight came, she cashed out with less than she'd had when he sat down.

"Where's she going?" Wingate asked Ed.

"Not everyone likes the roulette," he said. People all over the space were standing up. The games were ending. Some people were cashing in their chips, others were colouring them up to larger denominations and putting the chips away in their pockets. Maybe you could pay with the chips.

When the people who were going to play roulette were the only ones left, the back wall of the casino began to shudder as the partitions separated and turned perpendicular to the room. Behind it was a smaller section of the space they had been in. The roof of the riverbed encroached here, making the space more intimate. There was a single roulette table standing in it.

"Gentlemen," said the hostess, "Midnight roulette. Please step forward and place your bids."

Back in the Dublin Community Policing Office, Hazel said, "Bids?"

] 23 [

Midnight

His mind was turning over at top speed. Five people had left, including the woman. The remaining seven men were to place their bets, but he saw, as he approached the roulette table, that there were nine spots around the table and four chips in front of each spot. Each pile was a different colour. He had been playing blackjack for quarters, but how much were *these* chips worth?

The men gathered around the baize, and the croupier – a man Wingate had not seen before – started the wheel spinning. The space was closed, but there was another particleboard wall to his left, and there was a door in it. Space was tight in here, and the river in its gulley twisted at their feet before vanishing behind the second wall. As he approached the baize, he saw this was not a normal roulette layout. There were not thirty-nine squares and a couple for zero and double-zero, there were three identical strips, each numbered one to ten, in vertical columns parallel to each other. The wheel was on the right end of the table, surmounted by two walls of Plexiglas to keep people from touching it. Each man went to a monochromatic stack and waited. Wingate did the same. He was light-headed and worried a vein in his neck was visibly pounding.

"We've only got two lots tonight, sorry, gents. Shortage this week. Good luck to you."

He dropped the ball into the wheel, where it hit with a worried clack and jumped up onto the polished wooden rim above the numbers. The wheel was normal, but the numbers on the baize didn't match. How was the winner determined? Men were already putting chips out. They were only using the two numbered strips closest to the wheel. For whatever reason, they didn't think the third strip was a good bet. Wingate mirrored them. They were moving the chips around, too, changing their minds. Wingate picked up one chip and moved it. A man across the table from him looked at him strangely. Finally, one man put a chip down in the third rank, and after he'd broken the ice, a couple of other men did as well.

Then the ball dropped.

"Hands away!" called the croupier, a little more harshly than Wingate thought was strictly necessary. "Six ninety-eight is the winner, the winner is red."

And the man whose chips had been laid on those numbers, in that order, rasped a little *yes*, and the players retrieved their losing chips.

Plaskett came forward and shook the winner's hand. "Lucky you," he said. "Good price, too." And he led the man away. The man was happy to be led away. Plaskett took him through the door.

The wheel was spinning again. Wingate paid more attention this time. The ball falling into the wheel was the sand running out of an hourglass. The wheel was a timer that timed the bidding activity. And the three ranks formed a number. Had 698 been the highest combination of chips? It had been. The man who went away had bid $698 on something.

"Anyone going higher than seven?" one man asked. He was using the brown chips. Nobody seemed willing to advertise their strategy.

Another man said, "Do it."

Brown made a bid of 755. There was some approving laughter. The bidder's friend said, "I'm not going to get in your way!"

The ball was still spinning. Another bid went down, green chips on 780. Applause. Ronald Plaskett looked at the bet and smiled. "Someone's hungry!"

Who were these men, and what did they need so badly? And what would seven hundred, eight hundred dollars buy? Three ounces of pot? It wasn't enough for coke, and it wasn't heroin. These people weren't shooting anything. Maybe it was for pills. Hazel had said she'd found Oxys in Henry Wiest's medicine cabinet, along with the pot. Brown changed his bid to a flat 800.

"Pussy," he laughed at Green. The ball was clacking into the partitions now. The croupier was getting ready to sweep his hand and end the bidding. Wingate put his three blue chips down: 900. The ball dropped and the croupier waved his hand brusquely over the baize. There was an atmosphere of shock at the table. "Hands away! Nine zero zero is the winner, the winner is blue."

"Wow," said Brown. "Nice snipe, buddy. I hope you get your money's worth."

Wingate felt strangely numb. He was the winner. Nine hundred dollars. Plaskett appeared at his side.

"Way to go, rookie," he said. "Let's go see what's behind door number one." He led Wingate to the door at the side of the room. He felt eyes on him. Plaskett opened the door. The riverbed continued beyond it. It was cold again. The grade began to rise, and the ground here was a mix of solid, smooth stone and earth. The walls themselves were earthen now, and here and there a filament of dead root or a furze of mould told him they were getting closer to the fields again.

"So I just pay cash?" he asked.

"Cash or chips. This is for you, by the way – " He handed Wingate another ID. This one said René Arsenault. "I heard your card didn't work in the door. I got you another one. Save you a trip."

Wingate thanked him and pocketed the ID. He counted out nine hundred in twenties and fifties and held it out to Plaskett.

The man stopped dead. "Whoa," he said. "What's this?"

"Sorry?"

"This is nine hundred."

"What should it be?"

"You bid nine thousand, Mr. Lupertans." He looked at Wingate's face. Wingate imagined he'd gone white.

"Nine *thousand*."

"Feldman didn't tell you?"

"Oh, I guess uh, I wasn't totally clear on the procedure, you know?"

"Well, Chester bid eight thousand. I can't take nine hundred."

"I have more," Wingate said hurriedly. He had to make this buy. "I have about thirty-five. Can I just have a, you know, a taste?"

"A taste?" Plaskett started walking again. The cold, dark riverbed looked like it was going to go on forever. But then Plaskett stopped at what looked like an alcove in one of the curved earth walls. Wingate came up beside him and saw Plaskett was standing beside a giant concrete slab that had been set in the side. Someone had blasted or dug a hole in the earth and plugged it with concrete. "What the fuck, Pete? – René, sorry. That's one-third of your bid." Wingate's sinking feeling was only intensifying now. He had no idea what his depth was now, but he hoped his tracer was still transmitting. He might very well be on his own, and right at the moment when they were going to finally learn what was going on under these fields. Ronnie flicked his fingers at Wingate, and when Wingate didn't move, he shoved him with tented fingers against his chest and he stumbled backwards. "Who are you?"

"What?"

"Who the fuck are you? Why don't you know how this works?"

He looked down on the hand that was pushing him backwards. There was no point coming this far and having to go back. "Fucking mumbling Feldman," Wingate said. "I'm really sorry, Ronnie. I want to do this. But the fact is, I've just got thirty-five right now. Can I pay the rest tomorrow?"

"You want a taste, you ask for a taste. You don't come in and make a deal. You ask for a fucking taste."

"I know."

"Show me the cash."

Wingate removed the money as casually as he could. He had seven hundred in chips, too. Altogether he had thirty-six hundred.

"Fine, Mr. . . . Arsenault. You can have a taste. But don't fuck around, okay?" There was another card reader here and Plaskett produced a card of his own and ran it through. "Your card doesn't work in this one. In or out." Plaskett opened the door and went through and Wingate followed. He'd never done illicit drugs. Pot a couple of times in university. Now he was going to have to put something in him and withstand it, no matter what it was. He was starting to work on the odds of his getting out of here alive. He went through the door. Somehow, impossibly, he was standing in someone's laundry room. Enclosed with more particleboard at the bottom of a set of wooden steps. With his mouth as close to his cellphone as possible, he said, "I don't suppose you have a cigarette do you?"

"Gene'll give you one," Plaskett answered.

They climbed the rickety steps. At the top, they went through into a darkened vestibule. Someone flicked a light on, and Wingate came up to see that he was standing in a living room in someone's house. His mind was spinning. Whose house was this? There were farmhouses here and there in the fields. This had to be one of them, but which one? There were a couple of couches and a large-screen television on the wall, playing soccer mutely. There was another man here, and this one was armed with a gun of some type that was holstered on his hip.

"Hey," said the man Wingate presumed was Gene.

"He's just here for a taste."

"A taste?"

"Takes all kinds. René, this is Gene."

"Hullo," said Gene. He offered a hand.

"Hi," Wingate replied. He was in a movie now.

"Put him in that room over there," Ronnie said. "I'm just going to go downstairs."

He felt Gene's hand take him lightly under the arm and then he was walking across a wooden parquet floor. He felt a couple of the wooden pieces shift under his step. He couldn't calm his mind. "Mind taking off your shoes?" asked Gene. "There's a carpet."

Wingate slid off his shoes. An elaborate and illicit scheme was unfolding before his eyes, and he was taking his shoes off so as not to soil a carpet. The floor under his feet was cool. He held his shoes dangling from one hand. He had to be careful to keep the hidden transmitter with him. "Got a cigarette?" he said again, when Gene was on the same side as the pocket the phone was in.

"Menthols," said Gene.

"Oh. Never mind," Wingate replied, secretly grateful.

Gene opened a door and led him into a room. The lights were off in here; the man flicked them on.

They were in a guestroom of some kind. There was a fireplace to his right with two nice chairs in front of it, facing each other. A neatly made four-poster bed with some throw pillows on it took up the wall in front of him, and across from the fireplace, to his left, was a couch. He felt like he was in a hotel room. Gene left before he'd had a chance to get a look at his weapon, but he was pretty sure it was a little stun gun. The weapon that had killed Henry

Wiest and put his wife in hospital. The connections were manifesting.

Wingate tentatively sat in one of the chairs in front of the fireplace, and then went to the couch. The only light in the room came from a fixture in the ceiling, a frosted glass globe. There was no window, as there had been no window in the other room.

Gene opened the door a crack. "Just wait here."

"I'm not going anywhere," he said, and he had said no truer thing of late.

Both the trace and the phone call had dropped off in the temporary office in Dublin. Forbes and Hazel Micallef had heard the footsteps after Wingate had won his bid, and then the signals had started to fray. The last thing they'd heard was the word *hundred*, and then his voice was gone. The tracer fell off ten seconds later. James Wingate had vanished a hundred metres north by northwest of the corner of the Tenth Line and Sideroad 6. Hazel removed the headphones.

"Jesus, he's alone down there."

Forbes said, "We should go in."

"No." She tapped the screen and tried to will Wingate's location back onto it. "Let's give him twenty minutes."

Wingate heard footsteps coming closer to the door, and he stood. He couldn't stay seated. Whatever this was, it was not going to start with him sitting on a couch.

The door opened and he straightened, seeing a brief blur of activity in the doorframe, movement that resolved into the form of a girl. There was a girl struggling against Ronald Plaskett. She was on the end of his arm, his fingers clutching her wrist. He shoved her into the room.

"Don't go too hard on her, my friend," he said. "She's got a bruised cunt. If you like her, top up your bid, and you can have the fresh stuff." He pushed the girl into the room. "You've got fifteen minutes."

He closed the door, and Wingate heard the lock turn. The girl, dressed in a loose nightgown, stood in front of him with her eyes cast down, breathing hard. In his paralysis and astonishment, he could find nothing to say. The girl gave a deep sigh and reached down to the hem of her nightie and it was already over her head by the time he understood what she was doing, and what she expected him to do. She stepped forward and into him, pushing his hands away from the middle of his chest. Her eyes were empty and distant.

"I really need a cigarette," said Wingate.

Interlude

He lay on the bed watching her. She moved toward him slowly, shifting her hips from side to side. She knew how beautiful she was, what happened to men when their eyes fell on her. She liked the feeling. It was the one area of her life where she felt like she had complete control.

"You're beautiful," he said.

"Do you like me?"

"Yes."

"What do you want to do to me?"

"Whatever you'll let me."

She laughed and crept up onto the bed, catlike. "Maybe I'll only let you look."

"That would be enough," he said, reaching for her.

She collapsed against him and pressed her lips hard

against his. It was Reading Week, and they had nine full days in his apartment, the outside world was gone, forgotten. Exams had nearly killed her and she was ready to be coddled. She let Matthieu do all the cooking, he ran her bath, he read to her from Gogol in his rotten Russian, making her laugh, filling her with delight.

"How can you study Russian for as long as you have and still have such an awful accent, Matthieu?"

"It makes you laugh, my darling. If it did not make you laugh, I would do it properly."

"Your tutor does not approve."

"My tutor is off this week. This week I tutor the tutor. In other matters."

They made love in the kitchen, on the floor of his living room, in the bathtub. He fit the cliché of the Frenchman: experienced, fearless, possessed of immense stamina. He wore her out. During the school year she had to be careful: he left her drained and hollow and she hardly had the mind for her schoolwork afterwards. She was in her last year of nursing, and the final exams were in May. She'd kept a high average for all three years of the course, and she hoped that when she finished, she would find a good job in one of the rehab facilities in Lviv. She'd been a runner in high school and had missed a scholarship to the university when she injured herself, tearing a hamstring and blowing out a knee. She'd recovered excellently, and while going back and forth to her physical therapy, she'd met the most wonderful and caring people. They'd nursed her expertly and lovingly back to health. By the end of it all, eight weeks of going twice weekly, she had begun to run again, lightly, knowing she'd never compete.

There were many more patients much worse off than her, though, and it was watching these men and women – victims of car accidents, falls, industrial mishaps, diseases like ALS and Parkinson's – that gradually convinced her that she could lead another kind of life. She talked it over with her friends, and her boyfriend at the time, and he encouraged her. The next year, she enrolled as a student at the Lviv State University of Physical Culture.

She'd felt bad for her ex, Oleg. She knew they weren't going to last, and when she met Matthieu through the tutoring program in her second year, she let him down as easily as she could, but he'd been destroyed. Matthieu had helped her deal with the stress of having a depressed ex, and she'd appreciated it, but finally she'd had to be hard on Oleg and tell him she didn't want to hear from him anymore.

She was thinking of Matthieu as she lay on the hard bed in a motel outside of Kehoe River. She'd doubled back a ways and would have to be more in the open for her final act. She needed to rest again: despite her freedom, it only renewed her to a point. The weeks of mistreatment had worn her down. She didn't know if the nausea she'd been feeling was psychological – killing was not something that she'd ever imagined herself capable of – or just the fact that she'd eaten real food for the first time in more than two months. She was spent, mentally and physically, and she knew she was going to have to be sharp to get to the end of this. She had figured out where her next destination was, and it was close to here. It had taken forty minutes by car to get there from the rooms, but in this town, she was closer. She was going to have to have an airtight plan, or she was going to get recaptured, either by whatever law was certainly on her by now or, worse, by Bochko. Bochko would kill her slowly. He would hold her up in the air with one arm, as he had done before to her and some of the other girls, and crush the bones in her neck with his thumbs until she died, his inscrutable, curious stare studying her like she was a small, natural phenomenon. She'd get Bochko if she had the chance, but if it didn't come up before she got away, she'd have to live with it. Maybe one of the girls would get lucky one day and tear the eyes out of his head.

What was troubling her right now was the fact that, at the motel she'd stayed in, she'd finally had a chance to check her email and there was nothing from Matthieu, which confirmed for her the worst fears she'd had. Because, who writes to a dead woman?

How could she have been so blind? Something *this* ominous she should have been able to pick up in another person. How could she have been so blind with love for so long that he could have done this to her? The idea to come to Canada had been his, and he'd taken care of many of the details. He'd even paid for the trip. Now she wondered how well Bochko had repaid him. Even as she followed these dread thoughts, another arose: what if Matthieu had done nothing? And what if, to cover their tracks, her captors had harmed him? She swung back and forth between rage and anxiety. If he were innocent, his silence was ominous. If he were not, then one day she would confront him and know the truth. Just from the look in his eyes.

Matthieu was a problem for later, however, and she made herself focus on the present. *You are Larysa Kirilenko, you are a graduate nursing student from Ukraine. When you go home, you will restart your life, and none of this will have happened.* She was glad, for the first time ever, that her mother was dead. The thought that she would have to lie to her about her tribulations here was devastating to think of. Of course, her silence would have told her mother volumes. She imagined the nervous breakdown, and was grateful her mother wouldn't suffer it. She hadn't spoken to her father in years: her mother's death had accelerated his alcoholism, and she had given up on him in her late teens. She would not want to – or need to – rely on him for anything.

It couldn't have been Matthieu. She knew when she was loved. You don't spend almost a year with a person, sharing every intimacy, laughing and crying with them, and not notice some small detail that would make them capable of betrayal of the kind she'd suffered. That's not something that happens behind the scenes, something you hide from a person whose body you've treated with such worshipful attention.

A man had been at the airport in Toronto, in the arrivals area, holding a sign with her name on it. She'd been very impressed. "Was this Matthieu's doing?" she'd asked him in English as he opened the limo door.

"Of course," the man had said.

"Such a good man Matthieu is," she said in her still-rudimentary English.

As he drove her away to her fate, she could not have known that the man – whom she would learn to call Earl in the coming weeks – was driving her far from her supposed destination.

She had suffered greatly in the ten weeks she'd spent in the underground rooms, but nothing had preyed on her mind more savagely than not knowing if Matthieu was the person she'd thought he was. And it had been *his* memory that had kept her going all this time!

She pushed herself off the bed and walked hunched to the bathroom. What wouldn't she do for a nice bathroom, with a warmed tile floor and a bidet. Oh god, a bidet would be a blessing, better than a cold bottle of rosé, like Matthieu had promised her the first night they were in Paris together.

She'd chosen this rotten motel for a reason. She'd wanted to see it again. This was the place that Earl had taken her to, when he'd driven her from the airport. It was still there: *Dear Room 9, check-out is 11 a.m. Thank You. The Management, Forty Winks Motel, Kehoe River.* Room 9. Where the horror of her situation first became clear to her.

"Good luck," Earl had said to her, the same neutral tone in his voice that he'd had in the car when he'd informed her that she was being taken to her dormitory. He closed her in this empty room and told her to wait. Then, five minutes later, the door had opened and a powerful-looking, hard-looking man had stepped into the room.

Over the next few days, she remained in the motel room and the man came to see her. He told her to call him *Bochko*, which meant "father" in Ukrainian. But this was not a Ukrainian man. He was from this side of the ocean. He was strangely beautiful, and his beauty made him more terrifying to her. He began to break her as if she were an animal, coming to her unannounced at all hours of the day. If she resisted him, he struck her; if she wept, he would close his hand around her throat and choke the tears off. When she had stopped struggling, he trained her to please him, and to do it without being asked, and to pretend to enjoy what was done to her. By the end of the fourth day, she was broken and living in a horror-filled dream, a nightmare. He called her Kitty, and she did not correct him. That would be her name here. Larysa was gone.

She'd never once in her life been struck by another human being. An only child, she'd never had a sibling to beat up or be beaten up by. The blows stunned her. Later, in the mirror, she saw the weeping wounds on her face. There were bruises all over her legs and arms. When she washed her face, the basin ran red with her blood.

She was not allowed to sleep. Bochko was insatiable. He never slept, it seemed to her, was always ready to go at her. He did everything, even things she had once liked, and at every opportunity, if she flagged or became inward, he would remind her what the consequence was. Enjoying him meant moving her body, begging him for more, and when she could not do it, he punished her. When, on the morning of the third day, he appeared looking freshly bathed, she had begged him to kill her.

He had lifted her chin to bring her face to him, and his expression was sad and compassionate. "My darling," he said. "Do not despair! Transformation is painful! Imagine how it feels to push your way out of your cocoon, out of your egg? Your wings damp, your eyes blind, your stomach empty? Even the sparrows, who are nothing compared to you, fall before they fly."

At six on the third night, a woman had appeared with a tray. There was a bowl of pasta with two large meatballs on it and a glass of water. "Eat," said the woman without looking at Larysa. She'd spoken with an accent she recognized and Larysa answered her in Russian. *I don't want to eat. I want to get away.* But the woman had merely repeated the English word, "Eat," and pointed at the food.

Fear did not cancel out her hunger. She would have to eat to survive, to overcome. Larysa ate. The other woman was thin and her skin was sallow, as if she were starving. She sat the entire time facing away from Larysa.

"Vindow," she heard, and the other woman was standing by the curtained window.

"What?"

"Vindow," the woman said.

Larysa just stared at her. "I don't know what you want."

The woman crossed the room. "Door."

"Yes, that's a door. *What are you doing?*" she asked in Russian.

"*I have to learn English.*"

"*So . . . you come here to feed me and I'm supposed to teach you English?*"

"*Please, I don't know when he is coming. If he catches us speaking anything but English, there will be a punishment.*"

"*I've had his punishments. Fuck him. And I don't know much English, anyway.*"

"*You know more than I do! Look at me. This is punishment. I would not listen. I live in a dark room, no lights at all, and I eat nothing. When I faint, I'm woken with water and a piece of bread. When I think I have finally died of hunger, they wake me again. But one day, they will forget me in there.*"

"*What did you do?*"

"*I would not smile. With the men. I could not. I was a virgin in Saint Petersburg!*"

Larysa had no idea what to think.

"*He will have us both today. It is very popular, two girls.*"

Larysa went to the girl and held her. It was surely grounds for grave punishment, to be held, but the girl sank into her and began to weep.

"*Today he gave me breakfast. So I'd have strength*," she said.

There was a bag of apples that Earl had brought for between her meals. She was still in Bochko's good books, obviously: they were feeding her and she had chosen to take what was offered. She'd been a vegetarian at home, but here she would need her strength, and she ravenously ate the fast-food hamburgers and pastries they brought her, gulped down the bottles of water and the coffee, which was good coffee, and the apples. She offered the girl one now, and her eyes fell on it like it was a bar of gold.

"Apple," said Larysa.

"Apple," said the girl.

"My name is Larysa."

The girl looked fearfully at her. "No."

"Yes. My name is Larysa."

"Name is Kitty. My name is Timmy."

"What is your real name?"

"My name is Timmy."

Larysa reached for the apple and took it away. The girl smiled shyly.

"My name is Tania."

"Tania, I am Larysa."

She gave her back the apple. "But you call me Timmy, I call you Kitty. Kitty, we talk English."

"Okay," said Larysa. "Tania has been brave."

"*I don't understand.*"

"*You have been brave.*"

"*I have only been alive. That is all I am.*"

"Brave," Larysa said in English.

"Brave," said the girl called Tania, biting the apple.

She washed her face. It had been twenty-four hours since she'd put the knife in Terry Brennan's back. She'd bought a paper the last time she was out, and so now she knew it was Sunday, August 14. She found a station on the television that reported the local news, and she was the lead story on every channel. They had a sketch of her now, and although she didn't think it looked like her, it was enough to draw attention. Every hour she spent here regaining her strength was another hour forces were marshalling against her. She was going to have to be back on the move tomorrow, no matter how she felt.

3

Monday, August 15

] 24 [

Past midnight

"My name is Cherry," the girl said. "You must do what you like." She moved toward him, her hands already busy with his belt buckle. He put his hands on top of hers.

"Not yet," he said. He didn't want to break character in here if he could avoid it. Instinctively, he knew he was alone now, as alone as this girl was, buried somewhere underground in an unmarked place. Hazel was probably already dispatching the backup that would get him and this girl killed. And anyone else who was trapped down here with them. He felt sick with rage, beginning to process the information they'd drawn their wrong conclusions from. *Not drugs*. "Dance for me," he said.

He moved to the couch and sat, and Cherry stood in front of him, naked, and began to move her hips. Her arms were dead at her sides. "I dance," she said, and the look on her face expressed that it was as bad waiting to be raped as it was to be raped.

"Just keep dancing. Fifteen minutes of dancing."

She stopped moving very suddenly and looked toward the door. It remained closed. She came to him. "You must like me. I please you. You send me away, Bochko will come."

"Bochko."

"Just tell me what I do. I do it good."

"How many girls are here?" She was working his buckle again.

"Two. Three."

Yes, two now, he thought. That was who Kitty was. The third. He pushed her face away from his zipper. "No," he said. "I don't like that."

"*Please*," she appealed. "Cameras see you unhappy. Bochko *come*."

He hadn't thought of cameras. He grabbed her by the shoulders and pulled her up to standing. He pushed her backwards against a wall and stood very near to her. He pushed against her and put his mouth under her ear.

"I'm police," he said quietly. She stiffened beneath him. He held her hands down between their bodies. "I'm here to help you. How many men are here? How many guns?"

She grabbed his hair and pulled him away, spinning him off the wall and pushing him so hard against the bed that he thought he was going to have to defend himself. But then she had raised his feet and she was taking his shoes off. Her eyes told him he'd better cooperate. His buckle was still undone and she tugged his pants off and clambered on top of him. She kissed the base of his throat and spoke quietly and direly into his skin. "We both die, you *polis*. Both. You want?"

"No," he murmured.

"You fuck me." She began to unbutton his shirt, and he put his mind in neutral and focused on not getting them both shot. The girl helped him remove his shirt. How old was she? She looked nineteen. Perhaps even twenty. Maybe not. He prayed she was at least eighteen.

There was a hammering at the door. "Hey! What're you sittin' on the couch for?" came Plaskett's voice. It had taken him less than one minute to get from wherever he could see them on his monitor to the room. That was all the lead-time Wingate would ever have here.

"We're just getting to know each other," Wingate said.

"Nothing to know, Buddy. Just get in and out and fill out a customer appreciation form. What's the hold-up?"

Probably there were angles on the whole room. There was no hiding. "I just couldn't believe how fucking hot she was," he said as confidently as he could, and squeezing his fists together as he pulled the covers back. "Can I have some privacy now, though?"

"Well, get going."

"Come," said the girl impatiently. "Take off. All."

The thought that he *had* to get out of there – and immediately – was competing with the necessity to remove his clothing. If there was a signal coming from the device in his now-shucked shoes, he wasn't sure it was being picked up. The limit was seven metres, and the tunnel on the way to this part of the compound – the house – had gradually declined at least another five feet. It was possible no one was coming.

He would never be quite so naked in his life. He stood and took his socks off and threw them away. The girl had already tossed his shirt onto the couch. He went to the bed in his underwear, but she stopped him and slipped a finger into the back of his waistband. "Cameras," she reminded him. "Fuck and live."

She was going to find out exactly how impossible that was going to be, given all the circumstances.

He got into the bed and she came in after him, drawing the covers back for them both and then covering their bodies. She pushed him onto his back and lowered herself onto him, finding a discreet way to keep them on the safe side of intimate. He was grateful to her for whatever judiciousness she was now showing in her actions atop him. His forehead poured sweat. "I move, you stay still," she said, lowering herself to kiss him.

"I won't do anything."

"You will be okay." Her face came down beside his ear, and he felt the slow gyric motions of her body over his thighs as she enacted their travesty of lovemaking. She kissed his mouth and then along his chin, and she settled her mouth below his ear. The unbidden scurrying feeling in his gut that came with her mouth against his neck only confirmed the absolute absurdity of his situation.

She said, "My name is Katrina Volkov. I come from the city of Elizavetgrad, in Ukraine. I win a beauty contest, I fly to Montreal for Worlds. Next thing, I am here. They drug me. Put me in a van. Three months ago."

"Tell me who Kitty is."

"Kitty is dead."

"No. Kitty is alive."

"Alive? Ha."

"Shh," he said, and he held her close to his body. "Do you know how she got out? Did you know Henry Wiest?"

Someone hammered on the door. "Five minutes."

Cherry suddenly threw herself back, whipping her hair around in a circle, and she began making animal noises, pretending to revel in her pleasure. He now saw how very great the cruelty of this crime was. He pulled her back down to him and flipped her over, pushed her back against the pillows. She looked startled for a second and then smiled at him. Such a look of gratitude. He was going to save her.

She pulled him down to her, as if to kiss him, but she put her mouth against his ear. "Kitty is alive?"

Her breath was hot. "Yes. She's killed two men."

"Good girl."

"She's looking for something."

Cherry laughed softly. "We all look for something. Sometime, it make for trouble."

"Do you know where she's going? Who she'll try to see?"

"Mr. Sugar," she said. "She will kill Mr. Sugar, too."

"Who is Mr. – "

"Time's up," said Plaskett, throwing open the door. He strode toward the bed before either of them had a chance to adjust and ripped the covers off of them. Wingate leaped up and stood beside the bed, his police instincts telling him to have his weapon in his hand, and he stood with his hands apart and slightly bent forward, ready for anything. Plaskett laughed roughly. "Get enough, soldier?"

Cherry was calmly dressing and he patted her on the rump.

"Old Reliable," he said. "Gene'll take you back to your suite, dollface."

Wingate wanted to pull the man's eyes out of his head.

Cherry left without saying another word. Plaskett was facing him, his hands on his hips. "Well? She the goods?"

"She's . . . yes, very good. Expert. Are all the girls like her?"

"The other girls are young and firm and taste like peaches, pal. Not like this beef jerky. And there's more coming in all the time. Lots of turnover. Mind you, if you *like* Cherry, you can have her for the rest of the week. Make sure you like the service. But next time, you pay your bid like everyone else."

"When can I bring the rest of the money?" he asked, moving around the man to get his pants. He couldn't find his underwear and remembered that he'd stepped out of them beside the bed. This was overtime, danger pay, and a bonus all rolled up into one.

"You come back when you got it."

"Okay."

"I'll take you up."

He led him to the stairs that led down to the laundry room just off the river. He went back out into the riverbed. He was René Arsenault now. This new card would work in the reader. It would open the door to the river. Somehow, you made your reservation, then you showed your ID at the smoke shop, and you showed it again in the taxi. They would all know you were coming. He'd been lucky the security was so tight they could have faith in it. Or perhaps Thurlow would have thrown him to Plaskett. Because, certainly, when someone needed correction, Plaskett delivered it.

He walked back to the casino area, which then led up and out through the door in the river. He walked it out, pacing it and estimating the compass directions as the tunnel curved and then turned back to the hole with the stairs embedded in it.

Thurlow was waiting for him when he emerged, and without a word being exchanged, he drove Wingate back to the Eagle. Wingate transferred from the cab to the rental car he'd picked up in Mayfair, and which was parked in the same space Wiest's pickup had been left in. If the space was a signal, he'd wanted to trigger it. But Kitty did not step out of the woods looking for something she thought he had on her. She was still at large, and the OPS had a much bigger, darker case on its hands than anyone had imagined. He got into the car and then dialled in.

The signal had flickered back on where it had vanished. Two minutes later, it moved fluidly back to Queesik Bay, and she and Forbes held their breath as it stopped and then resumed its movement at a slower pace, back behind the Eagle. The blue dot on the computer screen reversed, then made a little turn, and then headed back out to the Queesik Bay Road. The phone rang. Hazel picked it up and heard his voice saying her name.

"I know who Kitty is," he said.

] 25 [

Mr. Sugar had been the first client to have her delivered. Terry Brennan was the second. But Mr. Sugar had been the worse of the two, and only serious deviants needed girls delivered. There in the privacy of their own homes, they could do whatever they wanted. She'd been told to call him Mr. Sugar – he was the owner of a profitable energy drink company – but she avoided speaking to him at all. He liked three things: Eating, gambling, and torturing girls. It got him off.

Anything could be an excuse for punishment. She was given cans and cans of caffeine-fortified power drinks but nothing to eat. They made her feel like an electrified wire had been run through her. He obviously drank quite a few himself: he was more than three hundred pounds. The first few times she'd seen him, in the underground bedroom, he'd been more or less gentle with her, although every inch of him disgusted her. He was a man of indeterminate age, somewhere between forty and sixty, but so ruined it was impossible to tell. Clearly an alcoholic, a smoker, and definitely a bad man. She'd been brought to him and Earl introduced him as their "favourite bachelor." There was no mystery to that. Some people took no care of themselves, but they had money and so they could do as they wished. Mr. Sugar was rich and he was a nine-year-old in the body of a debauched middle-aged man, greedily playing with his toys.

He'd come at the end of that first awful week in the rooms.

After six days in the motel, Earl had appeared and led her to the car he'd brought her from the airport in. She knew from talking carefully to Tania during their lessons that her destination was a place that was called "the rooms" and that she would stay there a long time. No effort now was made to hide her in the car or prevent her from seeing where she was going. Clearly, they never intended her to reappear in the world again.

She hadn't seen the outside world since she'd arrived in Canada a week before. Then Earl pushed her head down and put her back into the car. As he was pulling away, she saw the name of the motel. Forty Winks. Forty lashes was more like it. She hoped she'd never lay eyes on it again. Forty minutes south of the motel, he changed to narrower, rural roads and eventually into farmland.

He continued on to a house at the end of a long straight road. It was an older house, a nice brick country farmhouse set back from the road and surrounded by fields and other farmhouses. He brought her out, holding her wrists behind her, and unlocked a set of doors. There were two men inside, guards, she quickly realized, men she heard called Gene and Bobby. Bobby took her from Earl and led her downstairs. A door at the bottom of a set of steep steps opened onto the basement. There were rooms here, some with closed doors. There was a living room with two couches and a television attached to one of the walls. Two girls, one of whom was the girl called Timmy, were sitting on one of the couches. Evidently, Timmy's English, and perhaps her obedience, had permitted her re-entry into the general population. She looked beautiful now, and she had a new dress.

Bobby snapped his fingers and both girls rose. He made Timmy sit back down and passed Larysa to the other. "Show her to her room," he said, and the girl took Larysa gently by the arm.

"Come," she said.

"I am Cherry," she said.

"Kitty," she replied, knowing doing anything but playing strictly by the rules at this point would be suicide.

"Your English is good."

"I learn to speak in high school, and I take . . . I was take courses in English. French also."

"I wish I can speak like you." She led Larysa to a door that went into a hallway off the living room.

"How long have you been here?"

Cherry laughed softly. "My life. How it feels. But half-year now." She led Larysa down another set of steep stairs. The air became cold and musty.

"Here we are." Cherry opened a door and showed Larysa into a room made of dirt. There was nothing here but a row of doors standing in a wall that went from the floor to the ceiling of the earthen space. Someone had dug this room out. In the wall to their right, there was a concrete frame in which a heavy steel door had been mounted. "This was Gina's room," Cherry said, showing Larysa to a door. "Now is yours."

"Gina got out?"

Cherry just looked at her, and Larysa finally realized what happened to the girls here. Perhaps some of them, like Tania/Timmy, were pulled back from the brink by good luck, but now she didn't want to know what had happened to Gina. What happened to her was something Cherry knew, but it wasn't time to tell the new girl that. She would have a long time to live with the truth. Her heart sank farther as Cherry let her into the room. There was a filthy mattress on the floor, a steel rod that had some other girl's clothes still hanging on it, and a small side table with two drawers in it up against the wall. Here, the walls were made of earth, too.

"What do I do?" she asked.

"Wait. Wait until someone wants you."

"When?"

"Any time," said Cherry. Then, safe in the clay-walled room, she switched to Russian: "*If you cooperate, you eat. If you don't, you starve. This place is for men who do whatever they want to a woman. Hard or soft, gentle or vicious, you will meet them all. Outside, they are other people. In here, they do whatever they want. They come from all over. One day, there were Germans here. If someone likes you, they will deliver you to them. Hotels, warehouses, homes. Wherever they want you, you go. No one knows you are here. You may choose not to live, many girls have chosen not to live. But if you want to live, you must do your best and avoid pain and suffering.*"

"*How do they get away with it?*"

"*Nothing like this would ever happen in Canada . . .*"

She gave Larysa some threadbare sheets. "*Try to keep a part of yourself safe, Kitty. One day, they may find us, and it would be better to be alive then.*"

"My name is Larysa," she said in English, holding her hand out in thanks, but her gesture was cut short by a slap.

"My name Cherry. Your name Kitty. You never say name again. Your Larysa is dead." She turned smartly and walked back to the door. "*I wish you luck,*" she said in their mother tongue, "*and if you do not have luck, I wish you a speedy release.*"

She left and closed the door. Larysa heard her walking slowly back down the hallway. When the hallway was silent, she remained standing in the middle of the dirt room where a girl, or any number of girls before her, had once lived.

In the second week, she was visited on almost a daily basis by Mr. Sugar. He had her in one of the rooms on the floor above. Then, in the third week, he had paid enough to have her brought to him. Sugar did not let her out of the house, not that week, nor the next, nor the week after that: for almost a whole month he lay on top of her, tortured her, doing whatever came to his blackened imagination. Every inch of him imparted some awful scent or flavour, and it was all she could do not to vomit on him.

But she had decided she wanted to live. So she did what she was told to do. And she acted as if she liked it because that was the price of avoiding the rest of her fate.

After these three weeks, she was suddenly brought back to the rooms and told that Sugar had been outbid. Outbid? She was baffled by this idea. But with this, the whole depraved order of the place was laid bare to her. They weren't mere whores here, no. They were prize lots, given to the highest bidder, for a week at a time. Sugar had become complacent and missed out; Terry Brennan had stepped ardently into the fray and claimed her. But he would not have her at the house. For his two weeks, before Mr. Sugar won her back, Brennan came to the rooms, only once asking for Larysa to come to the house, a day, Larysa now understood, that his wife had been out of town. If not for that visit, she would never have found where Brennan lived.

She had worked hard at figuring out how she was going to find Mr. Sugar's house. He'd requested that she be blindfolded on the drives out, but he had never taken any care to hide how he made his money. He owned an energy drink company called Power Up Beverages. The motel manager had let her use the office internet and she searched for corporate information on Power Up. His fridge had been full of the products the company made, and he was always guzzling one down. The president's name was Carl Duffy. There was even a picture of him, the smiling pig. She plugged his name into a directory and found an unlisted number, but another directory turned up an address and Google Maps confirmed the topography she remembered from looking out the windows of the room he'd kept her in. The house had been high on an escarpment overlooking a lake. Gannon Lake. She was even closer than she'd thought: it was less than twenty kilometres from the motel. But to get there, she could not hitchhike, and neither could she dawdle about it. There was only one viable option: she would run there.

She hadn't run a distance longer than five kilometres since her injuries. A half-marathon, in her best days, would have taken her an hour forty-five, but she imagined a run like this, cold, would take her three hours if she wanted to have any strength when she got there.

She printed out the map and folded it up. She thanked the manager and told him she'd be back for another night. She didn't tell him there was little or no chance that he would ever see her again. But if someone was onto her, having someone else who could offer her pursuers a good lead might buy her much-needed time. In her room, she changed into the clothes she'd been wearing the night she left Henry Wiest in the parking lot, clothes he'd brought for her: a pair of sweatpants with the word CANADA on them and a T-shirt. She'd wrecked these clothes walking in the woods, but they were the best clothes she had for running. She set out, heading for the smaller roads behind the town, and before she was through the first kilometre, she'd taken off the tennis shoes and thrown them into the scrub. She'd trust her naked feet to get her there. Back when she'd been serious about running, she'd met a lot of barefoot marathoners who swore by it. It felt okay, if she stayed on the paved part of the road. By the time the sun was past its noon height and she was running past farms and fields, she had settled into a rhythm.

As she ran, she began to hear a voice in her head. Not a crazy voice, just her own voice, as if being broadcast directly into her mind from outside of herself. It was saying, *You are good, you are good. You have done nothing wrong. You are an angel.* She saw the killing she'd done in a new light and something inside her, like a weight, went down into her belly and settled and she began to run faster, with more power. The guilt and horror streamed off of her, and she began to understand why Henry Wiest had had to die, why Terry Brennan had to die. Why Carl Duffy, once he had given her what she wanted, would die. All of them had stepped out of the natural order, and removed her from it as well, and now they were all subject to new laws. Laws that did not obtain in the real world, where people had names and relationships. In this other world, the laws said she could eradicate anyone who had witnessed, participated in, or caused her shame. She had known love and obeyed *its* laws, which were trust, openness, abandon when it was called for, generosity, selflessness. The new laws demanded the opposite: secrecy, caution, selfishness, and righteous anger. She was a certain kind of angel. She ran in Larysa's body, but she felt with Kitty's soul. And in Kitty's soul, there was a surfeit of murder.

In her pocket, however, there was a folding knife. The good, heavy knife that Henry had given her. It was in her sidepocket and it tapped her as she ran, over and over, like a crop against horseflesh. The rhythmic urgency of her footfalls paired to the metronome of the knife pushed her. Along this road were little fruit and vegetable stands with trust boxes lying on the rough-hewn tables. She grabbed an apple at one, a bell pepper at another. She had brought a single bottle of water with her, and she drank from it slowly, pacing herself with the slap of her feet against the pavement, counting to a thousand and then taking a mouthful.

Within an hour, she had covered half the distance and it was mid-afternoon. She took a risk at a corner store at the base of the road that led up into the escarpment and stopped there for a sandwich and asked to have her bottle refilled. The man who served her noticed she was barefoot, but he didn't say anything, and she was in and out in five minutes. After that, the land began to rise at the base of the lake, and her energy flagged momentarily. Then she thought about how close she was to completing her mission here, and she drew herself up and ran harder.

She was running in cover, taking paths through the woods when she could still see the road, running on loam and moss. Somewhere she'd cut her foot on a piece of wood, or a stone, but she felt no pain at all. She was perilously alive. Maybe this was the end of her life. She was running to her death, rushing to it. She knew what Mr. Sugar – Duffy – was capable of. Her little hunting knife would be no match for him. She wouldn't be surprised if his arsenal extended beyond chains, locks, prods, and gags. When he'd won her back the week after Terry ran out of money, he'd turned up the torture, putting cigarettes out on her skin, slapping her, crushing her with his disgusting body. "Now Kitty is home," he'd said to her, and never before had the word *home* seemed so lifeless.

He was planning on keeping her forever, and he could afford it. There were special offers for people like Carl Duffy. People like Carl Duffy liked to have souvenirs. Who knows how many girls he'd had from Bochko before her, how many keepsakes he had. She had thought perhaps Terry had exercised that right before quitting her and she'd had to know for sure, which was why she'd visited him. But now she knew she'd gone to see Brennan because he had to be punished. Carl Duffy would have what she was looking for, and she would see the blood spurt from his throat before she took it away from him.

The map told her she was just a few kilometres north-west of Kehoe Glenn. She had no worries that she would fail to find Mr. Sugar at home; he ordered all his food off a website. It was brought to the door three, four, five times a day. He sent out for breakfast, for fresh coffee, for snacks. She had watched in raving hunger as he devoured pizzas, Chinese food, and burritos in front of her. He would toss her a crust or a noodle and she'd have no choice but to accept these scraps. After his meals and entertainment, the huge man would often lapse into sleep and leave her manacled for hours.

She'd only escaped the threatened permanence because Sugar had been careless and that Henry man had been a fool. Chance was the only way she was going to get out, and chance had favoured her. She ran up onto the escarpment, feeling her blood surging in her veins. She was an animal now, a machine, an agent of deliverance. Carl Duffy was about to die, and she was about to be free. It was August 15, a Monday evening in her twenty-sixth year on earth.

] 26 [

Monday, Auagust 15, morning

The morning after Wingate's underground ordeal, Hazel woke to a quiet house. She'd had a fitful sleep as her legs had jumped and woken her repeatedly. She'd wanted to go right back out, to mobilize whatever was needed to get those girls out of there, but both Wingate and Greene had convinced her they needed a better plan than that. And backup. And the aid of the Queesik Bay Police Department.

Cathy had gone to Greene's wife's B&B, but Emily would have nothing to do with it and insisted on sleeping in her own bed. Now, at 8 a.m., Hazel opened her mother's room and called to her. There was no reply: it was early, and her mother had taken to sleeping late. But Hazel noticed that her breathing was strange. It was shallow and raspy. She went closer to the bed and called to her mother again.

"Jesus Christ, Hazel, what time is it?"

"Eight in the morning. I have to go in."

"Fine. Go in. Have a blast. Leave me alone."

"You're breathing funny."

"Honestly, Hazel," she said, and her intake of breath was accompanied by a small whooping sound.

"Let me see you," her daughter said, but Emily just settled back under the covers. Hazel sat on the bed and reached for her, and started pulling, and to her surprise, her mother shot up in bed with an unbuttoned look of rage on her face.

"JUST GO TO WORK!" she shouted, but Hazel wasn't paying attention to her mother's words. Her skin was almost yellow and her eyes were lividly bright. She was in the grip of a high fever. Hazel thought she saw a tinge of madness in her mother's eyes.

"Oh my god, Mum. You're sick."

"I know I'm sick – "

"No, you have to get up. I'm taking you to the hospital."

"Get me a couple of aspirins and stop meddling. Where is your father? I work all week, I expect to sleep in!"

"Mother, get up!"

Emily shook her head in exasperation and threw the covers back. "Get out of the way."

Hazel got up off the bed, and her mother stood, surprisingly steady. She walked to the bathroom in the hallway. Hazel heard her peeing and flushing, then the water in the sink ran. When she came back in, it was clear the little journey had taken all of her strength. Emily sat heavily on the edge of the bed.

"What day is it?" she said querulously. Then she pitched forward and Hazel had to lunge to keep her from falling off the bed.

There was no choice about how to spend the morning, even though, at this moment, Forbes and Wingate were meeting Greene at the station house. Hazel was already forty minutes late for the meeting when she was able to call in from the ER. They'd told her to take her time, but that was the very thing it felt they'd already run out of.

"Ketones," Gary Pass had said. "That's the sweet smell."

"What does it mean? What's happening to her?"

He explained that she hadn't been getting enough nutrition, that her body had been cannibalizing itself. She'd come very close to being gravely ill, but they were pumping her full of fluids, and she would recover.

Had she missed *all* of the signs? Her mother had been tired, depressed, she wasn't eating much, but she'd been *present*, more or less. Hadn't she? *Or*, Hazel wondered, *was I too distracted with the case?* The diagnosis of myeloma had come in Saturday morning. Pass had called her with the news, and it was only two days later. How could she have declined that much in forty-eight hours? Pass reappeared in the hallway mid-morning and beckoned to her quietly.

"She's more alert now," he said.

"Is she happy about it?"

"Ecstatic."

He held the doors open to the ICU, and Hazel went in before him. He came around and led the way to Emily's curtained space. Her mother's eyes were closed, her head turned away. Dr. Pass left Hazel there and drew the curtain.

She called to her, but there was no response, so Hazel took the seat beside the bed and looked at the nape of her neck where the hospital gown drooped. Her mother had always had a strong neck, a neck to support her bull-headedness, and from where Hazel sat, it looked like a tiny machine shot through with cables. Small hairs stood up on it. Hazel had wrapped her little arms around that neck, she'd smelled her mother's cascading hair as she clung to her with her legs circling her waist. It was hard to imagine that body capitulating to anything. It had withstood so many insults, so many setbacks.

She leaned forward and put her hand on her mother's shoulder. "Mum? Are you awake?"

Emily shrugged the hand off her shoulder and Hazel withdrew it into mid-air.

"Don't be upset with me. What did you expect me to do? Let you die in bed?"

Silence. Hazel let her have it. She slumped back in the chair and waited. "I don't want you to die," she said, almost under her breath. "I could take . . . twenty more years of your mulishness, your forked tongue, your shitty cooking, your game shows, your wattled friends . . . I could take a lot more of it, Mother. All you have to do is sign on. Gary says the myeloma will move so slowly you could live to a hundred with it."

Emily sighed deeply. "I'm not a shitty cook."

"You burn tea, Mother."

Emily turned over onto her back, a compromise between ignoring her daughter and looking at her. "Your speeches must rally your troops to joyful insubordination."

In profile, her mother's face was like a broken half of something. Her nose was thinner and sharper, her cheekbones stuck out of her face like tiny elbows. "Are you feeling a little better?"

"They're pumping me full of chocolate malts."

"Something like that." She got out of the chair and sat on the edge of the bed. Her mother's eyes tracked over to her. "You're going to be eighty-eight in a week and a half – "

"Is this the pep talk continuing?"

"Let's have a party. Drinks and everything, screw Dr. Pass's injunctions. We'll get everyone together."

"A party of scarecrows."

"We'll change the mood in the house, Mother. Say yes. It'll be good for both of us."

Her mother shook her head slowly. "I don't want any bloody parties. Save it for the wake."

While her mother napped, Hazel waited for Greene, Forbes, and Wingate to arrive at the hospital, where she had arranged to use an empty chapel as a meeting place. Greene arrived with a large bouquet of flowers for Emily and left them at the nursing station, unaware that Hazel could see him from the window in the door. She wanted to hate him for trying so hard to seem like a good man. Then she remembered that he'd always *been* a good man. She was the one who had driven him out and only her shame and her pride prevented her from seeing him now the way she'd once seen him. This thought arrived whole, slipping in alongside her worries.

She opened the door to the chapel. "In here," she called to them.

"How is she?" Wingate inquired when the door was closed behind them. There were four pews inside the small room with an aisle running down the middle, a podium with a cloth draped over it, and a stained-glass window that was actually a glass box with a few lightbulbs in it. They arranged themselves at the ends of pews like four priests having a convocation.

"She's stable," Hazel said. She found she couldn't look any of them in the eye. "I stopped seeing her. I stopped noticing."

"It's not your fault," Wingate said.

"She doesn't want to live. How do you make a person want to live?"

The three men nodded, acknowledging her difficulties, but, like most people, they didn't know what to say.

Wingate said, "Cherry gave a name. She said Kitty would kill a man named Sugar. I've already looked through six Westmuir directories. There are, like, eighty people with that name in the county."

"Mr. Sugar."

"If that's his real name. I'm René Arsenault now." He dug into the inner pocket of his jacket and removed the laminated ID card in Arsenault's name. He handed it to Hazel.

"He gave you this?" she asked.

"Someone in that place could make a fake ID in less than three minutes. It looks real, too. There's even a hologram in it."

She held it up to the light and tilted it back and forth. "So they have a way of assigning memberships to false names and they generate their own ID. That's how they know who's getting into the cabs. They take reservations or something. Or there's something on the ID that confirms membership." She ran her hand along the surface, feeling a difference in textures, and held it against the light again. "You were lucky this Ronnie didn't run your own fake ID. Christ. He figured you got in legitimately, and he didn't check. Now you're in for real."

"But I have to reserve. Or arrange a time, or something like that. I don't think you can just swan in . . ."

"So how?"

"Wherever it is you sign up in the first place and they issue you your ID. There's probably only one way to communicate with them." He held his hand out for the card, but she'd slipped it into her pocket.

"Hold on a second," she said. "I know where it is. It's the casino. Five Nations. That's why they ask you for your driver's licence."

"Back up?"

"You go to the pickup window and they hand you back a brand-new Five Nations players card and your driver's licence. Like everyone else. The thing is, you never gave them *your* licence in the first place."

"The card they give you operates the door," said Forbes.

Wingate looked at him, a little sharply, Hazel thought. "I know that," he said. "And the name I registered with the service is on the card they made for me."

"So how do you arrange a second visit?"

By mid-afternoon, her mother's colour had returned. As far as Hazel could tell, they'd now pumped about ten litres of fluid and nutrition into her and damned if she didn't look fresh as a three-day-old daisy.

"How are you?"

"I feel reanimated. Like Frankenstein's monster."

"You just needed watering."

"Don't get too used to this. My miraculous comebacks."

"I'll take what I can get."

She spent the rest of the afternoon annoying the nurses at their station, reading the newspaper standing up, and making and receiving phone calls. She went back and forth to her mother, bringing water, magazines, and cookies. She was taking an early supper with her when one of the exasperated nurses came into the room to tell her she was wanted again.

It was Wingate, waiting out by the nurses' station. "How's she doing now?"

"They're still rehydrating her. She was like a dried-out old washcloth."

"Did you get what we need?" He passed her a metal-barrelled penlight. "Let's go over here."

He followed her into a supply closet. "I don't think this looks very good, you and me walking into a closet together."

"Shut up. Turn off the light." He did, and she snapped the penlight on and took the Arsenault ID out of her pocket. "There was a texture on the surface of the laminate," she said, and she shone the light over the card.

"What is it?"

"Nothing," she said. "Nothing I can see. But there's something there." She passed the card to him and he ran his fingertips over the laminate.

"I think it's just the texture of the plastic."

She turned off the flashlight and they were both silent in the darkness for a moment.

"I wonder if the cafeteria here takes big bills," she said. She opened the door and light flooded the little room. One of the nurses was turning a corner and saw them standing there, in the near dark. “We were playing with our two-way radios,” she told her, and the nurse pulled her head back on her neck and continued on her way.

They took the elevator down to the cafeteria and went directly to the cashier. “What are you doing?” Wingate whispered.

“Watch this,” she said. She went up to the cash. “Excuse me, but do you take large bills?”

“We do,” said a lady with a hairnet.

“Do you check them?”

The lady noticed Wingate was in uniform. “We’re supposed to. Do you have a bad bill you want me to check?”

“Yes,” said Hazel, and she dug out the ID again. “Check this.”

The woman looked at the ID, perplexed, but then she did what she was told and removed a little handheld device from a drawer below her cash register. Hazel took it from her. It was a banknote verifier with a UV light in it. Hazel switched it on and slipped the ID under the light.

“Oh, *well*,” said Wingate.

“Look at that.”

Struck out in ghostly purple, the image of a sparrow in flight floated over the printed data on the card. And below the form of the animal were five characters:

.info

] 27 [

Early afternoon

Hazel and Wingate went to visit Cathy Wiest at Ursula Greene's B&B. She was ensconced on the patio, sitting at a wrought-iron table and sipping an iced tea under a clear sky when they appeared. She froze at the sight of them. "It's okay, Cathy."

"Do I have to go home?" Her eyes darted back and forth between them.

"Not yet, not if you don't want to," Hazel said. "Ursula says you can stay as long as you like."

"Okay," she said, and she visibly relaxed.

It was terrible to see this proud woman reduced to a state of numbness, as terrible as it was to watch her mother begin to give up the ghost. So much of life was contingent. No one could tell you it wasn't, nor that you wouldn't suddenly be subject to its contingencies. Cathy Wiest's nerves were shot. It was going to take a long time to bring her back to the world.

Hazel hadn't wanted to come up and disturb her further, but they'd agreed that the prior connection between Jordie Dunn and Henry Wiest had warranted it. They had to know what Dunn had meant when he said that Henry was trying to help the girl they now knew as Kitty. How did Henry come into contact with her? Was Henry just another client of Sparrow's, one who had a change of heart? Or had he and Kitty somehow made contact with each other another way? Through Dunn, for instance?

They knew they were going to have to go back into that terrible place. But whether Wingate went in as René Arsenault or they just busted it wide open depended on what their options were. Maybe there was another way, a way Dunn had shown Henry Wiest.

Hazel sat down at the patio table beside her and put her hand on Cathy's. The grief-stricken woman looked at it like she'd never seen a hand before. Wingate stood a few feet away, trying to give them some privacy.

"We've made some progress," Hazel said. "We think we know what Henry was doing at the smoke shop in Queesik Bay."

"Oh?" A flicker behind her eyes.

"We think he was trying to help someone. A young

woman who had been . . . mistreated. The woman who came to your house."

"The girl who killed him?"

"Yes."

"Why did she kill him if he was trying to help her?"

"We don't know that yet."

"Are you sure he was trying to help her?"

"No," said Hazel quietly, sorry to have to tell Cathy Wiest the truth as she so far understood it. The truth was, they still couldn't tell the victims from the perpetrators. And it was possible, as it was always possible, that Henry Wiest had not been who he'd seemed.

Cathy's gaze tracked over Hazel's shoulder to Wingate. There was a low, gentle breeze playing in her hair. She looked like an old woman to him. "Have you caught her?" she asked him. "Is that why you're here? To tell me you've caught her?"

Hazel squeezed the woman's hand, bringing her back. "We don't have her yet. But we're getting closer. We just need to ask you a couple more questions."

She pulled her hand out from under Hazel's. "How is Beedle?"

"Beedle?"

"My bird?"

"Oh. Beedle is fine. He's at the station house."

"She," Cathy said distantly. "Beedle is a girl."

Wingate stepped forward and took the seat on the other side of her. "Cathy," he said, "do you know Jordie Dunn?" They had decided not to tell her that Dunn was dead, or that she was going to have to stay here, secluded, until the case was wrapped up. There was no point in upsetting her any further.

"Yes. Jordie worked for Henry. Sometimes."

"Did they know each other well? Would Jordie have shared confidences with Henry? Were they friends?"

"I don't know."

"So they didn't know each other socially then?"

"Maybe they saw each other at the bar, or a party or something. I just don't know."

"And Jordie didn't come up at all in conversation in the few weeks before . . ."

"No, I told you no." She pushed her chair back and stood. "I want to lie down."

They let her go back into the cottage. Ursula Greene was there, and she put an arm around Cathy. These were small-town graces, and Hazel was glad that the community had come together to support Cathy in her hour of need. But they were in their hour as well, and no help was coming. René Arsenault could go back to those dreaded rooms any time he wanted to now, but the phantom shooter on the roof of the Forty Winks Motel in Kehoe Glenn suggested that more eyes were on them than they strictly wanted.

"What if whoever killed Jordie Dunn is trying to keep our attention while they deal with their missing person on their own?" Hazel asked him in the car. "Clean up their own mess and keep an eye on us at the same time?"

"You must have been seen going into the Lorris Arms. They waited until you came out."

"It would have been hard to shoot Jordie in his apartment."

"But not hard to take a shot at him when he got back, or at you when you went in."

"Maybe not." They angled out onto the highway that led back to Port Dundas. "So they wanted us both, is what you're saying."

"Or him. And they just wanted to send you a message. *Stay away*."

"I wish them luck with that," she said.

They drove in silence for a while, each lost in their own thoughts. Then Wingate said, "Do you think it's possible they know who I am?"

"How?" she asked. "You haven't been down to the reserve on official business once since you came to Westmuir. Nobody knows you down there. But if you think you've been compromised . . ."

"No," he said.

"We can work another angle if you want. We just raid the place. Go in hot."

"Those girls in there die if you do that."

"Maybe not. And you don't."

"This can't wait," he said. "You have to send me back in tonight. Before they decide it's time to cover their tracks."

"Let me think about it," she said.

Wingate buzzed through on the radio just as they were pulling in. Howard Spere was waiting for them in the Port Dundas station house. He put his hand on Hazel's shoulder as she came into what was still, apparently, her office. "I'm sorry to hear about your mother," he said.

"Thank you, Howard. What have you got?"

"A leap forward. We stuck *sparrow.info* into a browser and got nowhere, so then Austin Franks – do you know Austin?"

"I haven't had the pleasure."

"You'd like Austin. He's a nice young guy. There's word that Willan might be moving him to the new HQ."

"Keep going, Howard."

"Anyway, Austin's got a good head. He tried a bunch of things: 'sparrow' in French, in German, in Polish . . . nothing. Then he asked some local birding association what kind of sparrow was on the chip."

"It's a house sparrow."

"How'd you know that?"

"I know what a house sparrow looks like. Don't you know what a house sparrow is? James?"

"I know what a house sparrow is."

"Fine," said Spere. "It was a house sparrow. So Austin looks at the Latin name. *Passer domesticus.* He puts that into a browser, and . . ."

He was done talking, and Hazel spun quickly to her desk. Wingate and Spere stood behind her, watching. She typed in *passerdomesticus.info*. The screen went blank, and then the image that had been on the casino chip faded up on the screen. Superimposed on it was a simple two-item toggle:

O Male
O Female

She looked behind herself and Spere made a gesture with his hand that said *carry on.* She clicked the second choice. The next screen said:

> Please create an email account
> in the name of
> **Fiona Emery**
> at hushmail.com.
> Click here when you are done.

She slid her chair away. "Do it," she said to Spere, and he leaned forward and hurriedly began typing in another window, one that had already been set up to take the name. In a matter of a minute, she was in the brand-new mailbox for Fiona Emery. There were two emails: one from Hushmail, welcoming her, another from Donnotreply@passerdomesticus.info.

> Pick up your membership card from member services after 3pm today. Deactivate your hushmail account now.

"Jesus," Hazel said. "That's it. Now the question is, how do you get an invite?"

"If someone goes down there this afternoon . . . ," said Wingate.

"There should be an ID waiting to be picked up by a woman giving her name as Fiona Emery."

She sent Wingate to fetch Ray Greene. He came into her office and closed the door. Hazel explained what they'd found to him. He came around the other side of the desk and looked at the browser windows that were open.

"Wow. That's a hell of an operation," he said. "We better send Bail or Jenner down to get that ID."

"Well, I can't go in there again," Hazel said.

"But you can send René Arsenault back into Sparrow's," Greene said.

Wingate nodded. "I can get in." Hazel looked at him. "There are two girls in there."

"But you need money."

"Fifty-four hundred."

"I'll clear it with Willan. When we get the false IDs at the Five Nations, we'll authenticate that it's the same production as the others, and then we'll shut it down."

"The whole casino?"

"Until we have everyone who's on the inside there, yes. When it's locked down, we'll bust the operation on Ninth Line. With you inside, we can communicate the timing of the bust."

"I had no reception down there."

"Can the signal be boosted, Howard?"

"I think so," said Spere.

"And what about Commander LeJeune?" Hazel asked.

"What about her?" Greene said.

She smiled at him. She couldn't help it.

] 28 [

Afternoon

This was how it would go down: Jenner, who was naturally more settled a person than Eileen Bail, would go down to the casino and walk calmly up to the pickup window at about five o'clock in the afternoon. There she would give the name Fiona Emery and see if it resulted in getting the ID. If it did, she would signal to Hazel, who would be in an unmarked van up on Church Bay Road, behind the Five Nations Casino, with Spere and Greene, and the operation would go live, with Wingate entering Thurlow's cab as Lupertans again, complete with Lupertans's ID. If it was possible, they were going to release the door in the riverbed from a distance with Fiona Emery's magstripe paired to a remote that could communicate on the same frequency as the lock and send three officers in. They were to secure the casino and leave one man there while the other two went deeper in to reconnoitre with Wingate, who would be "arrested" with the rest of the gamblers and the staff. Wingate had the number of employees at five, but he knew logically it had to be more. The forward group could neutralize the man who opened the door for him, as well as the hostess, and perhaps Ronnie, depending on his location. The guard named Gene would have to be taken down and whatever other guards might be present with the other girls. Wingate seemed sure there were only two. Another detail would take the Eagle simultaneously. There was also at least one other person in the Five Nations casino allowing the IDs to be distributed.

By four, there were unmarked cars in position at both ends of the Eighth, Ninth, and Tenth lines, as well as on RR26 at the entrance of the reserve, and Sideroad 1, above the Fifth Line. They were cutting off all avenues of escape. Wingate's tracker had been replaced by a device that would get a signal boost from a location a kilometre away from the grove. Willan signed off on it. It was going to be the largest police operation of its kind in Westmuir County, ever. There were a lot of moving parts, and much room for error.

By 4:30 p.m., everyone was in place. Wingate confirmed that Thurlow was driving and got into the man's cab in front of the Eagle. Cassie Jenner, in a pair of baggy pants and a golf cap, walked into the casino at 4:35. She got into a lineup that was three people long and waited her turn. There was no sense at all that anything more illicit than people wasting their money was going on here. The woman at the membership intake desk was all smiles and efficiency, and the woman behind the little Plexiglas porthole, the one who was fulfilling the memberships, seemed just as warmly businesslike. The two ID employees were in identical casino uniforms. Cassie reached the front of the line and gave them the name, as she was instructed. With no acknowledgment or fanfare of any kind, the woman handed the ID over. "Good luck," she said.

Cassie walked out and murmured "Got it" into her lapel mic. She was to walk now to the location of the unmarked van parked on the shoulder on a residential road behind the casino, where Spere would swipe the magstripe through a data reader. At the same moment, "Pete Lupertans" was being driven into the fields. She walked past the valet's podium and crossed the driveway that led into the first of the parking lots at the front of the Five Nations Casino. There was a woman in a uniform standing on the other side of the driveway, talking into a radio. She stepped forward and blocked Jenner's path.

"Madam, my name is Commander Ileanna LeJeune," she said. "I'm afraid you're under arrest."

Thurlow drove in silence, keeping his focus on the road in front of him, as Wingate went over in his mind the features of his own plan. Willan had supplied Greene with another fifty-four hundred dollars, which Wingate had in an inside pocket of his jacket.

He didn't care about the money. There were two innocent women in that place, kidnap and torture victims, trapped underground, and his only goal was to get them out alive. The three men (they were all men) Greene was planning on sending in after him were to take any and all parties they found in the casino, including the bettors themselves, and cart them off, but by the time the raid was two minutes in progress, he was pretty sure hell would have broken out in the other parts of the site. This meant getting out of that room, where he'd have the first chance to neutralize at least Gene. He had no weapon on him at all, though, just his wits and his training. It had been a long time since Wingate had taken a man down with his bare hands, but as he'd learned before, righteous anger tends to focus a person. He had no doubt he could put Gene down in a matter of seconds. He viewed his own actions in advance, in the training room of his imagination, and he saw himself coming out to ask for something – some rope, some whiskey, something credible – and before Gene could react to the request, Wingate would deliver a single fingertip stab to the throat, followed by a knee in the balls. Simple, direct, effective. Then he'd have the weapon before Gene could either react or notify any of the other casino employees. Especially Ronnie. He wanted to stay clear of Ronnie. Then Cherry would show him the door to where the other girl was being kept. There would be two more heavily armed officers with him by this point.

All of their energies were now dedicated to busting the brothel in the fields. The murder that had touched off the whole case was back-burnered now, the first salvo in a crime the dimensions of which they could never have imagined until they'd seen it for themselves. He was more or less in a state of rooted terror. He could think, but he was actively in fear of his life now. It was amazing to him that this Kitty, on nothing but her will and her wits, had gotten out of here. And then done what she'd done. This was a dangerous person, a desperate person. It had not been admitted openly, but her transit from prime suspect to victim during the past week made their attitude toward her own mission sympathetic, if not exactly collegial. If Henry Wiest and Terry Brennan had encountered Kitty the way it seemed they must have, then whoever was next on the girl's list was low priority at this point. If she found what she was looking for, she'd vanish and be of no further concern to them. Or, Wingate had to admit, at least of no further concern to him. If David had survived the beating that had killed him, Wingate imagined not one of his colleagues would have spent much time investigating the mysterious revenges David might then have enacted. Not that he was that kind of person. Wingate was that kind of person. Or at least he'd become it.

Thurlow arrived at the grove at 4:45, and the black Mercedes stood guard as Wingate got out the back of the cab. It was a pleasant August late afternoon.

"He's there," said Spere, tracking a small, hollow blue triangle on a screen in the remote van. Hazel watched the symbol move forward at walking speed now and then stop at where the metal door was with its card reader. She imagined the door in its concrete footing and saw a pale grey square with a heavy plate in it, something like the hole Alice went through to get to Wonderland. That, too, had been a tale of innocence full of strange perversions, but they were harmless ones. She remembered reading those books to Emilia and Martha when they'd been girls, and like all children who had heard those stories, the thrill and magic of hidden worlds had animated their imaginations thereafter. Hazel doubted, were she ever to have grandchildren, that she would read those books now. Especially after learning, some years after the girls had grown up, what kind of man Lewis Carroll had been.

"Where are Willan's guys?" she asked Greene. Willan had insisted on supplying Toronto SWAT-trained men for the raid. They'd arrived in Mayfair the night before.

"They're in place."

"I have to give them the signal," said Spere. "I have to run the card Jenner's bringing first. If I can't trip the door remotely, then I have Dortmeyer ready to run it out."

"Who's Dortmeyer?"

"One of mine."

"I'm going in myself if you can't trip it from here."

Greene put his hand on her wrist. "I have strict orders to keep you under my wing," he said.

"Is that the word Willan used? Or did he say *thumb*?"

Greene smiled at her. "Just sit tight. There's a plan."

She checked her watch. On foot, it was supposed to take Jenner ten minutes to get to the van. She had one more minute.

The triangle was moving again. Spere said, "He's in. He's at a depth of five feet. Eight. Ten." It stopped. This was the second door. A moment later, the symbol that represented him moved forward a millimetre on Spere's screen.

"She should be here," Hazel said, and she stepped past the two men to the front seat of the van, where a black and white screen showed four small squares of real estate on all four sides of the van. She looked at the upper right-hand corner, which showed the view to the rear, where Cassie Jenner should already have been visible. "I don't see her at all," she said.

"Take it easy," said Greene. "James is moving around freely inside the casino now. Give her another couple of minutes."

Hazel kept her eyes trained on the view out of the back. They were parked down Church Bay Road behind the casino, pulled off to the side. The outside of the van had been painted with the name *Wilson and Son Surveying*. There were even two men standing in the woods beyond with a compass and theodolite. They'd been Willan's idea.

Wingate was now moving in a straight line again. Howard Spere was working on the screen in front of him, clicking squares on a grid that overlaid the satellite image of the fields between the Ninth and Tenth Lines. It looked like a rudimentary computer game now, with glowing red squares marking where the triangle had been. According to the grid, Wingate had travelled now to a depth of five metres, and he was about a hundred metres southeast of the entrance in the grove. Now the pathway curved and he descended another eight feet. The signal was still strong.

It was 4:50. Jenner was three minutes late now. "I'm calling her," Hazel said. She got her cell out and dialled her constable. Jenner answered her phone after two rings, but it wasn't Jenner's voice.

"Who is this?" it said.

"Who is this? Where's Cassandra Jenner?"

"Who's Cassandra Jenner?"

Hazel tried to hide the alarm in her voice. Greene and Spere were staring at her. "I must have the wrong number." She hung up. "Fuck."

"What is it?"

"She's compromised," Hazel said. "We have to get Wingate out of there."

Before they could stop her, she'd thrown the road-side door of the van open.

"Do you believe me now?" said Cassie Jenner.

It took Hazel a moment to register who Jenner was talking to. She saw Commander LeJeune returning the cellphone to the constable. LeJeune came forward and looked into the van.

"Well," she said. "Isn't this a surprise."

Ronnie met Wingate at the inner door. "Mr. Arsenault," he said. "Welcome back."

The casino was almost empty. A couple of diehards, including the woman he'd seen last time at the blackjack table, were hard at work gambling. He guessed the operation also catered to people who couldn't stop, and for whom the will or desire to lose everything was strong.

"You brought the money?" Plaskett asked. Wingate handed it over. "Cherry's ready for you."

He led Wingate through the door in the roulette room that opened onto the continuation of the riverbed, which connected the casino to the rooms beyond, and Wingate followed him. He thought of the matchbook-sized device planted under the sole of his right shoe and willed it to send its beacon back to Howard Spere's computer loud and clear. His muscles were twitching in his forearms and his calves. For a moment, he wondered if he shouldn't try to take the man out here and now, between the two populated parts of the site, but if he went alone through the door that Gene was watching, he might not get another chance at Plaskett. He had to wait.

"After this, you can come back and try someone else," he said. "We're expecting some new stock as early as next week."

The sound of Plaskett's voice intoning these details so casually filled Wingate with rage. But as René Arsenault, he forced himself to say, "I can hardly wait. If Cherry is anything to judge by, you can expect to see a lot more of me."

"I like to hear that," Ronnie said. "We like to keep our customers happy."

They had reached the door in the earthen wall and Ronnie ran his card through. The door swung open and almost right away, there was a second sound, a louder one, and Plaskett flew backwards, a spume of dark red blood tracing his descent. He hit Wingate flat on, driving him backwards. Wingate twisted, scrambling to the side, trying to make himself as small as possible against the curved wall behind him. He heard footsteps coming forward.

"Detective Wingate?" came a woman's voice.

In a dark patch in front and to the side of the door, he was trying to control his breathing.

"I know you're there. It's okay, come out."

He waited a moment and then emerged. The woman standing in the doorway held a Ruger in her hands. He recognized it as a single-shot model of the kind that likely killed Jordie Dunn. "I'm unarmed," he said.

"I know," the woman replied. "I'm Constable Lydia Bellecourt."

"Thank God," he said, coming forward, breathing a sigh of relief. "Did you guys come in from the Eighth Line?"

"No," she said.

"Well, I'm just glad you came when you did. Do you have a radio?"

"What do you want a radio for, Detective Constable?"

Something in her tone made him realize he'd been operating under a presumption borne out of the fear he'd felt when her gun had gone off. Now he saw she was still holding the gun, and holding it on him.

"What's going on here?"

"Who do you think told Ronnie to give you a new membership card? And told her commanding officer that the casino might be doubling as an outlet for fake IDs? She has no idea what for, of course, but she's probably taken down the other half of your raid by now. No one is coming, Detective Wingate."

Hazel had wondered out loud if Dunn's murder had been a warning to them, and it had. But in reading the warning the wrong way, they had played into Bellecourt's hands. She'd been a step ahead of them the entire time.

"Come on in back," she said. "You can join the party."

] 29 [

She finished her run with the top of the house in view over the trees, and she rested. She didn't have any way to tell the time accurately, but judging by the position of the sun, it was coming up to five o'clock. If, for whatever reason, Sugar had gone out, he'd be back by six. It would be a good idea to find a vantage on the driveway and keep an eye out for the delivery boy.

She dipped back down below the house – the address was 175 Highland Crescent – crossed the road quickly, and ran back up to a position across from it. And like clockwork, about forty minutes later, a car pulled up the drive and parked at the top of the curve. A man with a large brown paper bag knocked on the door, and she watched Sugar open the door and pay the man in cash. She saw the delivery boy look down into his hand – no doubt Mr. Sugar was a poor tipper – and he got back into his little car and came out the other end of the driveway.

How much did that house cost? Why do people who have everything want more? They get bored. Money shows them what's available, and after a while, they start wanting what isn't available. She'd known wealthy people back in Ukraine, it was impossible not to at least know someone who knew an oil magnate. Ukraine was lousy with oil magnates, and they were obsessed with tax dodges. There was another story in the newspaper every week.

She waited for the lights to go on in the TV room at the side of the house she could see, and then she crept up through the trees and crossed to the other side of the house. There were doors and windows everywhere in this place. He'd spared no expense. But at the same time, he'd created about twenty ways into his home.

She'd checked just three doors and two windows before she spotted a slip of curtain flapping lightly in the breeze on the wrong side of the wall. A window was open a couple of inches. She listened for any sounds beyond, then raised the pane as silently as she could. When she was able to fit her body through, she immediately dropped to the floor and stayed still. This was a study of some kind. She'd never been in here. She could only presume that if Sugar ever got his way and kept her forever, eventually she would have been raped in this room, too. But this was the first and last time she was ever going to see it.

Sugar loved carpeting and walked barefoot everywhere in the house – this was an unexpected boon to her now. Barefoot herself and raw from the run, she was grateful for the softness and cool of the carpets. And, of course, they muffled her steps.

She opened the study door a crack and looked into the hallway. She could hear the drone of Duffy's television, a repeating cycle of intonations with just enough variety that you knew a human was speaking. The house smelled of pizza and her stomach wrenched. She was starving, but her body was craving real food: fresh vegetables, fruits, brown rice, good coffee, chocolate. The smell of fast-food cheese sickened her. In the hallway, she oriented herself to the sound and determined that she could get around the back of the house to the cold storage, and through it, into the back hall and then the TV room.

She moved down the hall toward the back of the house and realized she was going to have to pass Duffy's guest bedroom. He was strangely fastidious about his own room, and she had never been brought into it. It was the guestroom where she was attacked most frequently, and where he kept most of his paraphernalia. She went past it silently and didn't look into its open door.

Ten days ago, she'd had no hope at all, and now she was almost a free woman. They'd tried to trick her, or test her loyalty, but she'd been too clever for them. She'd heard that Bochko liked to test the girls, to see if he'd truly broken them. He tempted them. Those who failed weren't heard from again. Eventually, all of them were never heard from again.

A man had been waiting for her in one of the bedrooms, someone new. Bobby was standing in the doorway behind her, telling the new man to have a nice time. Kitty was still fresh, he said. Talented.

The man had been waiting on the bed, almost expressionless, looking out of place. She came over and sat beside him as she'd been trained, and took his hand.

"Do you speak English?" he asked.

"I do."

"Do you read it?"

He palmed a note into her hand and she looked down. It was a folded piece of paper. "Read it later," he said.

"What is it?"

"It's help," he said, and his eyes slid away from hers. It was almost as if he was ashamed of himself.

A good actor, she thought. "What do you want me to do?"

"Read the note."

"No," she said. "Now. What do you want me to do now?"

His face creased with pain. "Can you dance?"

She put the note deep in one of her slippers as she undressed for him. He was strange, but many of them were strange. Uncertain of themselves, wanting to be led, needing permission to vault out of their guilt so they could have what they'd paid for. Only Duffy and Brennan had taken her for a whole week and had availed themselves of every vile impulse they had. But the rest could not say what they wanted; some did not know, even. Only their lusts overcame their horror at themselves. So many of them, she could see, could never have had a woman the way they wanted, unless they paid. Here, no one could say no to them. That's what this place was: a place where you got what you asked for, no matter how romantic, no matter how depraved. The girls had been trained to please. Even when there was just a couple of them, one was always coiffed and made up and glassy-eyed with vodka, and the other was starving. There was demand for both. The ones in the dresses, who sometimes slept on the upstairs beds, eventually made the transition to broken-down and filthy. The ones who started beautiful would tell the ones who didn't that it was better to be beautiful, just like in the real world. For the ones earmarked for abuse and torture, it was always good to be a little beautiful, but also not too capable of putting up a fight. Their men had agendas. Some of the girls didn't come back.

The man, who told her his name was Henry, didn't want to go to bed. So she danced for him and he watched with a paralyzed expression on his features. She danced for him, telling him if he wasn't pleased, she would be punished. After fifteen minutes had expired, he knocked on the door to leave. Gene had come on shift and he regarded this "Henry" with a sly look, saying he must have been desperate if he only lasted a quarter of an hour. And Larysa had been taken back to her room in the dungeonlike space below the bedrooms.

She took the note out when she was securely locked in her cubicle.

> My name is Henry. A man you know as Caleb Merton came to me. He is a friend of mine. He gambles, and he came here, but he didn't know what was really going on here. I will come back tomorrow. I will help all of you if I can.

Her heart had sped at reading these words, but she knew well enough not to trust what she was told or what things seemed. There was no limit to the depravity of the men who had found this place. If he came back, she would see what he was made of.

She kept the note to herself, reading and rereading it that night. Right now, there were two others down in the dirt-walled "dorms" where the girls were kept when they were not upstairs, servicing the paying customers. Timmy was no longer there: she had been delivered up to someone for their personal use. That, or she was gone. Bochko took girls back sometimes, as he had already done once with Timmy. If a girl needed to be disciplined, they became

Bochko's wife for a period. Larysa had heard that sometimes the girls who were punished did not come back. But Timmy had come back once; maybe she would again.

At night, they pressed their mouths against the dents in the dirt where there was space at the ends of the walls and talked. No one knew how it had all begun; none of the original girls were still here. But the one who had been there the longest knew what had happened to some of them, and knew what would happen to most of them. Her name was Cherry. The other one was called Star. They had shared their real names as well, which they kept like secret coins and never used. There was a form of communal knowledge they had that had been passed down. They knew that above them was a farmhouse on a country road that no one lived on for five or six kilometres in either direction. Only three rooms in the rear of the house were in use: a living room, a bedroom, and a sort of guestroom that looked like an office. The casino itself was down the mouldy-smelling tunnel they brought them through blindfolded if they ever had to take a girl out. They had dug out the back of the house's basement into the raw dirt and made the three cubicles there as well as a fourth, big enough to hold all three of them. It had come down through the broken telephone that the machines used for the job had been "borrowed" at night from a construction site at a town nearby. But no one knew if that was true or not. It was hard to imagine how this place had been built, but clearly the ground had never been broken in the open. *Imagine creating this place in secret*, Larysa thought. But this part was a house, which meant there was an exit to the outside closer than the one at the end of the tunnel.

The capacity of the downstairs pen was four; they could manage four girls at a time. If one vanished, another would appear to take her place. Larysa had replaced the one called Gina. Gina had been another of Bochko's favourites. Cherry had already expressed her belief that Bochko chose which girl he wanted and then set her a test she would fail. Then she'd *have* to be punished.

As he'd promised (or threatened), the man called Henry came back the next day. This time, Gene was on duty. He let her into the room where Henry waited for her. Now he was in the bedroom, proper, with its high, four-poster bed. The wall that she presumed had once held a window had been planked up with gypsum.

She stood as far away from him as the room would allow, staring at him. He looked harmless to her now; his expression was of honest concern. Finally, she sat on the end of the bed and motioned with her head that he should sit as well.

"Did you read my note?"

"There is no reason to save me," she said.

"You *want* to be here?"

"We have to be careful," she said, "they are watching us." She slid forward off the end of the bed and kneeled in front of him, spreading his legs. She undid his belt and she had to hold him down on the bed with her forearms to keep his whole body from shooting forward off the mattress. She clasped his thighs hard and said, "Don't move."

"Please, I – "

He had responded to her touch. He couldn't hide that he was like all the others. She lay her hand in his lap. "How do you think you can help?"

"I can get the police to come. Just tell me how many girls are down here. Who has weapons and how many are there?"

She laughed inwardly. Bochko would kill her for just telling the number of girls. "I know nothing," she said.

"I won't hurt you, Kitty. But I can't help you if you don't trust me." Her eyes were briefly on his. "Upstairs, they were bidding on others. Where are the other girls?"

"There is no other girls. There is only me."

"Jordie – Caleb – said he was asked if he had a preference . . ."

"There is only me," she said.

"I have to call the police."

She raised her head off his lap. His face hovered like the moon against the dark ceiling. She felt cocooned with him. "If you tell police, I will be dead before they come. I promise you this. At first trouble, they shoot." She felt him tense up beneath her again. "*How* I can trust you? Huh?"

He lowered his head and squeezed his eyes shut. "What

am I doing here?"

"I thought you are saving my life. You want? To save my life?"

"Yes."

"Come back tomorrow. Think *how*. How will you do this? If I believe, I let you save me."

He already had a plan. She listened. He wanted to make it possible for her to escape. The look on his face. Once, he touched her hand. He was for real or he was a good actor. When she got out, she would come to him, and they would go to the police together. He told her to look for his pickup at the back of a parking lot, a place he was pretty sure no one would be looking for her. When she got to him, he'd have a blanket to hide her under in the cargo bed. Then they could go to the police. He made her promise she would come and not risk her safety any further. But why did he want her to *come* to him? Why not, if he could help her escape, would he just not set her free entirely?

If she did not go to him, he could not take her to Bochko. And he might be taking her to Bochko. This could be the test she would fail.

But she had to do it. The chance would surely never come again. If he could get her out, she'd go to meet him. She'd decide what to do about this Henry when she had more information. She still wasn't sure what risk he posed to her. Yet.

] 30 [

Late afternoon

"Take those bloody handcuffs off of my constable," Hazel Micallef said.

Commander LeJeune told her prisoner to present the cuffs. She unlocked them and Jenner rubbed her wrists together, looking sheepish.

LeJeune said, "Detective Inspector, do you think I have no idea what's going on in my own back acre?"

"I'm sorry your slow-moving investigation has been affected by my own. But you have no idea – "

"I know about this casino, Detective. There are illegal casinos everywhere. We've been gathering evidence on three of the local ones for almost a year."

"This one's different."

"You're to pack up your van and get off native land. You're lucky you didn't blow *my* case. Go."

"Take it up with OPS brass. We're not moving."

Greene and Spere were watching her from the side door of the van. Greene came forward and introduced himself. He even fished out a card.

LeJeune ignored it. Gone were the collegiate courtesies. "I don't care who you are," she said. "This is a treaty violation. It also shows a stunning lack of courtesy."

"Look," Greene said, "we're in place. I think you're going to want to see what happens, Commander. I don't believe you have all the facts."

"I will have them presently." She snapped the cuffs shut and replaced them in her belt. "Constable Bellecourt," she said into her radio. "Come in."

"Bellecourt," came the constable's voice.

"I need you to secure Church Bay Road at both ends."

"I'll put Arnette and Mastaw on it."

LeJeune keyed off. "If you insist on staying, then stay you will," she said.

"I'm glad we're on the same page."

"I'll be back in ten minutes."

When Hazel returned to the van, Spere planted himself an inch from her face.

"What are you doing?" she asked.

"Call her back."

"Why?"

"Call the commander back."

She looked at him like he was crazy, but she reopened the door. "Commander LeJeune. One of my investigators would like to talk to you."

LeJeune hesitated, but then stopped and turned to face them again. Spere replaced Hazel in the doorway. "Keep your eye on that screen," he said. Wingate's triangle had been motionless for about a minute. To LeJeune he said, "Could you come here and radio your colleague again?"

LeJeune approached and took her radio out.

"Just keep her on for a minute or so."

LeJeune wore a distrustful look, but she understood that something was changing. "Bellecourt, come in."

The other officer's voice came through. "Bellecourt." LeJeune looked at Spere, who was gazing over his shoulder. He rotated his index finger at her, to tell her to keep going.

"Have you called in the two cars?"

"Mastaw is on his way. I'm just calling in Constable Young."

The whole time she was talking, Spere waved her away from the van, frantically flapping his whole hand at her. She stepped away, five paces, ten. He waved her farther back.

"Good then," she said. "Are you off-shift now?"

"Just left," said Bellecourt.

Spere made the okay sign with his thumb and finger, and LeJeune said goodbye. "What the hell is going on?"

"I had to make sure," he said. "There was interference." He half-turned. "Did you see it?"

"It flickered," Hazel said, "Wingate's triangle."

"Every time your constable spoke. And the interference was as strong with you standing right beside the van as twenty metres away. So it's not your radio that's causing it. Or our equipment."

"Causing *what*," the commander said frostily.

"We have a man in Sparrow's right now," Spere said. "He's got a tracking device on him. When you were talking to your constable, the signal fluctuated. More or less in time with her transmissions."

"Why?" said Hazel, leaning in to look at the screen. "Oh . . . oh, shit." She turned back to LeJeune. "She's under there, for Christ's sake." LeJeune's radio was rising into position. "No. Put that down. Just go find Lee Travers."

"You think he's still here?" said LeJeune, her face registering new knowledge.

"Who's Travers?" said Greene, but Hazel was plunging past him with her hand out.

"Give me your keys," she said to LeJeune. Spere kept calling to her from inside of the van. "Hazel – *Hazel* . . . you better come here."

"Tell me what is going on," LeJeune said.

"*Girls*," Hazel said to her. "That's what your constable is involved in, with her hunky fiancé. Kidnapped girls. Now give me your keys."

"Shoes," said Reserve Constable Lydia Bellecourt. They were standing in the laundry room with the stairs that led up to the house. Wingate kicked them off and she leaned over them. "Which one?"

"Which one what."

"Are you carrying a tracker up your ass, Detective? Because I can check there."

"Left."

She pulled up the insole from the left shoe and unpeeled the tracker from its underside. It was a sticker with a tiny metal transmitter stuck in the middle of it. A small red light shone along its rim. She put it on a step and smashed it with the butt of the Ruger. "Anything else I should know about?" she asked.

"The second that signal fails, they'll be on their way."

"They'll be at least twenty metres off. Anyway, it doesn't matter what they do. Come on."

She held her hand out in mock gentility, and he walked ahead of her. "Did your partners find you in the police service," he asked, "or did they put you through the academy to get you in place here?"

"Not partners."

"What?"

"Partner. I'm monogamous. Not like these sluts and the garbage that fuck them."

"Sorry, my mistake. Partner. Did he make you what you are, Lydia?"

She held the gun on him as he ascended the stairs to the television room. Then she steered him down the hall that had the bedrooms in it, and to another door. It led down to another part of the basement. "The way people honour each other is different from relationship to relationship. Watch your head."

He walked down to the bottom and she nudged him to the right with the end of the rifle barrel, and he turned and waited beside another door. She opened this one with a key and flicked a switch. He was hit with the stench almost at the same moment the light reached his eyes. It was a smell that made him recoil. She led him in, and he put his hand to his mouth to filter the air. The guard named Gene was lying on a packed dirt floor, the earth around his head stained a wet purple. "What will happen, Detective, is that I'm going to radio my skip in a couple of minutes and tell her and your people to come on up here. And they're going to wait at the distance I tell them to until I'm satisfied everything that needs doing is done. And then you can come out and dust yourself off. How does that sound?"

"Sounds like a lot of moving parts, Constable."

"I'm a multi-tasker. Here we are."

He'd been trying to inscribe on his memory the

desolation of this hopeless pit as she moved him through it. There were paths of cardboard on the ground, criss-crossing the little space, leading to a wall with four doors in it. These were the holding pens, he gathered. The whole space was perhaps four hundred square feet. The wall to his right had a steel door set in it.

"No expense spared," said Bellecourt. Someone had dug out this space. Just a small borer and a conveyor to the surface would have moved the dirt out. Probably it had been spread in the fields. The fields and the underground river had offered them perfect cover.

Bellecourt unlocked the heavy steel door. The moment it was open a crack, a pair of thin arms shot out of the space and scrabbled along the thick wall. Bellecourt smashed the arms with a downward swing of the rifle and a piercing cry shocked his ears. "Get back, whores," she shouted. "Get back or get shot."

She pulled the door open further. Wingate saw two women within, blinded by the sudden light. Both shielded their eyes and cried out. He recognized Cherry. Bellecourt had the gun at his back.

"Get in. We'll sort you all out later."

He walked into the space. It was ten by ten. The door closed behind him and he heard the workings of a heavy lock rotate the deadbolt into its concrete pocket.

"No . . . no . . . ," whimpered one of the voices. He felt a hand on his arm.

"It's me," he said, covering the hand. "Cherry, it's me."

"We are dead. Dead now."

"I'm Detective Constable James Wingate," he said, reaching out to the girl he didn't recognize. "I'm going to get you out of here."

"No," she said, avoiding his touch. "We will never leave here."

Hazel was already in LeJeune's cruiser, waiting with the window down for an opportunity to get moving. LeJeune had placed a call to someone she trusted in the casino and as they feared, Travers was nowhere to be found. They'd had the drop on them all along, Bellecourt and Travers. They'd controlled their every move. And now Wingate had gone silent, and the woman was down there, holding all of the cards.

Hazel put the key in the ignition. Greene was watching her blankly. "Now give me your radio," she said to Commander LeJeune. The woman appeared to be in shock, her mouth held in a small moue. She was lost in thought. "Radio," Hazel repeated, and LeJeune passed it to her silently. She put the car in drive. She raised the radio to her mouth and depressed the call button. "Bellecourt, come in."

"Ah, Hazel Micallef," came Bellecourt's voice. "Good to be on the same page at last."

"If you harm him, you die."

"Dammit," said Bellecourt. "We should have spoken before now."

"I want to talk to him."

"He's unreachable right now."

Hazel pushed the gas pedal down. This woman was going to die in pain. "Well, I guess I've played my part excellently, haven't I?"

"You did what any good detective would have done, Hazel. Don't get down on yourself now."

"Where's your fiancé?

"Taking care of business."

"I gather you know you're already surrounded by police?"

"Of course. I've had access to your frequencies since you came up and visited us last week. I know everything. Where are you right now, Hazel?"

"I'm coming to see you."

"Company! How nice."

"Will you come out and meet with me?"

"I'd love to, but I have pressing business. Can I propose we postpone?"

"I'm on the 26. I'm going over the speed limit."

"Well, you should know your James Wingate is in a hole below one of these fields. There's a hole poked in it so he can breathe, but I can stop it up anytime, if need be . . . are you still there, Detective?"

"I'm here." She tried to keep the relief out of her voice. Maybe he really was still alive.

"So let's do this my way. You go back and wait a spell with your colleagues. I'll call you when you can come and collect your friend. And you might want to tell everyone to use their cellphones from here on in."

Bellecourt disconnected. Hazel pushed the accelerator to the floor. She got Greene on her cell.

"Where's LeJeune?"

"We've asked her to stick around and 'aid' the investigation."

"Put her on." LeJeune was on the other end in an instant. "Mr. Sugar. Who is Mr. Sugar?"

"I don't know a – "

"It's not his real name. If Travers is involved with this, then maybe there's a link through the casino. Find out."

She didn't wait for LeJeune's response. She slowed down to forty for a stop sign.

Where the light was, there were also thin jets of air. It provided the only fresh oxygen they were getting, but it also contributed to the cold, which was wearying. Wingate ran his fingers over the opening of the steel pipe that ran to the surface. The bottom of it was closed over with a steel lattice that appeared to be screwed into place. Not that any of them would be able to climb up the pipe if he could get the lattice removed: the opening was five inches in diameter.

The two girls were holding each other to keep warm. It was hard to imagine that either of these women would ever recover from their trials. Only Kitty had been strong enough to survive. Perhaps Bellecourt and her accomplices deliberately chose women they thought they could break. They'd been wrong with Kitty.

He saw a fluttery movement in the corner of his eye, and it was Cherry reaching out to him. They needed his bodily warmth. Where before he had recoiled from the horror of the fact of her imprisoned body, now he went to her willingly. He found his arms were long enough to enclose them both.

] 31 [

The sound of the television was louder in the back of the house. She would have to pass through the kitchen. She pushed the kitchen's side door open slightly, the one that led into the dining room and from where she would have a vantage on him.

Through the crack in the kitchen door, she heard a voice – a TV anchor reporting the news. She saw the colours of the television program reflected on Sugar's eyeglasses. He held a bottle of red wine in his lap, his screwcap wine. Matthieu had taught her how to appreciate wine. They were going to drive through Bordeaux together. That was another of her futures she wasn't sure would happen now.

She let the door swing closed quietly and then opened it in toward herself so she could slip into the dining room. She quickly tucked herself against the wall to her right and began slowly tracing the wall to the corner, then along the side of the dining room, looking down the long wood table that never got used, and to the other corner where the wall turned to the cut-out between the dining room and the TV room. She held herself tightly up against the edge here and collected herself. She felt in her back pocket for the hunting knife that had paced her run.

It was a good knife. It was a curved, heavy one made entirely out of steel. Four inches closed, and heavy and balanced in her hand. It was spring-loaded, and small enough to hide. The night he'd given it to her, she'd sat in her dirt room weighing it in her palm. It seemed like a thing with a mind of its own. It wanted to kill.

The night she'd gotten out, shift change had come at around eleven as usual. She'd been hearing Gene's voice outside. Bobby would come in and replace him and he'd be there the rest of the night. Nothing unusual happened down there in the rooms, and whichever guard sat on the couch beside the single heater in the whole space usually fell asleep within minutes. Bobby snored. She waited in her locked cave for the sound that would tell her she could use the tip of the blade in the door handle. There was some shuffling without; she listened to it through her door. Bobby was a big man with a huge, round belly. She knew him to be careless and soft-minded. She could probably convince him to let her out to use the bucket that was in the corner of the dug-out room. But it would be better to take him asleep.

She didn't have to wait long. Soon, his deep, rumbling

snores filled the room. The noise would disguise the sound of the blade working the latch bolt. She pushed it in slowly, but the sharp tip wouldn't release the latch. The curved edge faced away. There was no handle on the inside to work.

She imagined "Henry" was already back at the Eagle, the name of the smoke shop he said was connected to Sparrow's. She'd never heard these names and she had no idea if what he was saying was true. But he told her where he'd be waiting for her. In that parking lot, at the back, near the trees. She wanted nothing more than to be on a plane heading over the ocean to home, but the more she went over the details in her mind, the more she realized there were things to be accomplished first. Housekeeping. Bookkeeping.

Cherry had told her that there was a market for their passports. A real passport could bring many thousands of dollars on the black market. But, she told Kitty, what she'd heard was that some of the men who patronized Bochko actually bought the passports as souvenirs. It was less risky for Bochko that way. You didn't want the passport of a missing woman floating out there in the world. It was better off in someone's underwear drawer, a fond memory.

Maybe Henry was the sickest one of the lot. Not only did he have the passport already, he was indulging himself in being a part of her further corruption. If Bochko could use Henry to help her escape, then Henry could use Bochko to torture her at a remove. Maybe that was the source of his apparent disgust when she had been brought to him in one of the rooms. He did not want to touch her, but he would be pleased if Bochko did.

The door's strike plate had been screwed into a flimsy frame. She could feel its wood splintering under the blade. If she could pry the plate out, she'd be able to carve under the hole that had been chiselled out for the latch bolt. It took fifteen more minutes to jimmy the plate loose, and another fifteen to get the tip of the knife under the end of the bolt. She leaned on the door and levered the bolt open and then she was free. She stood silently in the cold, open space. The other two girls had stirred and Star had whispered to her, but Larysa did not answer. She crept over the dirt floor to the couch where Bobby was sleeping and neatly sliced his jugular open. Her anatomy classes had come in handy after all. A geyser of blood burst from his throat with a sudden gush, and the big man lurched upright, grasping his throat and making a high squealing sound. He lunged off the couch instinctively, reaching for her in the near dark, and she snatched the weapon he kept in his belt from him before he crashed to the floor. The space came alive with sounds: Cherry and Star calling out in Ukrainian and Russian in panicked voices. Larysa did not answer them. She pounded on the outer door with the handle of the knife, knowing that Gene was taking his turn sleeping in one of the real beds upstairs. She didn't know how the gun she'd taken from Bobby worked. It had a handle like a gun, but the barrel was a square plate made out of plastic and metal. A cartridge of some kind was stuck into the end of it. She'd never seen a gun like it before. There was the sound of rushing treads outside and then a key turning an outer lock. She stood five feet back from the door and kept the gun at arm's length, her finger on the trigger. The door opened and she flexed her finger. A pair of wires shot out of the end of the gun and suddenly Gene was standing taller. His hands opened and the keys as well as a gun, identical to the one she was holding, dropped to the ground. He fell in a heap on top of them.

"*Shut up!*" she called out in Russian to the girls in their cubicles, and silence fell. Larysa stood, listening to the dark. No one else was out there.

The spent cartridge had ejected from the mouth of the weapon. A new cartridge had chunked into place. Gene lay on his back at her feet, but he was breathing. *Nice weapon*, she thought. *Not lethal but effective*.

She stepped over the man's insensate form and looked back at Bobby's. He wasn't dead yet, but to judge from the bubbles subsiding against the dark earth, it wouldn't be long before he died with his sins on him.

From there, it was easy to find her way out of the house. The front rooms were completely vacant. Bochko must have purchased the property and left it empty except for the spaces they needed for their activities. She had to break a couple of locked doors on her way to the front hallway, but then she simply unlocked the front door from inside and stepped out into the night.

It had been two months and nine days since she'd last stood alone and free in the night air. Their meeting place, according to Henry's map, was six kilometres away. At a good walking pace, it would take her just over an hour to make it. She stepped away from the house and began walking with long, strong strides south from where she stood. It was dark enough to walk between the fields of soy. Even at night, the peace of the deep green fields overwhelmed her with their beauty and the secret they held. She dropped to her knees and wept. But only for a minute. Then she stood straight and high and continued walking. Henry's map showed her how to avoid the main road on the way to where they would meet. She kept to the inside of the treelines along various sideroads that led in a disconnected, jagged line to her destination. A sign announced that she was entering Queesik Bay Reserve, a native territory. She heard the traffic for the first time.

Henry had told her to keep her eye out for a big red neon sign – THE EAGLE – that would be close to the main road. Now she saw it, and she crept toward it, still staying within cover, and keeping her eye out for her supposed saviour. He was at the back of the parking lot, standing beside a red pickup, waiting just as he said he would be. She emerged from the woods and he immediately dropped his arms and came toward her.

"Oh god! You made it . . . do they know you're gone?'

"I am sure everything is going as you have planned," she said, and the expression on his face changed.

"I don't know what you mean – "

"When you wake up," she said, and now he stepped away from her, seeing the gun raised before him, "tell Bochko I am not such a good girl as he was hoping. No, in the truth, I am very bad."

She fired at his face and he crumpled to the ground beside his truck.

"Am not stupid," she said to his quaking form. She was still holding the trigger down. Larysa yanked the leads out of his face and crumpled them up around the spent cartridge and stuck it all into her pocket. He had brought her a change of clothes, as he'd promised. It was all in a plastic bag on the front seat. Nothing too fancy. What did he care, when he was planning on having her out of them for most of the time anyway?

She dug in his pocket for his wallet. She rifled through his ID. One of the cards had the name of *Doug-Ray Finch*, but the rest gave his name as *Henry Wiest*. So he had told her his real name. Not worried, since she was never going to be able to use it against him, if he'd gotten his way. Sly fox. His home address was on one of the cards. She memorized it. She would have to see what he really was.

Now Mr. Sugar was sitting on a couch just a few feet away from her, utterly unprepared for what was about to happen to him. She took a deep breath. Then she turned into the room and faced Carl Duffy.

Bochko was sitting at the other end of the couch. He

was wearing a suit jacket with a white silk T-shirt under it. She could see a wall of muscle beneath the shirt.

"Hello, Kitty," he said. "You almost missed pizza."

She realized that Duffy's head was smoking.

"Say hello, Carl." He waited and then leaned over and knocked on the man's forehead. Larysa saw the tidy black hole there. That's where the smoke was coming from. "You didn't hear the shot?"

"No," she said.

"That's amazing. I bought a new silencer and they say you can't hear it past six feet. I guess it works." He rose and she took a step back. "Don't worry about Carl. You didn't need him in any case."

"No?"

"Of course not. I'll take care of you, Kitty."

"I bet," she said. "Anyway, is good. Saves time."

"See? You have an excellent attitude. Come and sit."

She hesitated and he raised the front of his shirt over his muscled stomach and showed her the butt of a gun that was tucked into his waistband. She had the urge to throw her hand out and pull the trigger on that gun. But she sat instead, across from him in an upholstered chair.

"I know what you are looking for, Kitty. And I am going to give it to you."

"Why would you do that?"

"To reward you. For all your effort. And, anyway, what am I going to do with it? I have to get rid of it. You might as well have it back." He tilted his head at her, but nothing in his two tiny eyes showed the least hint of compassion. "Come here. Come to me, Kitty. Look, here it is."

In his hand was the dark blue booklet with the crest of her country on it.

"Why didn't you just go to the police, poor little Kitty? They would have taken you in, they would have brought you right to your warm cozy consulate in Toronto and they would have worked it all out for you. Now, instead, you are back with me," he said, smiling. "And I am a little upset with you, you know."

"Do you want to know why I do not go to police?"

"I do. I do *very* much," he said, smiling warmly at her, as if he were proud of her.

"Because I get myself in this," she said. "I get myself out."

"I don't see that happening" – he opened the passport and looked at the photo page – "Larysa Kirilenko. I almost – "

At the sound of her name in his mouth, she lunged without thinking and knocked him sideways off the couch and onto the floor. But he merely lifted her off of him. He had not defended himself or even gone for his gun. He just stood and straightened himself. He held the passport out again. "Do you want it or not?" he asked.

"I want it."

She stretched her arm out and snatched it. She flipped through it quickly and saw that it was complete. Complete, but useless to her now. He would not have given it to her if there was any hope of her using it again. But she had it in her hands, this document that said she belonged somewhere, existed somewhere, had rights somewhere. She knew this would be the last victory she would ever have.

Bochko was studying the hole in Carl Duffy's forehead. "Bullet's still in there," he said. "These things break apart like the instant they meet any resistance." He looked back at her. "You'd think Carl Duffy's head wouldn't offer much resistance but – " He held his fists together in front of him and then pulled his arms apart, spreading his fingers wide. "You know? *Boooomm!* I bet it looks like pizza in there now." He laughed and leaned down to kiss the top of Duffy's head. A thin rill of red glugged out of the hole. Standing behind the dead man, Bochko looked over at her.

"So, Kitty. Where should we do this?"

She knew what he meant.

"It is up to you. Where you wish to die."

He smiled at her again, a wide-open, devouring smile. And he was about to say something else when they both heard a woman's voice coming from the street. It was small and tinny, but it was clearly saying a name. It was saying, "Lee Travers." He retreated carefully to the window, walking backwards, and lifted a curtain a little. Then he crossed the room again and grabbed Larysa by the wrist. "We have some company," he said. "Let's go."

] 32 [

Late afternoon

The burning in her cheeks and neck had subsided, and Hazel had suppressed the urge to smash the steering wheel with her fist. They'd been stupid; thorough but stupid, and the whole investigation had been tainted from the start. She tried to identify the point at which she could have seen the devil on her shoulder, but the case had been so opaque in places, and her life beyond the case so nerve-wracking . . . Had she been distracted? Had she dismissed a warning sign anywhere that might have drawn her attention back to the leak? Of course it had never occurred to her that Lydia Bellecourt had simply slotted Hazel into place in *their* plan, but that is exactly what had happened. It was shameful and horrifying. She had asked the questions *What is the girl running from?* and *What is the girl searching for?*, and these questions had been so worthy that at no point did she ever wonder if there was a fatal flaw in her point of view.

The sideroads swept past as she came closer to the Ninth Line.

What would she do now? Bellecourt had congratulated herself for staying one step ahead of them the whole way.

But now, finally, *they* were ahead. She knew where both the girl and Lee Travers were headed. She'd already dispatched cars. It had taken LeJeune less than five minutes to decipher the name Mr. Sugar. Everyone in high stakes knew him. He was a whale, not just to the casino, but in stature as well. He was allowed to eat at the tables because he bet a minimum of a thousand dollars a hand. He tipped well, too, especially the waitresses, who found him disgusting. He told them to call him Mr. Sugar. He'd made his fortune in energy drinks.

His name was Carl Duffy.

Now she didn't have to fake having a plan. She could gun for Bellecourt and let the woman find out for herself what kind of rage Hazel was capable of. Nobody put a hand on anyone she cared for.

Bellecourt planned to keep Hazel occupied with the fate of her lieutenant; she was going to keep Bellecourt occupied with the fate of her fiancé. This was their endgame. Bellecourt would have to get to Lee, or wait for him in those fields. Hazel wasn't about to let her choose, though.

She had to *not care*. The problem with a threat like the one that had been issued was that if you allowed yourself to be governed by the fear of the outcome, you might end up with nothing but the thing you feared. She had to push past it, keep Bellecourt in her sights. It was probably the only way to save Wingate and get Bellecourt and Travers into custody. She fumbled with her cell and dialled Ray Greene. "I'm not stopping," she said to him. "In five minutes you'd better have half your hands on deck up near Duffy's place and the other half on the Ninth Road. You're going to need a heat sensor to figure out where James is."

"Where are you going?"

"Straight through," she said. "I'm going to go get her. Then you move in and get Wingate out, and anyone else who might be under there."

"I don't know, Hazel."

"I don't know, either, Ray. But the longer she's roosting on top of them, the greater the chance of an outcome I don't think either of us can live with."

"Stay in touch with me. And be careful."

"I will. Just get James out." She ended the call as she passed the Eighth Line and continued up Sideroad 1 toward the grove. She might have been driving over the body of her detective constable; she focused herself on the task at hand and powered LeJeune's dark blue Maxima over the hardtop toward her destination. As she crested a low rise, she saw, in the distance, the black Mercedes that she'd seen before, coming slowly toward her, and she reached for the radio. "Bellecourt? Come in. We're alone on this frequency."

She waited. The black car seemed to be slowing. Then it turned and blocked the road sideways.

"Bellecourt?" she said into the radio. "I'm not stopping on this road."

"Hazel," came the constable's voice. "I thought I gave you my instructions."

"I know where Lee is."

"You don't."

"There are cars heading to his location as we speak."

"Please do stop. I don't want to have unnecessary blood on my hands. That's Earl Tate up ahead in the car. Do you see him?"

"I do."

"He has a rifle on him with a range of almost four hundred metres. I lent it to him. He's a good shot, too."

"Well," said Hazel, pulling the car onto the verge, "I'd better avoid him, then. Your commanding officer's cruiser has got quite a bit of horsepower." She drove far out into the field, beyond range, she thought, and then cut back in. She kept a wide berth behind the Mercedes as she drove back toward the road, through the vibrant soy.

Gunfire erupted from the passenger window of the Mercedes as she bored down on the road and pulled LeJeune's cruiser back sharply onto the hardtop. The cruiser hit the road with a jerk and a heave and fishtailed around a little, or appeared to fishtail – the fact was, Hazel was now pointing south on purpose. She was a hundred and fifty metres above the black Mercedes. The driver was no longer visible in the front of it. Protecting his head from a shot. "Last chance to catch a lift with me," she said into the radio.

"You put too low a value on life," came Bellecourt's voice.

"I have a sliding scale," said Hazel, and she put the car in first and floored it. That's when her hunch was confirmed and she saw Bellecourt pop upright in the front seat of the Mercedes. *Yes, my dear*, she thought. She remembered the Mercedes's driver had had long black hair, and she knew from Forbes's report that Tate was bald. She was already going forty kilometres an hour when Bellecourt began to hurriedly back the Mercedes up. She wasn't talking now, was she? Hazel closed the distance between the two cars, angling the cruiser to make contact with the front side of the Mercedes – fifty, sixty kilometres an hour, and she could see the determination on Bellecourt's face. She was retreating as fast as she could, dust kicking forward from her front tires, and Hazel had the whole front right panel in her sights. She collided hard against the black car and she saw Bellecourt's body leap up and toward her, but then the world went white and something punched her with incredible force. It took a moment to realize that the impact had triggered the airbag in LeJeune's steering wheel, and even as Hazel punched it down and coughed out a lungful of the white powder that now filled the car, she could see the Mercedes rolling slowly away toward the ditch, smoke and steam flowing upwards into the summer air, its rear facing Hazel. The pain in her neck told her she was going to be popping anti-inflammatories later, but job one was getting out of the car. She pushed herself out of LeJeune's cruiser and drew her weapon. There was no movement inside the black car, and the spent bladders of three airbags were hanging from its dashboard and doors. Hazel moved carefully around the back. The driver's door was still closed. She wrenched it open and found Bellecourt lying awkwardly against the passenger seat, blood dripping from the side of her head. She had something in her hand – the radio. Bellecourt's standard-issue Glock was sitting on the floor below the passnger seat. "Do it," Bellecourt said into it the radio and dropped it. She lifted her head to Hazel and gave her a small, pained smile.

"Boom," she said.

The fields behind them jumped and Hazel landed on her hip three feet from the car, skidding.

She shot to her feet and looked out to where the dust was settling within the soy. Something had been detonated, but there had been no sound, only the sensation of the earth bucking and all the air in the county rushing past her. She forced herself to focus on her prisoner: the constable was struggling to get herself upright in the front seat, and Hazel leapt out with her empty hands – the gun had gone flying – and wrapped them around Bellecourt's head to pull her out and to the ground. The constable was bleeding freely from the temple. The look in her eyes suggested Hazel had plenty of time to retrieve her gun. She grabbed it and then stood over Bellecourt, peering down the barrel at her.

"Didn't you wonder where Earl Tate *really* was?" Bellecourt asked her.

"Aren't *you* wondering if you're going to die today?" Hazel replied.

"I don't worry about that anymore."

"You should," said Hazel. She leaned over, her back protesting, and grabbed the constable by the front of her uniform and yanked her off the flattop into the base of her kneecap. Bellecourt's nose exploded against the bone and a jet of blood described the arc of her head as Hazel dropped her back to the pavement. "But I can hurt you. A lot."

Bellecourt smiled at her.

"What have you done to Wingate?"

"He's with the virgins now."

Hazel dropped the gun now and fell to her knees, straddling Bellecourt around the waist and trapping her arms. "Whatever they do to you in a court of law isn't going to be enough," she said.

Bellecourt spat blood at Hazel, laughing. "All you can do to me is shake a finger. The law is nothing, not compared to other laws."

"You're right about the law we both supposedly serve." She suddenly punched Bellecourt in the mouth, splitting both lips. "It lacks certain elegance." She punched her again, and again. Bellecourt, with her arms pinned, could do nothing to defend herself. "How do you think Lee will like you without your beauty?" Hazel asked, and she rained blows down on the constable. She stopped short of knocking her unconscious. "You thought I was bluffing, didn't you? I know where the girl has gone. I know where Lee is headed."

"You know . . . fuck all," Bellecourt rasped.

"175 Highland Crescent on Gannon. Carl Duffy." She lay her palm down flat against Bellecourt's clavicle and levered herself to standing. Bellecourt's face was swelling as if someone was pumping air into it. Hazel told her to get up.

She leaned over to retrieve Bellecourt's gun. She tossed it out the window and onto the road. "Let's go find your man," she said. Then she dragged Bellecourt back to her Mercedes and shoved her into the passenger seat. The cruiser was toast.

] 33 [

Star was asleep under Wingate's jacket, a thin windbreaker he'd decided to wear, recalling the cool of the tunnels. Now, as the cold seeped into every part of him, he wished he'd brought a parka. She'd more or less panicked herself into exhaustion, and Cherry had translated her keening wail: *Now there is no one to help us.* He'd tried to reassure her that the law was steps away from releasing them, but as time passed, her anxiety consumed her, and finally, she had slid down the wall in a heap, her eyes unseeing, and Wingate had settled her on her side. Cherry had given the younger woman the windbreaker earlier. She was made of sterner stuff, but he could tell how cold she was now. She paced, trying to keep warm, beating her hands against herself. They'd been trapped for more than an hour now.

His eyes had adjusted and it was like dusk in the underground pit. Looking up through the pipe, he saw daylight hovering high above him. Thin filaments moved back and forth over the mouth of the pipe twenty-five or so feet above his head and he realized they were leaves and stems of the soy plants in the field above. In the tomblike room, everything had a greyish hue, but he could make out details in the wall, on the ground, and he could see Cherry's expression. The muscles in her face were slack, but she was alert and alive. He felt a bond to this woman, whose real name he finally knew: Katrina Volkov. From Elizavetgrad.

"I am worry for Stoya," she said, using Star's real name. "She is smaller."

"I'm going to get you both out of here alive," said Wingate. "You're going to go home."

"In a box," she said. "Silly to take us out of one grave and put us in another."

"My people know where we are and they're coming. All you and Stoya have to do is not panic." But she knew what he knew: the room was inescapable. The door set in concrete was four inches thick and had to weigh half a ton. The room itself had been excavated from within and the structural integrity of the earth on all sides and above and below made it almost as hard as brick. The seams of the room – its edges and corners – were slightly loose from being disturbed, but there was no chance anyone could dig their way out of here. He'd already tested the wall at various points with his fingers and only where three seams met was there any give at all. These were the eight sort-of corners: four rounded ones on the ceiling and four on the floor. It was overall hopeless.

He kept examining the steel lattice that held the pipe closed. It was level with the roof of the room. Why would they have put a grille on that pipe? He'd been worrying this question for an hour now. There was no way up the pipe, of course, but closing the bottom of it off could present the possibility that someone would drop something into it. They were meant to die slowly in here, but the pipe could ensure a quicker demise in an emergency. There would be no escape from water or gas, and an explosive tossed into the pipe would sit at the level of the ceiling and bring tons of earth down on them.

This case had gotten worse and worse. He'd heard of things like this happening, and there had certainly been cases *like* it in Toronto during his time there, but this operation had been so rustic that its cruelty and deviousness took his breath away. Literally. The illegal casinos were a fact of life everywhere, but to hide something else inside of one, like an afterthought? This was more than a sideline, though. It was the work of a person who could convince others to follow. Wingate wondered now if he would survive to learn if this case would be solved. It would be a pity to die in an unsolved case. Hazel would see to it, though, that his body was recovered and given a proper burial.

When he heard something land in the lattice with a dull clank, he realized, ruefully, that his surmise had been accurate. He'd been good at his job. It made him think ahead. He'd had about half an hour to prepare, but it wasn't going to be enough. He'd used his belt buckle, but he was fairly sure, when he heard the fuse sizzling in the ceiling, that he was passing his last moments on earth. He thought of David.

Ray Greene had a force of ten men and two mechanical teams descend on the soy fields. Helicopter support had been ordered in from Mayfair, and he could hear them in the distance, closing. The incendiary team blew the door in the grove open and five men went in. The other mechanical, using the gridmap Howard Spere had created, brought an excavation digger to the place they believed the underground hold was. There was no need for Spere's map: there was an indentation in the wave of soybeans and it led to a small cave-in about two by two metres and ten centimetres at its deepest point. A little scoop in the field. Dust and smoke was still floating up from a circular opening they found in the middle of the plants. Greene called in his other team and told them to collect evidence, but not to enter the tunnels. He sent a second team into the farmhouse. But if Wingate was under the soy, they were probably going to have to dig him out. He sent three more officers to the grove and told the other two to go up on Sideroad 1 and see what LeJeune's cruiser was doing in the middle of the road.

"Try to go easy," Greene said, and the guy in the digger gestured at the giant metal scoop he was operating. "Well, try anyway!"

The man let down the head of the digger and scraped a groove in the dirt. Greene winced. When the operator dumped his load, it looked like a beach pail's worth. Anyone who was down there had a long wait ahead of them, unless they were already dead.

LeJeune rang him on his cell. "Are we still radio silent?"

"As far as I know."

"And is the detective inspector there?"

"No," he said, "but your car is."

"My car? Where is – "

"She traded up. She's in your colleague's Mercedes. They're headed north in it."

"She dumped my cruiser?"

"Did you know Bellecourt drove a Mercedes?"

"No," she said, after a moment.

He took a few steps toward the road, where he could see LeJeune's car better. The two officers were circling it, and one of them was putting his firearm away. The other kneeled at the front of the crushed hood. "It seems to be shorter now."

"What?"

"We'll have to work this out later, Commander. I'm trying to dig a hole here."

"Seems the one you are standing in is deep enough."

The digger was down almost a quarter of a metre in the middle of the depression. It scraped something, and the operator came out onto his step. "Skip?"

Greene came back to the excavation. "What is it?"

"There's a pipe down there."

He waved the digger back as well as the two men returning to the middle of the field. He tested the surface of the indentation as he walked across it to where a plain five-inch pipe was bent against the dirt. He leaned down to it. "Fried banana."

"Meaning?" asked one of the returning officers.

"Dynamite," Greene said. He put his eye to the opening and then pulled back, blinking furiously. Before anyone could inquire what had happened, he'd put his face back down and was talking into the pipe. "My name is Superintendent Raymond Greene. Can anyone hear me?"

He turned his ear to the pipe. After a moment, he repeated his message.

There was a faint whisper in his ear. He bolted upright, then anxiously settled himself again. The voice was faint and weak. "My name . . . Katrina . . . Volkov."

"Hello! Hello! Can you hear me?"

"I hear . . ."

"Are you injured?" he asked. "Can you see or hear anyone else down there?"

But there was no further reply. Greene stood and backed away from the opening. He waved the operator back into his cab. "Get going," he said. "Do it as quickly and safely as possible."

He made room and drew his other officers back with him. There were voices in the distance, men emerging from the stairway that led down under the grove.

Wingate had not been alone down there. He'd either been put with other prisoners or he'd been trying to effect a rescue when the place had been blasted. Either way, he was due for a commendation. Greene only hoped he wouldn't be giving it to him posthumously.

] 34 [

Approaching dusk

Constable Lydia Bellecourt slumped in the passenger seat of her battered Mercedes. Hazel had thought of putting her in the back, but the woman was surely capable of doing something that might have killed them both. She wanted to keep an eye on her.

She alerted incoming cruisers not to go all the way to the house; she wanted to be left alone with Bellecourt as the sole bit of stimuli. But officers were to cut off every point of exit from the escarpment, including sideroads that led down and away from the lake. There were to be no sirens. She was relaying her play through Wilton, who conferenced in Ray Greene as well as five cars on each of her calls. She had entered the escarpment. Bellecourt, who had become moribund with defeat, now seemed to rouse, a faint but rapt look on her face. Hazel had never made a large-enough allowance for the madness of others. She had been subject to any number of moods in her life, but never had she been anything but bitterly sane. Surely there was a place in every person where the spark of their insight into what they *really* were was present, and viable.

"You need to face what's happening," Hazel said.

"Go left here," said Bellecourt quietly.

The topmost road on the escarpment was Highland Crescent. Now Bellecourt sat up in her seat. She drew the back of her hand shakily over her lips and tucked a strand of hair over her ear. Hazel watched the house numbers go by. She stopped well short of number 175.

"I'm going to get out of the car now. You stay there until I open your door and then you get out. I have you in a beam of light right now, do you understand?"

Hazel got out, the gun trained continuously on her passenger, and she came around the front of the car. Bellecourt sat calmly, the eyes in her wrecked face tracking Hazel. She pulled the door open and shot a fast look down the street in case Lee Travers did have some powers she'd not yet encountered in another person, but the street was empty. Bellecourt slid out. She was holding her head at an angle, and the blood still seeped from her temple. Hazel marched her prisoner in front. "Don't give me a reason to react quickly."

"You don't want to go up to the house," Bellecourt said.

"Why?"

"You might get in his way."

"What has the girl been looking for?"

"The same thing we all are. Something that will prove we were here."

Hazel grabbed her under the armpit and spun her around. "I'm going to have three different shrinks testifying to your fitness. You can get as kooky as you want, Bellecourt." She let go of her. "Walk in front of me."

Bellecourt began to move up the street, leaning forward as if magnetised to something. "Now call him," Hazel said to her as they approached number 175. "If he's so sensitive, surely he'll hear you out in the street."

Bochko muscled her out of the house Carl Duffy had lived in. Carl Duffy was dead, and Bochko was in a hurry now. She wasn't sure if he'd planned to kill her in the house or move her, but now he was sped up. The webbing between his thumb and forefinger held tight against the tendons at the back of her neck. She was being forced down the stairs and although she stumbled, his grip on her neck, like a clamp, kept her from falling to the bottom.

"You are going to die, Bochko," she said.

He spun her around on the landing and crashed the back of her head against the wall. He pressed his kneecap into her pubis and she roared in pain. In her front jeans pocket, he roughly dug the passport out. Pinning her so ferociously meant there was no chance of his finding the knife in her back pocket. It pressed on a point high up on her buttock and lit up her nerves, connecting her pubic bone to the back of her knee in a lightning arc of pain.

He slapped her with the passport. She was surprised how much it hurt, like the end of a bullwhip. "I gave you what you wanted, Larysa Kirilenko. Now I will get what I want. I'll give this back to you when I have it."

"Even when you have it, it will not be yours."

His mouth widened into a bright, cheerful smile. "Come and see what I am." He let her step away from the wall, and she went down the stairs in front of him.

She felt the first threads of the cool evening as he led her down and out of the back of the house, and the air through the door carried the scent of the unseen lake behind the house. Under it all was the fragrance of lavender. A perfect August night. He took a handful of cloth between her shoulderblades and shoved her forward into Duffy's car, a white Porsche 911 Turbo Cabriolet. She fell into the passenger seat with a heavy thud and he walked around to the driver's side. The car smelled of leather and tobacco. Bochko slid his huge, sleek body in, like a knife into its sheath.

He put the car in gear. She lay back against the seat as if resigned and exhausted, her empty left hand hanging down with its palm up beside the gear shift.

He powered the Porsche toward the road and turned left onto it, hard, in the direction of town. The blood was shoving through her head and then he stopped suddenly and her face struck the dash above the glove compartment. A flare of orange burst behind her eyes. She smelled dried blood, cold steel, ocean. "Look at this," he said.

She raised her head to see two cops walking slowly toward the car. The one in back had her gun out, pointed straight at them.

"The door is open," he said to her. "Why don't you run?"

She heard her name being spoken loudly by both women – one calling her Kitty, the other Larysa.

Bochko rolled down the window. "Hello, Lydia," he said. Now there were cars closing into the space behind the women, moving slowly into position.

"Get out of the car, Travers," called the woman behind, and she fired a warning shot into the air. "I'm Detective Inspector Hazel Micallef."

"We've met," he called back. "You're just in time for the wedding." He levelled the gun against the bottom of the windowframe and fired a single shot, which lifted Bellecourt off her feet and threw her backwards, her right arm flying lifelessly up behind her. He pushed the accelerator down and Larysa allowed her right hand to slip into her back pocket where the knife was hidden. The steel was warm from lying against her body and she closed it in her fist and jammed her hand against her thigh. The car bucked and squealed: he was making a sharp right onto another road. Now there were more gunshots behind and the car began to go even faster. She stole a look at the speedometer. It said 130 kilometres per hour. Some kind of centrifugal force was keeping her pressed hard against the back of her seat. The road was a hardpack of dirt and a plume of dust enclosed the car, but inside it was silent. There was a loud, thrumming sound in her skull, though: the sound was electrical, atomic, seismic, a hum like a huge machine powering up, and the skin against her cranium had tightened like a glove on a fist. The car jostled right and then spun and turned left, and out of her window, she saw a second phalanx of squad cars coming toward them. Larysa saw, however briefly, that the one in front had *another* woman in it bearing down over the steering wheel. It seemed fitting to her that she would die now surrounded by women. Bochko wrenched the wheel again and now they began to pound over the ruts in an empty field, heading toward distant trees. Larysa released the catch on the knife handle and felt the blade spring open in her hand and lock into place.

"You better put your seatbelt on, Kitty," he said.

She shouted, "*Mena zvut' Larysa!*" and swung her arm up in front of his eyes. The blade – a gleaming comet, a natural force – arced before her as she plunged it into the middle of his chest. He sucked air violently as she sank it and tried to turn it, one of her hands on the handle and the other reaching under it. His own hands had gone instinctively to the knife, releasing the steering wheel, and Larysa grabbed it and dialled it down like she was closing a safe. The car leapt into the air and then there was silence for what felt like a long period, the two of them suspended as the field spun counterclockwise in the windshield. Then it vanished above her head and they were inside a small bubble of silence, airborne, and she kept her other fist clenched around the knife handle to brace herself, the blade buried to the hilt under his ribs. Then the car landed upright and charged across the field jumping and alighting, twisting and crashing.

And then they stopped and she was alive in the clenched steel. And he was alive as well, clattering in his skin, slamming himself back and forth in the three pinned inches he had between the steering wheel and the seat. Words bubbled up through his wet mouth, sputterings spoken through a bloody mist, but she could make none of it out. Her native tongue had been a mystery to him, and now his deathwords were a language she had never heard before. She kept the knife in its place, even as his blood-slicked hands tried to pry hers away. The women were coming, the women who meant to kill her or stop her or rescue her, they were coming from all sides, she heard them crying out her name, and he was still alive.

She grabbed the gun from the front of his pants and left the knife buried in his breastbone. She could end it for him, but she didn't want to. He could suffer and die or suffer and live, it didn't matter now. He'd be dead or in prison forever. She kicked the passenger door open and reached back to grab Bochko's jacket lapel. She yanked him toward her, pulling his face down over the gearshift. He grunted in pain, his animal eyes full of hate, and blood frothed in front of his teeth. "Give me my passport now, Bochko." He said nothing and she put her hand on the knife handle again, and pulled it slowly down, like a lever. "Just look with your eyes what pocket it is in." He was beginning to go. His eyes drifted down, toward the floor of the car, but then they ticked right and she shoved her hand into his breast pocket. He clamped his fist over her forearm.

"You're not that girl anymore," he whispered, struggling to keep just one eye open. "You are Kitty. Forever you are – "

She spat in the eye. And then she was out, and into the field, under the rising moon, stumbling desperately toward the safety of the woods.

] 35 [

Hazel was the first one to the car. They'd seen the girl burst from the passenger side and she was still hobbling for the treeline as the two forces converged from the road. The Porsche was about two hundred metres in, sitting like a ticking bomb in a cloud of smoke and dust. "Get Travers out!" Hazel called to LeJeune. She was crossing the field toward the commander and her officers. "I'm going after the girl!"

As she ran, Hazel kept twitching her head over her shoulder and she watched the officers of the QBPS yanking at the handle behind which Lee Travers was sitting in a pool of his own gore. She saw his giant chest clearly, still moving up and down. The radios had come to life again. An ambulance was coming from Kehoe River, and a SOCO team was on its way to catalogue the mess in the house and in the field.

Larysa had reached the treeline and Hazel was going to have to follow her into the dark.

Bars of light from the edge of the woods lay across the uneven forest floor. They stretched out like pathways into the trees, where they joined other shadows and became a mass of variegated grey and black.

Hazel stood within the cover and listened. She had to shut out the sounds behind her now – voices calling to each other, and, in the distance, sirens. She closed it all off and focused her listening toward the dark. She expected to hear the sound of Kitty's footfalls fading in the distance as she plunged forward. How injured was the girl? It would have taken a few moments for her eyes to adjust, as hers were doing now, and then she would have to pick her way through the fallen branches and the moss-covered boulders that hunched in the larger darkness.

"My name is Hazel Micallef," she called out. "I'm a detective with the Ontario Police Services. I know what's happened to you. I know what you had to do. I want to help you." She listened for any sign, any movement. There was nothing. She moved deeper into the trees. There was no order here – it was old forest, an ancient forest that had forever lined the backside of the Gannon escarpment, a thick carpet of brown and green. The trees here had never been harvested or cleaned out, and eons of growth crunched and moaned underfoot. Deeper in, the trunks of the oaks and chestnuts thickened and crowded one another.

She was about a hundred metres further when she saw the glow of a grassy patch beyond the next line of trees, and she stepped onto the edge of it. The last of the light was filtering down and the clearing sat in a disk of metallic light. Ten metres away, on the other side, the girl who had been called Kitty was standing calmly in the half-light, a reedlike figure in a hoodie and sweatpants. Lit by the dusky sky, she looked phantasmal, like an image out of Grimm's. A maleficent Goldilocks. She was holding what appeared to be a gun fashioned out of red metal. It was only when she realized it was covered in Travers's blood, did Hazel begin to realize what this woman had accomplished, to be standing at liberty in these woods, alive, and only one more person standing between her and freedom.

Hazel took two steps into the dusk-tinged light and stood where the girl could clearly see her. Larysa was ceding the light to Hazel. Her face was not totally unlike the police sketch that had been made of her on the Wednesday night, but almost. It was a like a face remembered out of the distant past.

"Are you Kitty?"

"No," the girl said. "I am Larysa. I have been rescued by Kitty."

"I am not going to try to convince you that I can fix what has happened to you. But I know there were other girls. You can help the ones who have survived. You can tell us what you saw."

"Cannot help. Cannot tell." She was half-holding the gun on Hazel. Now she pulled her arm backwards and lobbed it toward her, and the gun described a gentle parabola and landed in the loam a metre from her feet. Hazel leaned down to pick the weapon up with her thumb and index finger. It was another Glock; Travers's gun, cadged for him by Bellecourt. The girl was unarmed now, but she came toward Hazel, covering the distance between them quickly, and Hazel instinctively took a step backwards, raising Travers's weapon in front of her. Larysa grabbed the barrel of the gun and drew herself into it, steadying it an inch from her eyes, eyes that were concentrating the last of the August light into two sharp beads. "Choose," she said.

They stood together, connected by the gun. Larysa's fingertip balanced the muzzle in front of her own face.

"Who is this girl?" Larysa said. "Whatever then, now she's murderer. Why not she go to *polis*, for the *polis* to help her? No, she go and hunt. She can SAVE girls but does not! The dirty girls in the dirty hole, she leaves them. Takes her revenge!" She tugged the gun in toward her forehead, and Hazel felt it bump against the girl's skull. "Choose."

"There's no choice," said Hazel. She pulled the gun away from the girl's forehead. There was a perfect red circle of Travers's blood imprinted on Larysa's forehead. "I have to take you in."

"Shoot the gun," Larysa said. She began to walk away.

Hazel was not going to shoot the gun. Her feet were rooted to the forest floor; she had become one of the old maples here, that had seen everything for a hundred years and been incapable of action. "Please stop," she said.

Larysa stopped. She turned around again and faced Hazel. "Do you have child, Miss *Polis*?" she asked.

"You have to come with me."

"You have daughter," Larysa said plainly, stepping backwards, away from her. "Imagine, your daughter, this happens to her. Imagine."

The fabric of the girl's shirt was catching concentrated lashings of light as she slid away into the cover of the trees, and soon Hazel only heard her footfalls softening in the distance. The decision was too complex to make under these conditions. The girl was dangerous. The girl had suffered and done what anyone else in her position would have done. But Henry? Why had Henry known this girl? "Wait, wait a second. I want to ask you a question. Was Henry Wiest trying to help you?" She couldn't hear the girl's footsteps over her own voice. She called out, louder: "*Was he trying to help you?*"

But she was gone. The girl had vanished into the forest.

When Hazel emerged from the woods, an ambulance was already in place on Highland Crescent and two men were marching a stretcher over the field. She walked up to it and she saw the extent of Travers's injuries. She could tell that his survival would take a miracle. The paramedics carried him back across the field carefully.

She realized that her shoulders were up around her ears. So much of this case had been fugitive in nature that she had begun to mistrust her peripheral vision. She was expecting the ground to jump again, was braced for it. Even now, with the apparent kingpin dead or dying; his accomplices dead, gone, or perhaps even trapped underground; his victims silenced or missing, she still worried there was more to come.

When Travers was safely inside the ambulance, she looked for LeJeune. She found her standing with some of the men and women of the Ontario Police Service, Central Division. "Anything?" LeJeune asked.

"Nothing. She's gone."

"Where is my car?"

"Not now, Commander." She stopped as she was passing LeJeune and turned to face her. "I'm sorry. This has been a very unpleasant case for me, as I imagine it must be for you too now. If I'd known more sooner . . ."

"There were unexpected complexities."

"Yes. There were." There was more to be said. But she couldn't take her hand off her radio. "I need to talk to my people right now, Commander. Your car is smashed up on Sideroad 1, right near where all this stuff was going on."

"This stuff with girls."

"Yes. I'll come see you tomorrow and explain it. As best

I understand it."

LeJeune let her go. The ambulance was pulling away from the curb, its siren silent, its beacons off. Travers was dead.

Hazel raised the radio to her mouth.

4

Tuesday, August 16–Wednesday, August 17

] 36 [

Tuesday, August 16, midnight

By the time she returned to the soy fields, they'd brought in two more excavators and a flatbed-mounted bank of klieg lights and they were excavating from the side now. They had been communicating through the pipe with a girl named Katrina Volkov. She was trapped in a corner of the room, where "James," she said, had told them to crouch and pin themselves. The roof had come in. She was alive, and she could hear breathing from somewhere else in the pit, but just one breathing.

Hazel stood by helplessly, watching the machines. She thought of the girl, probably still on her way toward them through the woods. Somewhere to the west, she'd pass them later that night. Probably on her way to the States, or another province. Maybe she would try to go home.

At three in the morning on the sixteenth, they extracted a dead girl from the pit. Her body was still warm. Above, through the pipe, Ray talked to Volkov. "I still hear the breathing," she said. "And I hear the machines."

"We're almost there."

"You know who is breathing?"

"No," he lied. He tried to listen for the breathing, but he could only hear her voice, thready and faint, scraping against the inside of the steel tube.

"I want to shake the hand of your *polis*man. For what he did."

"I hope you will," he said. Then the excavators were through again and they called to them and both Hazel and Ray Greene went over to see what they had found. Wingate was face down, half buried in an inverted cone of earth, but his upper half was free; his head wasn't injured. But his pelvis was crushed, and his pale skin suggested he'd lost blood, although there was not much blood in evidence. The paramedic who'd been waiting in the field since eight o'clock pronounced Wingate in hypovolemic shock. More than 40 per cent of his blood was floating around inside of him. The rest of the excavation was rushed: he was too close to death to be careful getting him out.

He was "alive." This is what Hazel heard when the doctors talked. It seemed to be a matter of opinion. Some people made it out of this kind of thing, some didn't. It was better to be young.

He lay in the ICU of Mayfair General bundled up like a baby with layers of gauze. Allowances had been made in his wrappings for IVs and tubes and he appeared to be something that had been caught in a web and bound in silk. The spider took the form of the machines that stood sentry beside and behind him, unspooling their webbing on screens in shuddering lines of red, green, and blue. The doctors had induced a coma to keep him deeply asleep, and in the hour Hazel sat in the chair beside him, six doctors and three nurses paused within the curtained space to mark something on a chart, or adjust a drip, or just to gaze at what was the day's most interesting case.

Touch-and-go. That was the term they settled on. Greene checked in over the phone. There was an active collection of evidence going on in the field and below in the river and grove, and he had to stay on top of it, although she could hear his anxiety and concern. He'd been there the day James Wingate arrived in Port Dundas. They had not worked together long, but he'd liked James, and Hazel knew he was looking forward to working with him again. Greene filled her in on what they were finding. Katrina Volkov had been successfully extracted, and she was in another room in Mayfair General. That room had been a rough dirt chamber with a heavy door in a concrete frame in one wall, and not much else. It appeared that Wingate had used his flat steel belt-buckle to carve out shallow crawl spaces, about half a metre wide, in two of the corners. Volkov had tucked into one; the girl called Star had been found close to the other one. Wingate had just started his when the roof came down. Volkov kept saying she wanted to shake his hand. She was in love with him, she said. She was in shock.

Hyperspecialized specialists were being sent in to register their opinions. She overheard one doctor discussing the value of removing the top of Wingate's skull to "give the brain room."

No one would give her specifics. She was not his next of kin. She knew Greene was trying to look into it, but Wingate had never spoken of siblings or parents. She called Jack Deacon at home, and an hour later, he came into the hospital just as they were taking Wingate away for surgery.

"They have to do some work on him," he told her after talking to a colleague.

"Do I want to know?"

"I don't think so." He put his hand on her shoulder. "You know they'll do whatever they can."

"That's what they say on TV shows before someone dies."

"He's strong. He'll fight. But it's not good."

"Give me a number. Chance he'll survive."

"He's going to have a long road."

"Chance he'll survive."

"I don't know."

"Better than fifty?"

"Sure. Better than fifty."

"How much."

"I don't know, Hazel. I wish I could tell you."

They were bringing someone else into what had been Wingate's bed. An elderly man with a grey face. She began to explain that the space was taken, but one of the interns told her they needed the bed. The man who'd been here was going to be in recovery for a while, when he got out of the ER.

"Come on," said Deacon. "You should go home. I'll call you if I hear anything. Go home."

But she couldn't. She stayed in the hospital waiting room and read magazines and fretted. When Greene learned where she was, he called her and ordered her to go home and get some sleep. She snorted at him and hung up and then turned the cell off so no one else could suggest she do something else with her time. Twice, hospital employees came out and asked her if she was Hazel Micallef because there was a phone call for her. Both times she declined to accept her identity. She knew her mother would be asleep and any other news from the outside world she had no interest in at all.

She was woken by a hand on her shoulder gently shaking her, and she opened her eyes and it was James Wingate. He looked fine. It was possible she wasn't awake. Maybe the surgery had worked and it wasn't so serious after all. Or this was a dream and he'd come to tell her he was dead. She held his hand down on her shoulder, and the hand was corporeal and she was awake. "What time is it?"

"Seven in the morning."

"You don't sound like James, but—"

"I'm Michael." He took his hand off her shoulder. "I gather you don't know about me."

"I don't."

"It's a complicated story. But I'm the next of kin. I got a call."

"Well," she said, unsure what role she was to play here, "I'm sorry you're being . . . reunited under these circumstances. What did they tell you?"

"Severe internal bleeding. Broken pelvis, broken legs, two broken vertebrae. *Eight* broken ribs, lacerated spleen, lacerated liver, varied vascular damage. Swelling of the brain. Cuts and bruises. Coma."

"Not good."

"Not good."

If not for her deranging exhaustion and worry, the fact that James had a twin might have disturbed her. But in an odd way, it was comforting now. To have that face in the room. "Where did you come from?"

"New York City. I drove."

"Oh, god," she said. "Do you want a coffee or something?"

"No. I'm fine. I ate on the road and got a room near the hospital and showered. So I'm good for the day. But if you want to go home and rest or something, I could call you if anything changes."

She thought about it for a moment. "Okay," she said. "I'll give you my number." She wrote it down. "Is there anyone else coming?"

"It's just the two of us."

She didn't want to press him. She'd always known that Wingate had depths and secrets she knew nothing about. She hoped she'd have a chance to learn more about him. She realized, as she left the hospital and emerged into the dull morning light, that in the brief period of time he'd been with the detachment that she'd come to care for him a great deal. In fact, she realized, she loved him like a son. And then she sat behind her wheel and wept for him.

She showered and changed and went into work. The detachment was quiet. She entered through the rear door, but as soon as she was inside, she realized she had nowhere to go. The door to her office was closed and she heard voices within. She crossed the hallway and went into the kitchen to fix herself a cup of coffee. The Wiest bird – christened Willan, née Beedle – was still in its cage against the wall. They were going to have to call Cathy some time in the next few days and arrange to bring it back to her once she was comfortable enough to return home. She poured her coffee. It seemed the bird was getting used to everyone. It looked on her with a bored expression.

"I hear they named him after me," said a voice behind her. It was Commissioner Willan. "He seems pretty laid-back."

"Maybe they chose the name because he deserves to be in a cage."

"I'm happy to see you looking well, Hazel."

"I only look well, Commissioner. I gather you've heard about DC Wingate?"

"I have," he said.

"A lot of paperwork if someone dies in the line of duty, huh?"

He twitched his head to the side. "Not to mention the grief," he said.

She had no response. This was not the day to discover that her surfer-dude commissioner also had a heart. "In any case, I'm well enough to give you and Inspector Greene a full report when you're ready for one."

"*Superintendent* Greene."

"Right. Sorry. He abandons ship eight months ago, then goes and takes the exam, and now he's back, crowned in glory."

"Something like that. Can we live in peace?"

"What's that?" Hazel said.

He smiled mildly at her. "You know the new regional HQ is going to be here, Detective Inspector. The province is going to put twenty million dollars into straightening out the 41. Port Dundas is going to get a bigger dot on the map."

She lived among obliterators. “You straighten out the highway, Commissioner, traffic bypasses the town. You turn it into a backwater.”

“Not if at the new exit there’s a terrific new mall with stores people *will* visit, and the new Westmuir Police Headquarters is right there on the other side of it. Then you turn it into a gateway. *The gateway*,” he said, leaning forward with a finger raised, “of all of Westmuir. You’ll be top dick in the whole county.”

“After Ray.”

“Well, you can think of Ray however you like.”

There was no point in responding. Willan could carry on a conversation with himself at a dinner party. He was opening cupboards. He found some soup crackers and broke one in half for his namesake. The bird took it from him and then opened its beak and dropped it to the floor of the cage.

“I think he prefers seeds,” she said.

“If there were crackers in the wild, they’d never eat seeds again.” He brushed the crumbs off the front of his suit and held his arm out toward the hallway. “Shall we?”

] 37 [

Tuesday, August 16, late morning

The meeting took two hours. Howard Spere was present. Greene and Willan asked them to run down the entire investigation, from the discovery of Wiest's body in the smoke shop's parking lot to Spere's report on the body they found in Carl Duffy's house. The body was Duffy's, and his relatives, trickling in from parts distant, were being briefed on the circumstances surrounding his death by Roland Forbes in one of the interview rooms.

The squad cars that had staked out the Eagle the night before had found it abandoned; Hazel remembered Bellecourt asking her where she thought Earl Tate had been. They'd now determined he'd been the one to drop the dynamite into the steel pipe. Then he'd vanished. Finally, Travers was lying on a metal bed in a drawer in the

Mayfair General morgue. He'd died of his wounds, but the cause of death was Larysa. Hazel didn't say that part, however, when it came her turn to speak.

Her superiors listened with interest, and occasionally one of them took notes. After an hour, they dismissed Spere but asked her to stay. Step by step, they walked through her decision process during the investigation and took more notes. Her erstwhile office began to take on the atmosphere of a courtroom, and she wondered now if her "promotion" and the respectful nature of their questioning tone wasn't the framework for a gallows of some sort. But at the end of another hour, Willan thanked her and said, "That should do it."

"Do what?"

"Complete our records."

"Of what."

Willan smiled. "You know, Hazel, there was a regime change in the middle of this case, some unusual tactics were used, some jurisdictional irregularities were noted, and there are five dead bodies, plus, as you tell it, an unknown number of *other* bodies that I presume will not be turning up anytime soon. Then, in the hospital in Mayfair, we have a member of your force clinging to life, and a woman who was kidnapped, sexually abused, and regularly assaulted, who needs to see her consul but who is currently in a state of shock. We have a store licensed by the province of Ontario to sell native cigarettes that was the portal to an illegal casino that in turn was intimately tied to the rape and torture of kidnap victims. And Ray here let you spend a lot of money. Oh, and did I mention that you kept a witness and possible suspect – you never ruled Cathy Wiest out, did you? – ”

“Oh come on, now – ”

“But you didn’t and she lived in your home. With you.”

“Where is this heading, Commissioner? What’s it about?”

He stood up, and she remained where she was. She’d save standing up for when it would have the most effect. He said, “What it is *not* about, Inspector Micallef, is just you.”

“I know that.”

“What happens if this girl kills again?”

“She’s finished. She got everyone.”

“Are you sure?”

“Yes.”

“How. How can you be sure?” he asked. His tone had become ever so slightly heated and it was frankly disconcerting.

“If you had investigated this case, Commissioner Willan, you would have drawn the same conclusion.”

Silence.

“Am I fired?”

“What about future charges?”

“What future charges?”

“How many warrants were issued? Who was notified

that a covert investigation out of our jurisdiction was being undertaken?"

"This was too serious to announce our intentions!"

"It was," he said. "I agree."

"We acted with the best information we had."

"You're right. I'm here to say you did a good job."

"What?"

"Even though there *is* the matter of whether the man who shot Lydia Bellecourt also beat the crap out of her from inside his car, twenty feet away."

She'd gotten to the point where it felt unwise to speak at all.

"Any of this could be a problem at some point, Hazel. If you need to be covered, I'll cover you. And if there's anything I don't already know, I need to know it."

He offered his hand. She screwed up her eyes and looked at Greene. He chucked his chin toward Willan. *Shake the man's bloody hand.* She shook. Tentatively. He pumped.

"Thank you, Commissioner," said Ray Greene because she hadn't.

"Yes, thank you," said Hazel.

"Do it again, though," he said to both of them, "and it won't be difficult to fire either of you. Or suspend you without pay, definitely or indefinitely, retire you, reassign you to deskwork, send you on a teaching mission to Kapuskasing. My options are actually almost endless. Superintendent?" Greene stood. "You're her boss now."

"Yes, sir."

"Inspector?" Hazel tightened her chest. "Ray Greene is your boss. Everything you do from now on is hand-stamped, green-lighted, and approved, and not just in principle, by Superintendent Greene. Is that unambiguous enough for you?"

"Yes, sir."

"And when James Wingate gets out of hospital, we'll have a party for him and give him a commendation in front of the whole town. *When* he gets out."

"Yes, sir," she said, and this time, when he offered his hand, she took it.

He left them together in the office. Greene sat.

"That was interesting," he said.

She couldn't think of what to say. "I better get started on my reports."

"Good," he said.

"Is Cathy still at – "

"She went home last night. Are you going to see her?"

"Maybe. Not right away, though. I don't know what to – "

He was writing something. She strained to see what it was. He was making figure eights with the tip of his pen.

"Can I go?"

"I'll be at the hospital this afternoon."

"I'll see you there then."

That was the extent of it for now.

After trying to write her report, Hazel went back to the house in Pember Lake. It was mid-afternoon. There were a lot of loose ends now; matters she'd left unattended. There were some plates in the sink and she washed them. She flashed on her memory of Cathy standing at her own sink, washing her entire house with that look in her eye. She thought she knew now what Cathy had been feeling. Like the world was floating away. She noticed her mother's pill organizer still had its morning doses in it. Emily was upstairs taking a nap. A little wave of anger suddenly went through her.

She took a glass of water and the pills up the stairs, with a plate of Coffee Breaks, and went into her mother's room. She was asleep with her face turned to the wall. The covers were pulled up to her ears and the sheet barely moved with her breathing. Hazel turned on the bedside lamp, but the sudden little flood of light had no effect on her mother's wakefulness. A jolt of fear went through her and Hazel reached out and touched her mother's shoulder and shook her lightly. The shoulder was warm, and her mother shuddered beneath her touch and said something, and Hazel shook her a little more.

"It's okay. It's just me. Can you sit up?"

Her mother inhaled deeply through her nostrils and sat up, blinking and confused. "What time is it?"

"It's four o'clock in the afternoon. I'm sorry I woke you. You forgot to take your pills."

"Oh, for god's sake," her mother said, fully awake now. "I'm not going to die in my sleep for lack of pills."

"You don't know that. Now sit up and take them." Emily pushed herself up farther in the bed and held out her hand angrily for the medications. Hazel lay them in her cool, leathery, white palm. "I know you're not pleased with this situation, but this is the way things are. Take these pills, and take all your pills, and eat food, and stop acting like you have a date with the Grim Reaper. You never gave up a fight in your life, Mother, and you're not starting now." Her mother swallowed the pills without the water and then held her hand out for the glass because they wouldn't go down. "Jesus Christ," Hazel said.

"Am I allowed to go back to sleep?"

"Not yet."

Her mother blinked slowly and Hazel told her what had happened in the last few days. Wingate's injuries. The reappearance of Ray Greene. Willan laying down the law. Her long reign as interim CO was over. Emily had been summarily turfed in her fourth term as mayor, by a blinkered town council. Worse than what Hazel was going through now, but it was a commonality, and Hazel had lately been having the instinct to seek out as much connection with her mother as possible. And she'd appreciate her daughter turning to her . . .

"Well, now we can both curl up and die," her mother

said. "You want me to move over?" Hazel laughed. "What're you chuckling at?"

"I thought maybe you'd pat my head and tell me everything's going to be okay."

"I've never told you everything was going to be okay. In fact, if I recall, I've spent most of my life warning you that things go to pieces as a matter of routine. How come you haven't learned that yet?"

"I know it in my work life. I just thought . . ."

"You thought that if you could convince me I still have work to do as your mother, I wouldn't die yet?"

Hazel's smile faltered. "Well, when you put it like that . . ."

"I'll take my medicine, Hazel," her mother said. "If you'll promise not to make both our lives impossible when it's time to make important decisions."

"Gary says you can live with myeloma for years."

"But not forever."

"No," said Hazel. Emily swivelled her body on the mattress and slipped her frail feet out. "What are you doing?"

"I'm going to the hospital."

"You don't have to take me *that* seriously."

"No, dummy, I want to see James. Get me my grey slacks and something warm."

"Oh . . ."

"Your timing stinks, though. I was just skiing with your father in New York."

"Really."

"Ellicotteville, 1941. Two years before you were born."

"Simpler times."

Hazel got her mother's clothes out and told her she'd make some tea and then they'd go. But for herself, she didn't want any tea. She went back down the stairs and got a half-full bottle of J&B out of the cupboard and sat in the rocking chair with it. She listened to her mother in the bathroom and she took one good glug out of the bottle and then another. Then she put the cap back on and put the bottle away. She filled the kettle for her mother and then went back out into the living room to wait. The Weather Channel was on silently – her mother only muted it when she napped, but she couldn't be bothered to turn it off. Looking at the weather was perhaps a sign that the old bint was planning on continuing with life, pointlessness and all. Hazel stared at the screen. Weather systems were soundlessly pouring sideways across the province, forming and reforming like fog. Rain was coming from the Soo, but it was two days distant.

Her mother was taking the stairs slowly. "Every system in this body is shorting out but my hearing," she said. "And there's no mistaking the crack of the cap on a whiskey bottle."

Hazel turned the kettle off.

] 38 [

Wednesday, August 17, afternoon

Over the Tuesday and into the Wednesday, as Katrina Volkov began to recover from her ordeal, the heartbreaking and sickening details of the case began to come to light. Volkov knew of a total of five girls, but the cramped history of the place suggested the operation had begun three years earlier. The story came down as oral tradition – from the girls who had once been there to the ones who were still alive. Two women Volkov had personally known had died before Kitty's escape, and she had thought Kitty was dead as well. Now she was the only witness to a crime so horrifying that media from as far away as Miami were waiting in the parking lot of Mayfair General, hoping to get a word with somebody, anybody. Deliverymen were being handed wads of cash. LeJeune had dispatched every free body she had to the hospital on the Friday morning and her uniforms took up positions every thirty metres around Mayfair General.

Friday afternoon, a Russian-speaking officer was bussed up from Toronto, in case he was needed. But Katrina's English was good: she put her captivity at seven months. She'd been there long enough to learn English.

They connected her to her husband in Elizavetgrad.

"She is saying she was not in school," said the interpreter.

They left her alone, and let her rest. They had as clear a picture of what had happened under that little grove of trees as they would ever get. The last piece of information Hazel had really wanted had come out as well: Volkov had given Larysa's last name as Kirilenko.

The OPS and the QBPS had each sent a forensic team into those underground rooms on Wednesday afternoon. The two forces worked together. They'd found a basement that had been lowered and enlarged, like a giant tomb. There was a body there; later it was determined that this was the Ronald Plaskett that Wingate had earlier identified. He'd been shot dead. A long white wall with four doors in it ran against the longest wall. Each door had opened on a tiny eight-by-four "room," with a dirt floor and at least one dirt wall, the one at their backs. Most of the chambers had a foam mattress and a blanket or two. The heavy door still stood in the north wall of the crushed room beyond it.

Volkov's stories filled the space with suffering bodies and whispering voices. The rooms had been freezing cold, even in the summer, and they discovered that it was warmer sleeping on the dirt itself, especially if you could loosen it up a bit. You could also loosen the dirt in the back walls and there were sometimes bits of sharp rock that were good for digging with. But at this depth underground, digging through the dirt with a little stone was like trying to scrape a hole in the sidewalk with your fingernail. "We make a broken telephone, you know? Before I am taken away from my home, in that place, the girls before us make a system for talking. They have make small holes in the dirt at the end of the wall, where the wall touches. Always, you make these holes filled with dirt, but every week, same time in the middle of the night, anyone who want to talk, digs open the hole.

"And then we say short things. We learn names. When a new girl comes, someone shows how to use telephone." She said something in Russian, and Lenkov translated it.

"'This is how we got to know our neighbours.'"

"*Neighbours*," said Volkov. "Yes, our neighbours in hell. This is how we know our names, where we are from, what we did there, how it happens to us that we are bring to this place. That men rent us for a week."

"Did Larysa ever talk?"

"She was there shortest. But she *is* alive?"

"James told you that?"

"Yes."

"You got to know him a little."

"I only see him twice, but yes, I know him now. He is also . . . ?"

"He's alive. He was badly injured when the roof of that room fell in."

"Where is Larysa?"

"I don't know. But she's alive. I know she's alive." Volkov went into herself, her eyes tracked down. "It must have been just as hard to choose to go on," Hazel said.

"I wanted to live to thank . . ." she broke off and put her forehead in her hands. Then, a moment later, composed: "And to know about Bochko . . ."

"Bochko?"

"Big boss."

"Did you ever meet him?"

"Yes. Big man with muscle."

That was him. "His name was Lee Travers," Hazel said. "He's dead now."

"Good."

"Larysa . . . Kitty . . . killed him."

Katrina didn't say anything. After a moment, she withdrew her hand from Hazel's and used it to press the button that lowered her bed. Her eyes were closing even as it went down. But a very faint smile played on her lips.

Hazel left the room and started for the ICU, where James was still under heavy sedation. She and Emily had come the day before and sat with Michael in James's curtained nook full of machines. In the intervening twenty-four hours, part of the investigation had begun to focus on who Travers *was*, and already details were coming in. They traced him back to Michigan and discovered that it had been true that he'd taken casino management at U of M. But his picture, and not his name, had confirmed this for them. He'd taken his degree under the name Judson Carmichael, and he'd matriculated in *1994*. He'd worked in other casinos. Each employment lasted fewer than four and a half years. Some were less than a year. They had only just started to disseminate the details of their case to other agencies when the phones began to ring. In Perrysville, Maryland, Carmichael had gone by the name Harvey Kellog. He'd been an assistant manager in the casino there, and his *boyfriend* had met with a suspicious end. Kellog had left the state, and six months later, a man seeding his field had found a pile of partially burnt women's clothing. That had led to a terrible discovery in a derelict barn. That was after just one day of spreading the information. They dreaded what else would come up. Ten years was a long time to be a freewheeling psychopath.

Now, on Thursday afternoon, she entered the cordoned-off space where Wingate's body was still being operated from without and said hello to Michael. After half an hour of silence, he said, "I can tell you a little about myself, if you want."

"Only stuff I could find out by Googling you," she said. "I don't know what the rules are here."

"That's fair. Google would tell you I'm a props master for film and TV. I handle all mechanical props, like appliances, weapons, devices – "

"Devices?"

"You know, the box with the switch and the light on it that's in every other episode of *24*?"

"I don't watch TV."

"Anyway, I make that box."

"Okay."

"And I live in New York, and I have for thirteen years."

"And you are . . . married? Single? Kids?"

"You wouldn't find that on Google," he said, and he offered her a conciliatory smile.

They sat on either side of Wingate's bed for half an hour after that, not saying much. The machines breathed for him, and the monitors watched him, and it felt like it would take a long time before anyone could tell her what his fate might be.

Normally, she'd just have taken it. But she was going by the books now: she requisitioned it out of evidence. Then Greene had asked her about it and told her he'd have to check with Willan. He told her to come back after lunch. She had two hours to kill then, and she decided to use them wisely: she decided to take in the late August air and try to settle her jangling nerves. She had the thought of driving somewhere and just sitting and watching the leaves move around in the wind. But instead she stayed in town and walked down Main Street a ways, and then up, north, into the oldest residential streets of the town. She'd known that part her whole life, and she looked at some of the houses she'd been inside. On some streets, she'd been in all of the houses; she'd known the names of successive generations, successive owners. It was like she could pass through the very walls. Although some of these houses had been the homes of childhood friends, most of her experiences within them were adult ones. After thirty-five years on the force, she'd had cause to be in many of these houses.

After her walk, she went back down to Main Street to The Station House Grill for lunch and let herself have a BLT. She'd eaten lunch in the Station House at least a thousand times. It had been on this same spot for eighty years, forty years more than the now-demolished train station it had been named for. It had never changed. Dmitri Agnostopolis had opened it, his son Jim took it over, and Jim's daughter-in-law, Grace Wong, owned it now. Grace made a coconut cream pie almost as good as Cathy Wiest's.

But the Station House and the houses in the old part of town were among the few things that weren't changing here. Not only were the crimes Port Dundas was seeing becoming more serious, but the outside world was truly infecting it now. When she was a kid, no one particularly cared for this part of the province in the summer, with its bug-infested waterways and its tiny towns with nothing to recommend them except for a few guesthouses on the water for fishermen. It changed slowly at first. The urban middle class learned how to swim. Motorboats became affordable. The moneyed crowd figured out it was prestigious to have a summer place in the same province they made their money, a place of their own they could go to all summer, forever.

And towns like Port Dundas couldn't say no. Not to all that commerce, all that foot traffic. People got rich off it. But the gargantuan houses that were built on the new lots lasted a lot longer than the money did. Westmuirians had been squeezed out of their own countryside. It made her angry, but she'd accepted it by now.

What was left of the town of her childhood she felt fiercely protective of. Main Street was the map of her life. She was eleven before her parents decided she was old enough to walk to town on her own, but the moment she was allowed to go, she was there all the time, running in and out of her father's store, "helping customers," going to the bank for change, looking at the river under Kilmartin Bridge, following the leaves skirling in rainwater in the gutters, buying sodas at Ladyman's. (She looked at the venerable old restaurant now, through the window of the Station House. It was badly in need of three coats of paint both inside and out. The great old sign that poked out over the sidewalk, and famously had 109 lightbulbs in it, had been gone now for twenty-five years.) When she was eleven, the heart of the main drag had been O'Connor's Stationery, the S. Baker Pharmacy, L'il Folks Shoes (and beside it, the more solemn, leathery-smelling Famous Footware), Micallef's, The Station House, Ladyman's, the Riverside Café, Porelli's Grocery, Porelli's Meats, the Red Door Bakery, a Stedman's, and the cinema – The Beverly – which had been her favourite place in town.

By the time she was thirteen, she felt like she owned the town. She knew every inch of it, was a repository for its dailiness, its history. People used to joke that the mother was in City Hall and the kid was directing traffic out on Main Street. There wasn't a soul who didn't know her on sight.

Now her mother was coming to the end of her life, and her own personal Port Dundas was vanishing. Charles O'Connor had died in 1965, the Porellis closed up both their shops and moved to Kitchener in the 1970s. Stores came and went, although the ornately carved keystones above their doors, and the beautiful lintels and soffits were still there if you traced your gaze up the rain-softened stone. She had truly kept watch over this place her whole life, and now she felt the first moment of the final act beginning. Ray Greene was in charge. Willan had anointed him. And they *were* going to straighten the 41 so it ran east of the townsite, that was surely going to happen. They'd connect Mayfair in a straight shot to Port Dundas and Fort Leonard without actually running the highway through the middle of town. It was going to miss Dublin entirely. She wondered if the investors in Tournament Acres knew anything about that. She suspected not. Then again, maybe that town would be saved. Maybe only Port Dundas would die.

After lunch, Greene gave her permission to do what she'd asked to do, and Hazel filled out the rest of the paperwork. She waited for Wilton while he was in the evidence locker in the basement, and then she drove down to Kehoe Glenn with the knife they'd found in Travers's chest.

There was a little cool sting in the air now. Summer was not officially over until September 21, but this always happened in the second half of August, this sudden encroachment into the heat. It never stopped shocking her when the summer began to end. You wait so long for it and then, like a switch being thrown, the cold makes its appearance.

Cathy looked at Hazel through the screen door and then opened it, and Hazel walked in past her, touching the widow softly on the upper arm. She went into the kitchen and sat down, placing a paper bag on the table. Cathy came in hesitantly, seeing the bag and not liking it. But she took a seat.

"I hope those are french fries," she said.

"No."

"Then I'm going to have a drink. Do you want one?"

"Whatever you're having."

Cathy went to make the drinks and dropped an ice cube in each glass. "This is going to be an unpleasant experience, isn't it? I can feel it." She was weaving a little, side to side, against the counter.

"Maybe you shouldn't have another," Hazel said.

"This is my first, Officer. But I *am* stoned. I presume I am not arrested."

"No."

She brought the drinks to the table. "So, why are you here?"

"The girl's name, the one you saw, her name was Larysa Kirilenko."

"Is she dead?"

"No. And we haven't captured her. Yet," she added and reached for her drink.

"So I have to leave my home again?"

"No," said Hazel. "I promise you, she's gone. You'll never see her again."

"How can you be so sure?"

"Because I know what happened to her now."

Cathy didn't want to know, though. Hazel could see the fear in her eyes. Now was the moment she would learn how her husband had earned his death.

"What's in the bag, Hazel?"

"I told you Henry might have been trying to help her. She was in a place . . . a place there was no way out of. I saw it. I do think that Henry was trying to help her. I think he found out somehow through Jordie Dunn and that's why he went there. Somehow Larysa was able to stab a guard with a knife and she took the guard's stun gun. That's how she got out. But she was six kilometres from where Henry's truck was found. So either she tracked him, with an intent to kill him, or he told her where to go, to meet him."

"And what was he going to do with her when she showed up?"

"Bring her to the police? Get help? But she killed him instead. She used the stun gun, which she had probably seen used down there. They're not supposed to kill, not even this type. It was an early kind of stun gun, called a Lea Stinger. Russian. She must have known it wasn't lethal. And she had the knife, which she did use to kill with. Twice."

"So she didn't *want* to kill him? They were friends? She *did* kill him!"

"I want to show you the knife, Cathy. It came out of evidence, so it's pretty awful. We can't clean it yet. Do you think you can look at it?"

Cathy was shaking her head *no* but looking anxiously at the bag. "Why?"

The question was enough. She had to see it. Hazel removed a ziplock evidence bag from within and lay it on the table. The hunting knife they'd removed from Lee Travers's chest was inside, still in its open position, and encrusted with dried blood from its tip to the end of the handle. "This is what killed that guard and also Terry Brennan and Lee Travers, who ran the whole thing. It's a brand-new Buck knife. Your husband's was the only store north of Mayfair and south of Sudbury to sell this brand of knife. This particular one is a Buck/Simonich Raven Legacy, a top-of-the-line knife that costs almost four hundred dollars. Someone at the store confirmed for me yesterday that the one they had in the case is missing. He hadn't noticed it until I asked him. Henry gave Larysa this knife, Cathy. Because he wanted to help her escape."

"You said she was looking for something."

"We still don't what it was."

Cathy picked up the clear plastic bag. It had a date and a code scrawled on a white patch in permanent black marker.

"And you think he gave her this."

"I believe he did."

"And is this supposed to make me feel better?" She fell silent and dropped the gruesome object to the tabletop. "This isn't proof my husband was a good man."

"No, you're right," Hazel said. "It isn't. But if you can believe he was, then proof is nothing."

Epilogue

Late August

The man at the customs desk at Kiev Borispol stamped her passport and handed it back to her. Her visa had been for a full year. He asked her why she came back so soon. "I didn't like it in Canada," she said. "I got homesick."

She'd paid cash for the cheapest flight: a one-hopper from Toronto on Delta and Aerosvit. When she stepped out of the airport at noontime on a Friday at the end of August, it was hotter than she ever remembered the summer being. She hadn't eaten real food in three months, her *own* food, and she stopped in the first decent place she could find and ordered smoked whitefish, potatoes, and a Heineken. Afterwards, she purchased a package of Yava

Golds and had the first cigarette she'd smoked in ten years.

She'd exchanged the rest of the Canadian money in the airport and received a total of almost ten thousand hryvnia. This was a lot more money in Ukraine than twelve hundred Canadian would have been in Canada. She could be independent for three months on that money, thinking through what her next move should be, planning how to execute it. She did not have to stay in Ukraine. She could opt never to be found by emigrating to Russia. In Moscow, she could change her name, her looks, her life. This was very appealing. It was desirable. But she could not leave Ukraine without *knowing*. For a week she lived in a cheap hotel and thought, and ate, and smoked, and slept.

When she felt stronger at the end of that week, she paid 350 hryvnia for a ticket to Lviv and arrived in her hometown late one afternoon. She walked from the station to her and Matthieu's flat on Doroschenka strasse and simply rang the bell. She did not expect him to answer. She did not expect to find him there. But if he *was* there, she would know from the instant she saw his face whether he had played a role in what had happened to her, and she would know what to do.

She buzzed again and this time, she heard his voice. "Yes?"

"Matthieu?" she said, feeling an unexpected thrill in her stomach. Maybe it had been a mere terrible dream, a life gone temporarily off course. It could not have been him!

Just hearing him say the simple word "Yes" convinced her of this, and she said her own name. There was silence. Then he released the door and she walked in and up the stairs to their flat. He was waiting on the landing, looking perplexed and delighted all at once.

"Laruschka? Oh my goodness, my goodness – " He opened his arms to her and stepped forward to grasp her tightly. Now she could not see his face, and she pushed back to look in his eyes.

"Hello, Matthieu."

"I don't understand. Did you . . . did you quit school? Come in, my goodness, my love, come in! Why did you not call?" He threw the door wide, but she saw he had a worried look on his face, and she could not interpret it. She entered, keeping her eyes open, and she went into the kitchen, where she dropped the satchel she had bought at the airport in Toronto and sat. The kitchen smelled good. Matthieu was making a stew on top of the stove in one of her crockpots. It was an innocent scene. He stood on the other side of the kitchen, in the doorway, studying her. "I don't understand."

"You don't ask me why you haven't heard from me in ten weeks?"

He pulled his head back sharply on his neck. "What do you mean? We've been emailing every other day. Sometimes *every* day."

She looked at him with lowered eyes. "I have, have I?"

"What is going on, Larysa?"

"I did not quit school, Matthieu. Does this surprise you?"

"It does. If you did not quit school, then I don't know what you are doing in our kitchen. I was not expecting you back until the beginning of January!"

"You were not expecting me back until the beginning of January," she said with a sneer. "How were you expecting me to appear, when I returned at the beginning of January?"

He came to the table and sat down, deeply confused, and took one of her hands in his. "What's wrong, Laruschka? I'm very happy to see you, but you are angry, and I don't understand. Tell me how I have upset you."

His eyes were filled with real concern. "When did I tell you I was coming home in January?"

"My darling, you said if you could get an inexpensive flight home for Christmas, you would come home. You asked me to make you kutia. I said I would."

She erupted out of her chair. "When? When did I say this? When did we have this discussion?"

Her outburst shocked him and he flung himself back in his chair. "Larysa! What is wrong! You're frightening me – "

The knife block was standing on the counter, where it had always been, and she pulled a fish-boning knife from it and held it in front of her. "How much did you get paid, Matthieu? How much did they give you? To treat me like garbage and make me a whore?" Now his face changed, he trembled in his seat with terror; his hands flew to his mouth. He was caught or stunned, she couldn't tell which and the tears that suddenly flooded his eyes seemed to give her the answer she sought, but could he fake such tears? He stood and she backed away, brandishing the knife, but he was weeping now, wildly, his mouth wide and wet.

"What are you saying!" he wailed. "Laruschka, *please* tell me what has happened to you!"

He came toward her, fearless of the knife, and his eyes glistened and flowed with feeling that had to be real. She put the knife down and let him close his arms around her. He said quietly in her ear, "No, no, please, what has happened to you?"

It took the rest of the evening for her to tell him her story. When his face was not in his hands, he listened with a terrible, rapt expression. She had forgotten how intensely he paid attention to her. She felt like she was murdering him with her story, but he held up bravely under the onslaught, and emboldened, she told him everything. How she had been treated, her many resolutions to take her own life (and how his face, with authentic grief, had collapsed at this admission), and then, afterwards, what she did when she was free. What she felt she had to do. What she *needed* to do.

He was moved by the awful choices she'd had to make, for her survival, and he absolved her – as much as a person who loves another person totally can absolve them of a mortal sin.

Then he showed her what she had been to him in the nearly three months she'd been captive. It had not occurred to her that when they had taken her laptop and her phone from her that they would have access to a rich supply of personal information they could use to cover their tracks. Email addresses of friends, colleagues, and family. Her password was saved in her browser, all they had to do was collect her email, pay any bills that came up (it was nothing compared to what she was bringing in for them), and reply to messages that clearly needed replies. He had almost sixty emails from her, and more than a third of them came with pictures of Toronto, supposedly pictures of school and her friends, a couple of images of herself taken by Tate or Bochko in which she had been told to smile and look happy or else. She'd understood these images were going to be used for the website, but now she saw their application had been much wider. It was astonishing to think of the difference between her life and that of her virtual doppelgänger.

"Do you understand?" he asked her, holding her on the couch. "Don't you know I would have done anything to help you if I'd known you were in trouble? My god, my god," he said. "I can't stop thinking about it – "

"Don't try," she said. "I can't be alone in my memories."

"I am here, Larysa," he said, and he kissed her eyes.

He had made the stew to last him a few days, but he served it with reverence to her that night, putting heaping spoonfuls of it onto her plate. He went out and got the best vodka he could find, and they ate and drank themselves into a stupour. They went into bed almost comatose with food, drink, and relief, and Matthieu fell asleep right away. He was never one to hold his vodka. He had not touched her at all, except to hold her and console her, and now she lay in his arms and felt his warm breath on her neck.

Despite her full belly and her drunkenness, she could not sleep. Or perhaps because of it she remained painfully wakeful. She lay in the bed, alert, feeling the city of her childhood go through its nighttime motions, cars and the voices of people in the street, the slightly yeasty smell of the bread factory nearby, and the cry of the soccer fans in the stadium on Kleparivs'ka strasse. She hadn't grown up here, but she knew the streets like she knew herself. That thought led to another one, as she lay on her side with Matthieu's arm around her belly, looking at the streetlight coming through the window. The thought was that she could not be that person anymore, that *self* she'd known like the streets of Lviv. There was no actual life to return to. She was a victim of crime and a criminal herself. She would not be able to escape this truth, even if she told no other person than Matthieu about it.

The real question now was could she trust herself? Her feelings had, in the past, led her astray. She saw the good in people. But no more. It was possible that Bochko's agents were already aware of her presence here. It was possible that Bochko had alerted Matthieu and Matthieu had already made contact with the people who would come to deal with her. And then written sixty emails to himself.

What did a capacity to deceive look like? It would mean a talent for hiding yourself, for expressing feelings you didn't have. The truth was that if Matthieu's heart had been broken by her revelations, or if he was a liar who had sold her into slavery, his reaction to her homecoming would have been the same. The performance would be as credible as if it were real. It would have been simple for Bochko to tell Matthieu that she had escaped. Matthieu could have been preparing for a while now to perform his shock and horror at learning the "truth."

And so, in the end, it was impossible to know the truth. As it had been with Henry Wiest, for that was his name, the name of her first victim. Choosing to see the good in people was an invitation to evil. If she was wrong about Matthieu, then a life of wedded bliss awaited her. If she was right, she'd be dead before the summer ended.

She got out of the bed and paced nervously in the kitchen, lighting a cigarette and smoking it over the sink. *Do I have a choice?* she asked herself. *Do I not owe it to those girls I suffered with to be truly free? To start over? To really survive?*

She went back into the bedroom and quietly opened the closet where all of her clothes still hung, as if in tribute to her. She slid a suitcase out from inside and laid it on the floor and silently piled her things into it, pausing to ensure that Matthieu did not awaken. She would not need much, just enough to get her through a few weeks of instability, enough to keep her looking tidy until she found a place to settle and a job. She would have to be careful: her name was not uncommon and if Matthieu or Bochko tried to track her down, she would be found under that name. There were going to be a hundred little details to attend to. Another haircut, another colour. New clothes. She packed her toiletries and went into the front room, where the lights from a billboard across the road played over the bookshelves and she selected a few novels, a number of collections of poetry, and the collected works of Tolstoy and Boris Pasternak, and wedged them into her suitcase.

Matthieu kept sleeping. She took the suitcase into the kitchen and sat down to write a note. She began a number of times, tearing up her efforts and stuffing them into her jeans pocket, and on her fourth attempt, she was satisfied. She looked at the words she had written:

> My dearest Matthieu. I hope you will forgive me for doing this to you. I hope you can understand why it's necessary that I do it. I feel I don't have a choice but to protect myself from all danger, even, perhaps, imagined danger. I wish I could explain to you what it is like to lie in your arms and feel doubt about everything. I hope one

day I will be able to love and trust again, but for the foreseeable future, I don't think I can. The Larysa who loved you will never forgive herself for this. But that Larysa is gone, and so is her life, and Kitty must live. Kitty must live, no matter the cost.

I am Kitty.

This is Kitty.

Goodbye.

She folded the paper up tightly and pushed it down into one of her pockets and then she took the thin, gleaming fish knife out of its slot in the block and returned to the bedroom. He was lying on his back with his mouth slightly open, snoring quietly, his chest rising and falling. She placed the knife gently against the base of his throat and drew it across quickly, pressing down, and the flesh opened in a broad red grin. He didn't even open his eyes. A mercy.